*A Follow Your Heart Novel*

# Linda Phillips

MOON WATER
Copyright © 2023 by Linda Phillips

ISBN: 979-8-88653-123-7

Published by Satin Romance
An Imprint of Melange Books, LLC
White Bear Lake, MN 55110
www.satinromance.com

Published in the United States of America.

Cover Design by Caroline Andrus

*To author Sonja Gunter, a special thanks for inspiring this story and for the kindness and patience of working with me on writing skills. She deserves a medal.*

# Chapter One

F ollow your heart...Make a splash.

It was a perfect blue sky, mild-temperature kind of day in the Atlantic Ocean near Barbados. A father and son stopped and fished in one of their regular spots. A day of bonding. They stopped at their favorite spot and pulled in a couple of nice keepers. The son chattered endlessly about the catch.

But what happened next...

THUMP. Something hit the bottom of the boat with incredible force, causing the boat to rock violently back and forth. Grabbing the handrail of the boat tightly with white-knuckled hands, the man looked over at his son, who was beginning to fall out of the boat. With a forceful grip, he grabbed the boy and held him tightly to his chest. After putting life jackets on, he sat the boy in a safe place on the deck and pulled in the anchor.

The boat started swaying from the current developing, churning and pulling it almost in circles. The man glanced back and saw what appeared to be a whirlpool developing. Heart thumping, the anchor was now inside the boat and he started the engine. He had fished for years in this spot. *A whirlpool?* This just isn't a place for these conditions. His fingers automatically scratched his head.

The tidal conveyor belt was working against him, mighty and forceful, so he used small throttle adjustments to move forward. Thankfully, his experience in boating saved them and he moved away just in time before his boat was sucked into the vortex that was growing wider minute by minute. Beads of sweat poured into his eyes. The man used a cloth to wipe them, squinting because it left a stinging sensation. His head turned back and forth as he sped away, relieved. Boat journal in hand, he scribbled in the location, never to fish in it again.

The boy pulled himself up and sat on the seat, scanning the treacherous water they had just left behind, and noticed it had settled down. He jumped up and yanked on his dad's shirt, trying to get him to stop the boat. "Dad, look! You have to look at this."

But his dad ignored his request and drove as fast as possible to escape a potential disaster. The man would never be able to witness what the boy saw. A large whale's fluke came up out of the water and splashed the surface before it submerged into the ocean; at least that's what it looked like to the boy. But what is the rainbow of colors that keeps bubbling up onto the surface? And how could the boy explain it all to his father, especially since he didn't even know where to begin? They would never return to their best fishing spot ever again.

# Chapter Two

The aroma of coffee hypnotically pulled him out of bed. That's okay, because getting up for work wasn't something he dreaded. He looked forward to his job every day. It seemed he and his parents lived in the water, always collecting specimens, measuring seismic activity, and so many fascinating and important duties as oceanographers. They had seen things most people dream about, like a new sea creature or unexplainable formations under the sea. He couldn't wait to see what unbelievable things they would uncover each and every day.

It was completely silent, and the thump, thump, thump of his jogging down the steps echoed through the house. The sun shone brightly on the family portrait, as though trying to catch his attention. He stopped and looked at it. Mom takes it with them wherever they go. He smiled, thinking about his sentimental mom. Back home, he has an apartment on the beach, but his job working for his parents' diving company, takes them all over the world, so he ends up staying with his parents in temporary apartments.

He studied the portrait, seeing himself, Hagan Bennett, in

fourth grade, a snaggletoothed, string-bean boy. He giggled, glancing down at his body now. He looked nothing like that boy.

His dad tapped down the stairs and stopped beside him, placing his arm around Hagan's shoulders. Then he stares at the portrait with a smile. He squeezes Hagan's shoulder and walks to the kitchen.

A peculiar notion kept Hagan entranced, and the oddest thing started happening. In the portrait, he saw himself begin to fade in, then out. He was there and then gone, repeating over and over. He wiped his hands upward across his face and ran fingers through his hair, clutching the strands before releasing them. This was disturbing. Maybe he was dealing with a medical issue just beginning to materialize. Even stranger was how he felt excited and happy, but sad thoughts popped up in between them. *What could this possibly mean? Is God trying to tell me something? Am I about to die? Sheesh!*

Again, his hands feel around his head, face, shoulders, arms, even bending downward to feel his toes. *Ahh, all there.* Hmmm, *I need coffee*, he decides, tapping his head with his index finger.

The coffee was not made with some special, exotic bean, just a brand picked up from a grocery store. But it must be the fact that Mom still used a percolator to brew it. It makes the coffee smell heavenly. Hagan breathed in the intoxicating aroma. And who doesn't love hearing that bluh-bluh-blup sound? It gurgled as he entered the kitchen. Scratching his head, he still couldn't shake what happened with the portrait, but he was not about to tell his parents about it. No way was he going to spend the day in an office. *Ugh! Shoot me now! I'm an outdoorsy kind of guy.*

He picked up the paper and was glued to a story about how facts and evidence don't apply in all circumstances. He began to wonder if he could ever come to understand that ignoring *feelings* was dangerous, especially ones that alert us to a warning. It felt like he'd just got hit in the brain with a two-by-four yelling at him, *Trust me, do not ignore them.* Talk about a mental ouch! Fingers massaged the oncoming migraine. *What is happening to my sensibility? Get it together, Hagan,* he urged himself.

After breakfast cleanup, he and his parents head to the pier that the owners built for the apartment complex they are staying at in Holetown, of the parish in Saint James, Barbados. The owner allowed them to keep the boat tied up there for the duration of the time they will be here for work. They arrive at the boat. Now, involved with work for the day, how is it remotely possible to be sweating in his current circumstances? Beads of sweat slide down his forehead and into his eyes. No way to wipe them off. *Driving. Me. Crazy.* In his mind, facial expressions showed thoughts of fear, excitement, and sadness. Trying to get his focus back, his face revealed a mishmash of emotions that hit him like a brick, producing slanted eyes and a face that squished together with questions. Anyone who knows Hagan will testify that he doesn't trust a feeling. *If only I could splash my face with cold water to cool off.*

From the corner of his eye, he sees a shadow go by, and when he turns his head to follow it, thoughts overwhelm him. His body engages in the old dance called *the Shimmy*. Beautiful rainbow colors swirl and dissolve like the mist from the morning sunbeams. It was a Sci-Fi moment. There is an inability to process what this could be, something urging him to investigate it. People take it seriously when they have a feeling about something, while scientists have lacked reliable testing on the subject or any reason to be objective about it. Being "Hagan" he disregarded the warning begging for his attention.

The expedition begins like any other expedition. Their assignments on each job are relatively the same: Enter the water, collect sediment samples and specimens, research seismic activity, ecosystems, and their inhabitants, study attributes of the oceans, and so much more. So much to do and research with not enough time in the day to get it all done. But what promises to be a normal day proved to be anything but normal.

He's in the water when, wham! Out of nowhere, something just bumped into him, jerking his body with force. Bump. W*homp.* And another forceful hit. Like a fight scene from a *Batman* comic book. Pain in his face, doubling over, his body felt like a punching bag, the last strike more like an outright, full-force assault, causing him to double over in pain. He wrapped his arms around the stomach area for a few seconds. There has to be severe bruising, or heaven forbid, more serious injuries. He held one hand over the sore spot, using the other arm and legs to gain control back. *I am too rattled to think clearly.* It startled him because he never saw it coming. Scary, downright fear, entered his thoughts: sharks?

The water is nothing but turmoil at this point, so he remains still while it clears up. He looks for sharks, but there aren't any around. Anywhere. Then, it's difficult to make out what appears to be an elasmobranch or shark—fish. Now, far away, it's only a guess.

Feeling silly, because he actually starts to think he might die, he looks around for his teammates, but they aren't close enough to see what's going on. Could this be the reason he'd started dissolving in the portrait? These thoughts of death were anything but peaceful, as he feared he would be torn apart and eaten by sharks. Not a good way to end a life.

Memories flash through his mind of his family, closest friends and meeting the good Lord above, what is most important to him at the time of death—and his car, which he loves. That is what he would focus on as he took his last breath. They have been in several life-threatening situations throughout their lives because of this profession, but never once had there been this strong of a sense of dying. The fear inside him would not subside, and his body shook from being so nervous.

His love for being in the water is so profound that he wonders why God didn't just make him a fish. Sounds stupid, but it's strange just how comfortable in the water he feels. Even his parents agree. "You can call me a Thalassophyte," he tells people. But what had bumped into him with such force? What he saw was something about the size of a large dolphin. Feelings; schmeelings. He usually brushed them off and focused on the facts at hand.

Now came the moment of truth: facts or feelings. It felt as though a cement block, or maybe two cement blocks, lay on top of his chest. He noticed he was taking longer breaths; not good. In all of his experiences with not ever knowing what to expect, feelings never played a role in his thoughts, because they were insignificant and not worthy of our time or consideration; but with facts and evidence, they can never go wrong.

Until now.

He wondered if anyone else ever gave thought to what lay beneath. But whether terrifying, intriguing, or both, these emotions weren't making sense. This was uncomfortable for him and he became anxious, darting his eyes around, still taking too long of breaths.

Feeling frightened, the hairs on his arms and back of his neck stood up straight. And that had never before happened—ever.

# Chapter Three

Still rattled, he climbed inside the boat and tilted his head up to view the gorgeous sky to take his mind off what had just happened. The sky was like a painting with the bluest color you could ever see. He pretended to be Thomas Kinkade, the Painter of Light, acting like he held a paintbrush making brushstrokes across the sky. Good thing no one was paying attention. Such a brilliant, happy-go-lucky blue it is that his eyes couldn't help but stare with happy thoughts. A nice distraction from what he'd witnessed physically and emotionally minutes ago. *Thanks for the distraction, Lord.* His lips formed into a smile.

The Lord was on his mind. He may be somewhat of an intellectual—not meaning that in an arrogant manner, truthfully—but when he thinks about the Lord, all his loved ones, good friends and Dani, his girlfriend, he can't help but get sentimental. They mean the world to him. He would die to save them, if it ever came down to that. His relationship with the Lord helps him put things, people, and situations into perspective. Without Him, he probably would take the wrong path. Wondering if He is still working on him with how much time goes into his work, he rubbed his temple. *I fear it is a lost battle because I can't imagine giving up any of the time that goes into this profession. Don't give up on me, Lord.*

Occasional soft, fluffy clouds drift by just now intruding in his thoughts about marshmallows. He'll call Dani while toasting marshmallows tonight at the fire pit; couldn't help but lick his lips at the thought. He wishes she was here with him. An ocean breeze added the perfect complement, along with a perfect temperature to consummate this beautiful relationship.

Barbados has around three thousand hours of sunshine each year, and because of the northeast trade winds, it is not unbearably hot. Needless to say, the water is a pleasurable temperature. Hagan loves it here. The town of Holetown, where they are staying for the moment, is located in the parish of Saint James on the west coast. His mother loves to be here in February, so she can attend the Holetown Festival, which is well worth the time and proven to be a fun day in the past.

His mind is still filled with an unsettled feeling from what he'd experienced moments ago. Silly, but not even realizing it at the moment, he started humming Morris Albert's song, "Feelings". He's a trivia nerd—and a comic book one, too. His mother always listens to the late sixties and all of the seventies music, and it stays in Hagan's mind. Most of the time, his friends look at him like he belongs to a different time period because he's always humming one of the songs subconsciously. He's still working on that scream that only Steven Tyler can pull off. It's a head scratcher, because it actually adds to the song.

It was time to get back to work. It takes him a few minutes to put on his deep-ocean scuba gear, along with a safety check of the equipment. In the water, he drops.

Now that the danger had passed, and he'd completed his research for the day, he strongly sensed a need to explore; something their team seemed to never get the opportunity to do with such hectic and demanding schedules. But he had some free time, and probably being an idiot wanting to find out what had attacked him. Maybe it wasn't an attack; if nothing else, the mere fact that he was alive right now should signify as much. You better believe he was going to take advantage, especially since this anxiousness inside was still so explosive. He twitched from a nervous chill that traveled down his spine. Awkward.

Hagan nibbled on his fingernails. Obviously, he couldn't initiate that bad habit, so he focused elsewhere. A wahoo just swam past his face! Little surprises like that make his day.

He notified the team and provided his coordinates, then took off into the wild blue yonder. The water is a piece of art today. There is every color of blue, green, and even gold from the sunbeam's reflection in the water.

If he had to guess, being in the water was his real true love. That thought opened his eyes and caused a shudder throughout his body. Should he rephrase that to be that Dani was his true love? But whatever sent a warning signal with thoughts of dying, he didn't even think about her. But why? He loved her. He really did. This was very disturbing. What's even more shocking was that he would love to get married and even planned on purchasing an engagement ring. Now that he thought about it, marriage would force him to give up a lot of time spent in the water. Dani was always upset about how much time he'd spend in the water. His body literally cringed, stiffened at that thought. *How can we be married if I have to travel half of the time? She would be miserable and I would feel horrible.*

"Hold on a minute," he spoke to himself. In front of him, a rainbow of colors swirled around again. He leaned forward. It was astounding and took his breath away. Obviously, this was something he'd never seen before. *Just what unfathomable thing have I found?* The water was crystal clear at the moment, and that made his curiosity even stronger. How does someone produce goosebumps on their skin in the warm water? He felt the prickle run up and down his whole body. This was quite exciting.

Clearly, he needed to inform the team about this. They'd been in all of the oceans of the world and had never found something this magnificent and strange. Strange sea creatures, yes. This, no. But maybe he should get closer and investigate it before bringing the team over? A rainbow of colors was shooting out of this deep —looks—like never-ending hole. But how was there a hole in the middle of the ocean? Even a blue hole doesn't make sense.

Before diving down further and heading in that direction, he checked the decompression meter to see how much Nitrox was available to him. According to his reading, he needed to resurface soon. Sooner than he'd hoped. Not a smart idea to dive down deeper. His parents and other teammates were stationed close by with different duties, but he couldn't resist inspecting this strange phenomenon. He'd taken off many times on his own, just as long as he didn't go too far from them. Truthfully, his father didn't like it when he did this, but he was impatient, and if he didn't check it out right away, it could disappear. He just hoped this turned out to be something incredible, so he wouldn't get upset with him.

Light bulb moment: by pushing the Dive Alert Buddy Watcher, his dad would find him and force him to ascend, that much he knew. Plus, the fact that he had been in the water two hours ahead of him, so he wouldn't be put in any danger. This would give Hagan more time to explore.

His hope was that this could become one of the biggest scientific discoveries in his lifetime. Their team could finally have a chance to receive world-wide recognition as a well-established oceanic organization. Move over Jacques Cousteau. His parents had worked so hard all of their lives. They deserve an opportunity that will bring them this type of attention and notoriety.

Hagan swam cautiously toward the location for a closer inspection, stopping and starting, repeating the same moves, like it was choreographed. Was his hair actually standing up by the roots in fright? It sure felt that way. He wondered if he looked like Guy Fieri right now. He's just so cool and talk about the perfect job. The sight in front of him brought him right back to wondering what he was looking at.

Then a sense of awe calmed his nerves. This was unbelievably incredible—wait!—what... What is that coming towards him? He held his breath for a moment, and sort of treaded in one spot. It can't be real!

Struggling with his mental capacity at this point, just as previously, the hairs on the back of his neck stood up. Goosebumps, the size of golf balls, travel up and down his spine. Hagan checked his decompression meter again and, without any type of notice, a fast and powerful swishing of water spins around him, making him lightheaded and a little disoriented. Shortly after, he felt hands grabbing his wrists and pulling him up to the surface.

Now at the surface, team members pull him into the boat and he recovered quickly. A diagnosis is conducted to be certain he's okay or if he needs to be transported for medical care. Hagan was fine, thankfully, and he knew his parents would not be satisfied without the "checkup".

"What is your name?" his father asks him according to the manual he's following.

"Hagan Bennett."

"How old are you?"

"Twenty-six."

"And when are you getting married?"

Hagan can't believe his mother chose this time to pry into his personal and intimate life. *Well played, Mother.* He rolls his eyes.

"Good try, Mom. Good try." She scoffed at me and her eyes looked like marbles rolling across the floor. How does she do that?

The only injury Hagan receives from his encounter is a bruise about the size of a soccer ball. It is painful but no internal organs were damaged. He gently ran his fingers over the injury and shuts his eyes. "Ooh, it is really tender. Ouch!"

Now that the "checkup" was complete, and Hagan released from care, his mind revisits the discovery and the other thing he saw. Was he hallucinating due to a lack of oxygen or a situation with greenhouse gases? Revealing what he saw to the team was a chance he couldn't risk and wouldn't take. This discovery would be huge, and he refused to have to take time off for his well-being, if that's what they decide. That was not going to happen. No siree Bob. The team was coming back next Monday, and he planned to be a part of that momentous occasion.

Eyes glance around, and everyone is watching him, like they were analyzing his condition. His body stiffens, face somber, prepared for battle should they dare try to keep him from joining them in the investigation. They must have read his mind, because they each walked off in a different direction.

Down the hall, Hagan hears a conversation about a fishing story. Supposedly, a fisherman and his son were fishing in the exact location where his attack happened and they had an awkward experience with a developing whirlpool. This spot has no reason for such extreme conditions. Now his curiosity is even stronger.

They are trying to keep their voices down so he can't hear. They knew that he would have to explore it, more so now that he knew someone else had dealt with a disturbing situation in the same spot.

Hagan flew home for the weekend. Dani's parents were coming into town and their relationship dangled by threads. She'd asked him to be with her, so she didn't have to face them alone. They seemed to argue constantly. Why? He didn't really know. Dani was pretty easy to get along with, unless it was something she felt passionate about. Then she pushed hard. Her parents were pretty easy to be around, other than the constant arguing. She told Hagan that they loved him like a son. That made him happy, especially since he had plans to propose, but Dani has no idea.

He ponders for a minute as he drives a rental and speaks out loud to himself. "Here's the thing. Even though we don't ever seem to argue, something doesn't feel right. I would be devastated if she left me, but she's been a little uninterested lately. Asking her about it, she always said nothing was wrong, that I was imagining it. But I fear they are just words and that she is withholding valuable information concerning our relationship. I just don't know." He exhales a deep, discontented breath.

They are truly complete opposites. He was a risk taker. Hagan was the person who would stand on the plane's wings in flight. He loved the adrenaline rush extreme sports offered, like standing on the plane's wings while in flight kind of risk taker. And she's a let's-just-take-a-walk type of person. He's strictly facts and evidence; she's full of imagination and loves fantasy. He enjoys hanging out with groups of people; she likes staying in and getting cozy. But what works about their relationship is that they bring out in each other the characteristics they lack otherwise. That's what a good relationship should be about; compromise and bringing out the good in each other.

They had a really nice weekend together and there was no arguing or intense moments with her parents. Hagan took advantage and drove his rental to a jeweler. He had been planning to do this for quite some time. The only people who were aware of it were his two best friends. He had been admiring a particular ring for a while. It was expensive, but he thought she'd love it, so he did it. He bought it and gave the jeweler her ring measurements. She would be so excited the thought made him happy.

Just before heading back to the airport, they hugged and managed a quick kiss before he had to get to the airport and board the plane. She was never comfortable with public displays of affection, so he left somewhat frustrated. Hagan was back in Barbados in no time, and Dad was waiting to drive him to the apartment. He loved it here, although he missed Dani and his friends.

# Chapter Four

I t became the oceanic discovery of a lifetime. The non-profit organization NORS, abbreviated for the National Oceanic Research and Study organization, headed by Dr. Thomas Bennett, which included his wife, son, and several serious scientists, stumbled upon a most amazing revelation. Their team consisted of biological, chemical, geological and physical oceanographers. Fingers crossed that this would go down in history.

"Son, I want you to take this interview. You discovered it first and it would mean a lot to all of us if you would do this," he said with warm eyes as he squeezed Hagan's shoulder.

"Thanks, Dad. I'll do it, but I won't take all the credit. We are a team and we will receive recognition as a team."

"We couldn't be prouder of you. You know that I hope?"

"Coming from you, it means more than you'll ever know." He teared up because he has always admired his dad—and his mom. The whole team. They have done so much for the greater good and refuse to be acknowledged for any of it. They never want to lose sight of what they stand for as a team.

For clothing, it seemed appropriate for him to wear the team's polo shirt with the abbreviation of their organization imprinted above the pocket, and a pair of khakis.

The reporter, Curious Christine, she is called, began the interview.

"May I call you Hagan, Mr. Bennett?"

"Yes, that's fine. It is an old family name handed down through the years. Anyway, I am speaking for the team, which is headed by my father, Thomas Hagan Bennett."

"Of course. Now then, in your own words, tell us what happened." She stared at him with an odd look, blinking her eyelashes a lot, stroking her hair. Maybe I'm imagining it.

"During our expedition here in Barbados, working around some uninhabitable islands of the Atlantic Ocean, a very peculiar, but portentous and totally unexpected anomaly had been spotted by me, but it was the team that investigated it. Our team was studying continental drifts, varying magma densities, Rift, extensional tectonics—"

"Whoa there, Mr. Scientist. I have no idea what you're talking about."

"I'm sorry. My mom is always telling me to talk in lay person terms. Believe it or not, I loved learning all the scientific terminologies and just basic new and unique dictionary words during my college years. Let me continue and I'll keep it simple."

"From every movie I ever watched, you certainly don't fit the profile of an intellectual scientist. No glasses, your hair is way too long and you're big and muscular; nothing like what the movies portray. That is off the record, by the way."

She didn't even blush. "Forgive me. Please proceed," she said in a cool-as-a-cucumber tone.

Hagan didn't know why, but he felt she wanted more than an interview. Her skirt seemed to hike up way too much when she sat back down, and her shirt seemed to have missed a few buttons. She was twiddling with them, he noticed. His gaze shifted away from her, focusing on the enchanting merfolk underwater paintings on the wall to just get this interview over with. Something about her struck him the wrong way, and he didn't trust her. The fragrance she wore was actually titillating, he hated to admit, trying to hide the fact his nostrils were breathing in the exhilarating perfume.

"This deep hole gave the appearance of an underwater city. However, each time we went back to the location to explore, we were met with turbulent conditions that consisted of some type of a whirlpool and density-driven currents that made it too dangerous for further exploration. Rogue waves came out of nowhere, and I mean like they started and hung around just that spot. What is even stranger is that this isn't an area that would normally produce such conditions. My parents took photographs of this bright, colorful glow from a deep, deep hole that seemed endless. And I'll never forget what else I saw."

"Are you talking about something other than the deep hole?"

"Ye—No. I mean, a person could never forget seeing this. It is beyond thoughts." He dared not try to explain what else he saw. It was possible, after all, that a lack of oxygen did cause hallucinations. He can now admit to that, but at the same time, his mind kept bringing back photos of what he'd seen down there. It was as real as the pain of that bruise on the side of his body. Now feeling the pain, he readjusted his body to alleviate it.

The interview went on for about thirty minutes. Curious Christine invited him out for drinks and dinner and anything else that might present an opportunity. He declined. There was an untrusty warning buzzing in his head. Dani was the only girl for him. His mother pointed out how his eyes squinted, and he had a serious face, as though he were analyzing Christine's actions. It's been said his facial expressions often exposed his thoughts. His thoughts could shoot into outer space sometimes. Poor people, if that was true and his thoughts showed through his expressions, he hoped he hadn't offended her. But he couldn't explain what bothered him about her. She seemed really pushy and flirtatious and cuts people off all the time, rather in a rude way.

Photographs of the anomaly and the article caused an explosion of interest and publicity. It brought about many exploration teams, but each team was unsuccessful in their attempt to get near it. A few of the scientists and their associates lost their lives, because the area would suddenly become perilous.

Just out of the blue.

From being totally calm and easy to maneuver through to an immediate death trap.

No one could solve the mysterious reason as to why. Over many group discussions, the experts would agree that as soon as anyone got close to the deep hole, the water seemed to come alive and intent on fighting off any intruders. It was completely mind blowing.

The team had other studies to perform in the area, so they decided to retreat from this research temporarily, as much as it killed them, and try to figure out a strategic plan to enter the area in question.

Later, back at the house and sitting in his room, Hagan called Dani. She was distracted and couldn't hold the conversation. He knew he likely was imagining it, but he swore she was hiding her giggles. She's a special woman, good, trustworthy, and could be a lot of fun. *Please don't get bored with me,* he thought. Or maybe she's losing interest because it was taking him so long to propose. Since they were getting nowhere on the phone, he lovingly told her goodbye, then threw his head against the backboard of the bed. Eyes automatically closed, and he tried to figure out his emotions, but they refused to pull together. *What is happening to me? Will somebody please tell me what's wrong with me?*

# Chapter Five

At the Port of Bridgetown, close to the area of the Bennett team discovery, all was quiet and peaceful. It was in an area not visible to the prominent beach tourist attractions.

Two people, returning from a swim, perched themselves up on some rocks to meditate over the natural, serene beauty of this tropical paradise. And it was beautiful. Waves crashed on the rocks, tropical trees like Manchineel, coconut palms and mangroves hung down over the water. Tourists knew the fruit of the Manchineel tree was poisonous, even though the fruit looked tempting, like right out of the Garden of Eden. Beautiful coral rock, sandstone, clay or shale flirted with the pristine ocean, but that briny smell was the final ingredient necessary to compose this tropical paradise. The water was as warm as a baby's bath water.

But the beauty of the tranquil paradise was nothing compared to the beauty resting on the rock. Elbows propped behind her for support, she lay back on the rock, her head tilted up to feel the sun beat down on her face. Her long, radiant hair blew around like a mild whirlwind. There was something so breathtaking, mystical, and captivating about her, the man thought. No words could justifiably describe her. For treasure hunters all over the world, she was the treasure of all treasures. The man sitting next to her was of myth and legends.

And of your worst nightmares.

He stared at her face with no emotion, just a–this-is-business expression. For a second, his forehead wrinkled as he continued staring into her face. Then he turned his head away quickly.

He'd lured her to this location under false pretenses. As a dear family member, her uncle had no trouble coaxing her to take a swim. His plan was to provide her, the treasure, for monetary exchange. A woman men dream about and would search the ends of the Earth to find. There were so many beautiful women in the world, but why did her beauty seem to be right out of a fairy-tale story? It was unexplainable. There was something odd, a good, mystifying oddness.

But she wasn't for sale and nobody's path to fame and fortune. And she was unaware of what was about to happen to her.

Her uncle had tricked her into believing he'd found her long, lost mate-to-be and asked her to close her eyes to make the surprise special and memorable. The truth was, he had no idea what happened to her long, lost love. But the excitement of seeing him again was too much to contain, and she struggled, blinking her eyes while keeping them closed, and fidgeting like someone would if they had ants in their pants, body in a constant wiggle. But he was insistent that the surprise wouldn't be revealed unless she kept her eyes closed. She bent over and kissed her uncle's cheek in gratefulness and re-closed her eyes tightly.

What happened next was totally an unexpected surprise. Everything went silent, and she instantly fell over into a state of unconsciousness. The man looked down at the syringe he'd inserted into her neck that caused the instantaneous reaction in her body. He held the syringe up to his face in thought, then tossed it into the water. There was so much Propofol administered, it had to be by the hand of God that she survived. It took two days for her to become conscious again.

Later, she would learn what happened—learn about her horrible destiny, after a ship carried her to a private island that was a secret to the outside world. Only the rich and famous had enough money to visit this 'resort'.

Shortly after her arrival, she became conscious. Her eyes blinked open, and she was met with an audience of men and women, but she didn't recognize any of the people or understand any of what she saw. With her hands gripping rocks to keep her balance, she glanced around at her surroundings and all the people staring at her. She rubbed her eyes for clarity, confusion on her face. Her ocean blue eyes were black and narrowed, her forehead wrinkled. She kept swallowing, holding a hand over her mouth in a desperate attempt to prevent herself from vomiting. Fright consumed her very being.

The large group of people stared at her. Most of them were wearing white lab coats. Her uncle stood behind them all, and she would soon learn his part in the abduction, believing it would help to make the world a better place.

For whom, though?

As time went on, her uncle had been told it would be easier and easier for him to capture his own people to help save the world; foolishly, he'd bought into the idea. It would also afford him the opportunity to make gobs of money in the process, which had never interested him before. The influence of having a lot of money and to buy whatever he wanted, or never knew he wanted, was a misnomer of his loyalty to his own people. Once he saw for himself what it could do for him, greed naturally took over.

Now, he shuffled the money in his hand, staring at it. Looking around, he noticed the eyes of women blinking flirtatiously at him. He inhaled and let out a satisfied sigh, smiling wickedly.

It was as though his people came from a world of their own. He, too, was breathtaking, and men and women couldn't quit staring at him. They appeared to fall into some sort of trance watching him. It was the oddest thing, he mused, failing to understand it.

At the moment, it was uncertain, according to the person in charge, if she'd been captured for sex trafficking or was to be used as a specimen in their experimentations.

~

Face serious, the girl watched a group of what appeared to be leaders in their fields gathered together and speak in low voices, eyes growing intense and body language forceful. But one man took control and ended the whole discussion.

She had no idea who these people were, though she would soon learn they were composed of scientists, professors, government leaders, ichthyologists, veterinarians, pediatricians, and physicians with a background of embryology, biotechnology, and genetic engineering. The list of such highly qualified professionals went on and on.

The island was tropical and had some very charming areas, and some very scary areas consisting of two huge facilities. The one was an architectural piece of art, landscaped to perfection with suites and services fit for a king—or someone willing to pay that kind of money. The other facility was your basic white cement building. It was quite large.

Coherent now, she looked around to see a triple amount of chained fences that went all the way to the ceiling, and it was a room that could be observed from all sides. The sun reflected on a huge padlock secured to a gate. None of these strange amenities existed in her home. This room and everything in it were brand new to her. But she was smart enough to realize it was a trap. She was paralyzed with fear and couldn't scream or move. One of the men moved toward her to check her pulse because it looked as though she had stopped breathing, but then her mouth opened with a deep exhale. To her, it was becoming all too evident that there was no way to escape.

Naked. Groggy. Terrified. Confined.

What could they possibly want with her? The deranged looks in the faces staring at her caused mild body spasms, and other signs of extreme distress. Why were her arms and legs chained?

Why? She jerked on the chains and gasped.

She looked over to see the audience laughing heartily. They seemed to enjoy the powerful feeling of being in control, and for many of them, wicked intentions were clear and present in their stare. Some unconsciously licked their lips and breathed heavier, stuck in an incapacitated state. She bit her lip and her body shriveled up.

A man spoke, informing all of the people to leave the room. Even though she couldn't understand the languages being used, the way the people responded and walked out of the room quickly, it was obvious he ordered them to leave. One person stayed back to ask a question. She tilted her head toward the woman to hear her say, "Yes, Prince Raiatea."

The prince unlocked the door, the sound of swishing coming toward her, but yet keeping his distance. For some reason, he seemed hesitant to get too close. His eyes flickered with evil intentions as he scanned her body over and over, licking his lips and swallowing several times, then quiet moans escaped with lustful intent.

When her eyes met his, she cringed at the evilness looking through her soul. Fear in her eyes and body leaning backwards, she felt she stared into the eyes of Satan. Her eyes squeezed together tightly then, as she wrestled to free herself from the chains, but it was hopeless. She was too weak. Her heart had been pure and protected, but wise enough to analyze his looks.

She screamed and screamed. Squirmed and squirmed.

~

A month after her abduction, a guard was bringing lunch to her when an alarm blasted through the sound system for all personnel to report to the holding cells on the fifth floor immediately. This was a direct order.

The guard set her lunch down and, in a panic, ran out, forgetting to lock the chains back up before leaving the caged room.

She escaped.

It was a dangerous situation. One of the mutant creations had escaped, and if found to the outside world, would expose their whole operation.

Unfortunately, the woman was caught and held captive with stricter care and guidelines.

# *Chapter Six*

Hagan still hadn't proposed to Dani, after a three-year relationship. His mother was concerned he would lose her because of a fear, or whatever it was, of making a lifetime commitment. How much longer would any sensible woman remain in a relationship that seemed to go nowhere, after all? Work always came first. She and Thomas put in long hours working, too, but it was different. They worked every day together.

When home, it seemed Dani had too many reasons, appointments, whatnot for the two of them to get together. It was a little concerning, but he gave her the space she needed. After all, she gave him the space he required for work. He felt he owed her that much. So he did what any logical person would do: pulled out his comic books and read for hours. The idea of supernatural beings just fascinated him.

~

They were out with their group of friends when he asked her if he could get her anything else to eat or drink, and would she like to go for a walk or prefer to go home. Hagan's friends started up with their normal, at-his-expense, joking around.

"Hey, Dani, could I get you a million dollars or maybe take you to England? Paris? Or I will do whatever you want. It doesn't matter." Then they made the tied-around-the finger gestures.

She was *his* girlfriend. When he got the chance to be with her, he wanted to do things for her. Why was that so wrong? Regardless, he brushed them off, and they left.

One weekend, just before heading back to Barbados, they spent two days together. It was nice. They walked along the beach hand in hand, strolled through shops and, honestly, it was good. Really good. Maybe she had a lot on her mind previously. His cell-phone rang.

"Hi, Mom. Everything okay?"

"Of course. I am having difficulty with my computer and hoped my genius son would come over and take a look."

"Sure. Oh, wait, the gang is meeting at the pier on Fort Myers Beach in a little bit, but I can spare a few minutes. Hold on, Mom.

"My mom needs help on the computer. Would you mind if we stopped over there before meeting with the gang?"

"Well, I was going to run home and shower first, anyway. Sand and salt, you know."

"Yeah, I get it. Okay then, I'll meet you there in a little bit."

He bent down and kissed her on the lips, then headed over to Mom's. Before he walked away, he swore she rolled her eyes and a sound of "hhhwhoo" huffed out of her mouth, but Hagan couldn't tell if he was making that up in his mind. He didn't want to abandon Dani or his mother. It would only take a few minutes to help Mom, and Dani wanted to shower, anyway. He must be imagining it, he mused as he massaged his forehead. Doing a lot of that lately.

Hagan heard people talk when they don't realize he's listening, but not meaning to, of course. They would say things like he's the nicest guy in the world, and that he would help anyone anytime. They say he was easy to talk to and would strike up a conversation with anyone.

He doesn't care if they're financially well off or poor, attractive or not. He just enjoys getting to know people. Hearing how people feel about him makes him tear up. You never give thought to how people perceive you and when you stumble upon a conversation not meant for you to hear, well, Hagan never thought of himself that way. Who does? He felt choked up thinking about it.

The breeze was perfect as Hagan and his friends sat on the pier. They were all having such a great time. It always made him feel sad to leave his friends and Dani, but he loved his job too much to let that stop him from leaving. His arm was around Dani's shoulder and she leaned against his chest. This group was as close as you could get to each other. Dani would hang out with them even when he was away, which didn't bother him at all. He wanted her to be happy and not sit around waiting on him to come back.

Although, she and Adam had been getting really close lately. She spends a lot of time talking with him and they laugh a lot. It's not that he's jealous, because he really trusts her and Adam. Maybe Hagan was bothered that she could talk with him effortlessly, while many times he would have to force her to talk, sometimes feeling like he literally had to drag the words out of her mouth. He was sure it was all in his mind.

They parted that night on good terms. His friends hung around the pier, but Hagan had to get home and pack since their job wasn't completed in Barbados.

One day, as Dad's team was out at sea conducting studies and research, they found themselves in unsafe working conditions.

"That ship is coming straight at us. Let's get out of here NOW," Hagan yelled, just as his father dove into the water. All eyes widened and mouths dropped.

"I'll jump in and get Dad to safety while you move out of the ship's way. You need to move quickly. Hurry!" His voice kept elevating. They were in danger and so was his dad. Finally, everyone seemed to gain consciousness and began to execute survival strategies.

Hagan was rushing in a panicked state, fumbling with the regulator and flexible hose, finally getting it straightened out. His fingers were slightly shaking. Now that the mouthpiece was secure, he dove into the water. Trying to remain calm, he pulled himself together and searched for his dad. The dive computer on his wrist showed what the current depth was and now all he had to do was follow the coordinates in his dad's direction. His dad wasn't far away and was already engaged in gathering samples, dropping them into a container.

The ship was getting closer, the shadow of it close by, so he grabbed his dad's arm and motioned for him to dive down deeper, pulling him along. Hagan felt the ripples in the water as it passed over, water churning vigorously, fish darting in several directions.

As they moved away quickly, a dead fish, or what the heck it was, floated past churning below the water because of the ship's wake. It looked like a mixture of a fish and animal, but it was too dangerous to go back to it and try and identify what it was. It disturbed him.. He couldn't quit thinking about it until he saw the glow from the deep hole.

The rest of the team moved the boat away as fast as they could, but not quite fast enough.

The rumble of the loud engine snuck up quick. The team could see the ship's crew members looking down at them, waving their hands, yelling for the team to get out of the way.

There was no attempt on their part to steer the ship away. One of the teammates grabbed his cellphone and managed to contact the proper authorities to report the belligerent and dangerous operation of the ship. The wake of the fast-paced ship caused their boat to capsize. It was that close. The ship kept right on moving without stopping and no one offered a hand to help for the situation they caused. Instead, the team could hear their foul curses and calling them idiots for being in the way, except for the fact their team had been given permission to work in this area of the ocean, whereas the ship, they learned, after filing their report, was traveling on the wrong course.

The team, proficient in swimming, tried to gather as much of their equipment as possible before clinging onto the capsized boat while they awaited arrival of the rescue team. Soon the Barbados Coast Guard showed up. Their boat and all teammates were transported back to safety.

"It happened so fast that we couldn't identify the ship. Marcus only had time to call for help before we could maneuver our boat out of harm's way before the ship collided into us. We barely made it out with our lives," Hagan's mother, Melana, informed the authorities. She was quite shaken up, body trembling. Thomas wrapped his arm around her, snuggling in close to comfort those jittery nerves.

"This is outrageous behavior, and that ship needs to be held accountable. This incident could have resulted in fatalities," Thomas added in a take-charge manner.

"They had no intentions of moving out of the way. We had absolute permission by Barbados authorities to be conducting our research. I have the documentation at the apartment to prove it. Their ship should have been a lot further away from us by maritime codes and regulations," Hagan added.

"Without having a description of the ship to reference, there is no way to identify them. Do you know how many ships are out there?" Petty Officer Third Class Kenneth Klondike asked in frustration.

"There has to be a way to find this ship. I saw this giant of a man, but not close enough to provide you a better description. He had an awful, despicable look on his face. I bet I could pick him out in a crowd," Hagan responded. "It all happened so fast."

"Look, we'll conduct a search and maybe someone will have information. We can't promise you, though. I'm sorry we couldn't be more helpful."

"Thanks and please do try to find them before they truly hurt someone with their unethical behavior," Thomas pleaded.

The team gathered back at the apartment.

"I spoke with our clients of this assignment and we have been ordered to return home for the time being. They are very dissatisfied with the investigation and feel it would serve us well to return home until it is completed. Let's load up and head for the airport," Thomas said reluctantly. He was looking forward to completing their studies in the area and had never abandoned a project in the past. But this wasn't his fault and totally out of his control.

"I'll bet they were pirates," Marcus mentioned to anyone listening.

"*Aye matey*," Hagan humorously replied. "There is no way to determine that, but their horrific mannerisms and lack of concern for our safety surely could make you wonder.

"Oh, Dad. When we were diving down further to avoid any danger from the ship passing over, I couldn't help but notice that glow in the deep hole we discovered a few years ago. The glow seemed brighter and my curiosity is now stronger than before. You would think being worried for our safety would be my only focus, but that proves it is something so uncommon because it held quite an impression in my mind. There was a soft glow, like as if being in a plane at night passing over mountains and seeing the lights from a small-town glowing in the valley. I was so intrigued, but the shadow of the ship passing over us distracted my focus. When we come back here, we need to try and investigate it again. There has to be a safe way to get in there. I just have to know what is down there."

"Absolutely, son. I'm looking forward to it, but I won't risk any of our lives. It would seem the area is protected by something unknown and unseen. I can't even speculate an opinion because it caters to the imagination more than facts."

I started humming the *Twilight Zone* theme music, which Dad wasn't amused by.

"Heaven forbid we do something as frivolous as use our imagination." He smiled, having some fun with his dad. He hesitated and then smiled back at Hagan.

"What are you thinking it could be, son?" Melana asked with much interest, casting a solemn look with her index finger resting on the right side of her cheekbone and the rest of her hand clutched to her chin, covering her mouth. The other arm was wrapped around her chest, supporting the elbow. Hagan looked into her eyes and noticed her eager expression.

"I don't want to speculate either without getting a closer look at it, but honestly, it reminded me of driving through a forest at night up to a town or city and how the lights glow above it before you enter into it. My imagination is running wild with thoughts. Bet you never thought you'd ever hear me rely on "imagination". *Not to mention "feelings".*

"And one more thing: I felt like I wasn't alone. What I mean is, it felt like something or someone was staring at me, but I didn't have time to look around. A presence was causing the hair on the back of my neck to stand up. What it was, I have no idea. I do honestly believe something was watching me, though." Goosebumps developed on Hagan's skin as he contemplated. He looked down at his arm to confirm for himself. Yup, goosebumps.

"Don't worry. It's not the first time we saw something strange.

Remember when we all thought we saw a sea serpent?" Melana reminded them.

They all laughed.

"I think we all were running low on oxygen that time. Too bad we didn't have time to snap a picture. Without evidence, we would sound and look pretty foolish and never be taken seriously again," Thomas said with remembrance of that day in his mind.

It was beginning to look as though our discovery would remain a mystery until someone came up with a safe and tested method to enter. That was just messed up. So disappointing. The entire team all felt it. The opportunity to present a spectacular finding as this to the scientific world was right at their fingertips, but now they had no choice but to abandon it.

The team sat and sat and sat in the airport terminal, waiting for their flight. Some of the crew took advantage by catching up on some much-needed sleep, while the rest of them paced back and forth impatiently.

"What are you doing there, son?"

"Oh, hi Mom. Since we have loads of time to kill, I thought I'd review some diving techniques and calculations to see what went wrong the day I first discovered the forbidden, deep hole. We have the best and most advanced dive gear. These streamlined suits provide a much smoother way to maneuver through the water. I just love it. I'm going over the basic calculations. You know: VtxVC/T/P=SAC."

Hagan remembered that day, checking the pressure in bars of the average depth of the dive and the maximum depth before they dove into the ocean to be sure he'd calculated it correctly. He kept a journal for all projects. When they got back after his 'checkup', he reviewed the calculations again and they were absolutely correct. There still was enough oxygen to make it back to the boat.

"Maybe it was the shock of that hole and the other thing I saw." He made the "oops" didn't-mean-to-say-that expression.

"What do you mean 'the other thing you saw'?"

He formed a fist and knocked on his head at the stupidity of that remark. "I don't know. I'm just thinking out loud." He couldn't tell her the truth. There has to be solid evidence, or the team would just dismiss what someone thought they saw as conjecture.

Thoughts brought up a memory in my mind of something he tried to keep out; ignore. *What sea animal could grab my wrist with its hand? Something grabbed my wrist and tried pulling me before I fell slightly into unconsciousness.*

"Hagan. Hagan!"

"Sorry, Mom. My mind drifted away for a moment. Anyways, combined with running low on oxygen and the shock of what I saw is why I felt uncertain at the time. I keep more precise logs now. Dad is very wise to require the team to train twice a year in the latest and advanced diving techniques and gear, plus panic reenactment situations. I know I feel much more confident and safe because of it."

"Agreed. I will never forget how scared I felt that day at the possibility of losing my son. If your oxygen is running low, head up to the boat and replenish it after taking a rest period. Promise me. No life is worth any discovery."

"I promise, Mom. You have to admit, I've been very careful since then."

"You're absolutely right. Thank you for that."

"On a different note, maybe heading home early is a good thing. I can surprise Dani and spend some time with her for a change. Picture her expression of surprise. She'll probably faint thinking she is looking at an apparition. That acknowledgement makes me feel ashamed not making more of an effort to spend time with her. Her computer is in the shop so she asked to work on mine. I'm certain she'll be at my apartment when I get home."

"I think that's a wonderful plan. Son, you know I would never meddle in your private life, but I just have to ask." *Here we go*, he thought to himself. His eyes didn't mean to roll up into the socket. "Don't you think it's time to consider marriage?"

"I have actually been giving it some thought." Relief and a smile spread across her face. "I'll let you know either way, so please don't bring it up again. Promise that I am thinking about it."

"All right, son. I'll give you some time, but not too much."

He guessed she wanted to shake him up and yell at him, and he heard her exhaling a louder sigh than she meant to. He could imagine her thinking, *What is he waiting for? If he isn't careful, Dani will walk away, and rightfully so. Someone has to get through to him, and who better than his mother? But he put himself in this position.*

As she walked away, her lips pressed tightly together, he heard her snort in frustration, obviously not satisfied with his response. He was trying to analyze her thoughts, but even though she wouldn't admit to meddling, this conversation had happened at least three times now and with much more interest.

"If you only knew, Mom," he whispered as she walked off.

The phone kept ringing, and Dani finally picked up. With a frustrated voice, she almost yelled into the phone. "Hello!"

"Hey, it's Hagan. Did I catch you at a bad time?"

"Yes, I'm afraid you did. I'm struggling with getting my work done on a deadline. Sorry, I don't mean to take it out on you. I only have a minute. Did you call for any particular reason?"

"No, just to say hello. I forgot that you had a deadline for the end of today. I just wanted to hear your voice."

"That's really sweet, but I just don't have time to talk. I'm sorry."

"I understand completely. I'll let you go. I love you."

"Love you too, bye."

There it was again. That uneasy "feeling" yelling at him. How does he get rid of this new development—feelings? He had to admit, he wasn't a fan. She used to love talking with him for hours at a time. He understood the fervency of having to meet a deadline, but that wasn't it. Lately, she hadn't had much to say. The words felt forced, and she just acted bored with him. He couldn't blame her, because his work took him away...a lot. It was selfish of him to expect her to be happy about it. Could he give up a lot of his trips to stay around her? He couldn't answer that. His work was addictive and being away from it made him feel as though he was going through withdrawal. He got antsy and tense.

His head dropped to his hand and his eyes closed partially. Hagan felt his hand giving out from trying to hold up his heavy head.

# Chapter Seven

Hagan's mom was going to be so surprised to find out he'd purchased an engagement ring just before leaving for their assignment. Now, all he had to do was stop by the jewelry store on the way home to pick it up. Dani will not only be surprised to see him, but she has no idea he's planning to propose.

Frowning now, he wondered why he wasn't busting out with joy at the idea. It didn't feel any different from planning a trip to the grocery store. What really excited him was to see the look on his Mom's face when she saw the ring on Dani's finger. He knew that actually seeing the ring on her finger would be such a more meaningful surprise than just telling her about it.

Still lost in thought, Hagan reasoned with himself. *I have been with her for three years. Of course, I love her. With everything that has happened over these few weeks, it must just be exhaustion. That has to be the reason for my lack of excitement in such a huge step in my life.*

Truthfully, his job or Dani? He shamefully knew he would pick his job. What a rotten human being he must be, and he had to ask himself again, would he really choose his job over Dani?

As the team exited the airport, Thomas provided instruction:

"Listen up, crew. When we get our new assignment, I'll get in touch with each of you. For now, enjoy some much-needed leisure time. Good job to all."

"I'll talk to you soon," Hagan yelled, and took off running. He stopped for a moment and picked up a package that an elderly lady had apparently dropped and was attempting to pick up. She smiled, and he smiled back, asking if she needed any help to get to her car, but her husband walked up at the moment to help, so Hagan waved goodbye and took off like a cheetah.

Jumping in his jet-black Hennessey Venom GT, 270 MPH, powered by a 7.0-liter (427 cubic inch) V-8 engine fed by twin precision turbochargers, 1,244 horsepower and 1,155 lb-ft of torque, used, of course, was like a hot fudge sundae to him. Fun and so satisfying.

People laughed when he explained the meaning of "jet black" because they really could not care less, but he found it quite interesting. The fact is *Jet* is a type of lignite, the lowest rank of coal, not a mineral but a mineraloid. It comes from wood that has changed under extreme pressure, which, in turn, means as dark a black as possible.

Hagan was more than a little obsessed with the car, undeniably. He'd found a mechanic who could get it up and running, and he kidded people before riding with him. "A syringe of antivenom is in the glove compartment in case you get bit with the "gotta-have-one-of-these." After all, "venom" is part of the car's title.

How many times had he yelled at himself to be gentle in accelerating? His tires squealed and left a tire mark on the pavement. Anyone around looked over and shook their heads in disgust. "What, am I a sixteen-year-old?" he scolded himself, face flushing with embarrassment.

The realization of what he was about to do frazzled his nerves. So, of course, he started biting his nails in a steady typing beat to distract nausea—yikes, yes, nauseous feelings in his stomach. He had no explanation for that.

"There's no reason in the world why she wouldn't accept my proposal—was there?" For some reason, saying that out loud terrified him. He wasn't sure if it was because his macho self-image would feel deflated or because it sincerely would devastate him. Three years together. Three long years. Yikes again! He was pretty sure he didn't mean it the way it sounded.

Everything was good between them when he'd left for this assignment to Barbados. They'd laughed and cuddled a lot.

But that strong and powerful feeling came back and with a vengeance. It wasn't the kind of fluttering you get that tingles inside when you touch the person you truly love. To be honest, he'd never had those fluttery, tingly feelings with Dani. But the feeling that overwhelmed him now was uncomfortable, perhaps even disturbing. Nerves, he decided.

Feeling his forehead wrinkle, he began to think.

What was odd to him was that she never pushed him about the marriage thing. Never mentioned it. Could it be that she was just fine with their relationship as it was? That she doesn't want to get married? The times he casually brought it up, she would laugh it off and change the subject. Like it was a forbidden subject.

Now Hagan struggled with having second thoughts, but a little too late. The ring had been purchased.

"I just have to follow through and hope for the best." Hagan still can't figure out what was wrong with him, and why he felt trapped in this decision. "Oh well, here goes nothing."

# Chapter Eight

Pulling into his parking space, there was Dani's car parked in the visitor parking spot. "Here I go," he muttered. With the ring stuffed into his pocket, Hagan stepped out of the car and walked slowly to the door, purposely inhaling and exhaling for courage, anticipating in his mind how it would go. Before opening the door, he gave himself a pep talk to make this a very intimate and memorable moment. A three-year relationship deserved that much.

All was silent as he walked in and quietly hung his keys on the hook. Lifting his head, he sniffed candles. He saw the candles flicker romantically in the living room and his ears tuned in, listening to soft music playing on the stereo. The fragrance of a soft vanilla was perfect. Sensual and innocent. Actually, the setup was perfect for romance and he felt encouraged about his decision. When he thought of Dani, he would always picture this scene in his mind. Except, he would throw some chocolate candy into the equation.

It was the perfect setup for romance, but not for a proposal. When he found her, he was so flabbergasted it felt as though his breathing stopped, his body feeling like rigor mortis or paralysis had set in. This can't be his Dani, his sweet, kindhearted, innocent girlfriend. He took a deep, agonizing breath and got up the nerve to speak.

"Am I interrupting something?" he said, voice dripping in anger. He felt his face heating up, and he breathed deeply. He felt as though he'd been stabbed in the heart. He jammed his hand against his chest because of the physical heaviness. As the shock of what he'd witnessed passed, he was about to become unglued. *The green man* kind of unglued.

"Hagan!" Dani shouted in shock. Her eyes widened, one hand on her chest and completely immobile, hair tousled, strands hanging over her eyes.

Adam, his best friend in the whole world, jumped up off the couch, grabbing his clothes while he ran out the door, but not before apologizing about fifty times. "I'm sorry. I'm so sorry," he kept saying and then vanished like a ghost, abandoning Dani to deal with this now psychotic monster. She grabbed a blanket to cover herself up while gathering her clothes.

"Hagan, let me explain. Please...please forgive me."

"From what I see, no explanation is needed. Just get out. Get out!" he shouted, blood pressure shooting sky high and he could only imagine what his face looked like if it was painted red.

She ran to the door, stumbling to put her clothes on. Knowing her as he does, the one thing she wasn't going to do was let anyone see her nakedness. Believe it or not, something he hasn't seen yet. Long story.

Watching her through the front door window, he saw her face contorted with shame as she ran to the car, heaving out tears and gasps. He would never physically hurt her, but the shame and embarrassment of hers and Adam's actions was just plain wrong. Completely immoral. Her expression showed as much. Yes, she should be ashamed, and he had every right to be furious.

While she ran to the car, he threw all her papers and books out the door. They scattered in the wind and she ran like a chicken with its head cut off to gather them. He could hear the thud as books hit the ground. The paper rustled in the wind. Wondering, he mused, *would anyone blame me for acting like this? It's not as though I was prepared for something this devastating.*

~

Dani sat in the car bawling her eyes out and muttering to herself. "I'm so ashamed of myself for doing this to him. He doesn't deserve this. He's always been faithful to me, well, except for the other woman: his job. I told him many times I was jealous of how much time he spends with her. Now that I think about it, this isn't all my fault. I've been so lonely and he knew it but refused to admit his job was coming between us."

She couldn't quit thinking about how gorgeous he looked. How many times did her friends comment how lucky she was to have a guy who was incredibly handsome but kind, intelligent and good? The shirt he chose to wear had different tones of green and blue, highlighting the color of his beautiful eyes. So impressive and attractive, he turned heads and left a lasting impression. "What did I just do?"

Now angry, wiping all the teardrops from her face, Dani started her car and tore out of the parking lot, justifying her actions instead of wallowing in guilt. Right now the only shame she felt was what his parents and sister would think of her, not to mention, disappointment of compromising her morals and values. She spent more time with Hagan's family than with her own. They called her their daughter and sister. It all hurt terribly— agonizing hurt.

~

Hagan sat on his bed with his head drooping, and tears poured out of his eyes, something he couldn't ever remember doing since the time he lost his dog as a boy. That nauseous feeling before-hand must have been some kind of warning that something really bad was going to happen. Life changing, and boy was it ever.

"My best friend!"

How could he tell his mom what happened? This will devastate her. She loves Dani like a daughter. They have a very special bond. And Adam, how could he do this to him? He was going to be Hagan's best man.

More tears poured down his face and then the tears turned to anger. He didn't know what hurt more, his girlfriend or best friend betraying him..

Hagan paced his apartment floor all night with only about an hour or two of sleep.

There was no way to get around it. He had to call his mom but would not go into all the dirty little details. Not yet. But very soon there would be no way to avoid it. That would be the only way she would be able to accept that his relationship with Dani was over for good.

"Man, this is going to kill her."

# Chapter Nine

Instead of calling his Mom, he decided it was best to deliver the news in person. Dad was gone, but Hagan was kind of glad that he didn't have to deal with both of them at once.

When he got to his parent's house, his mom walked into the living room, and he said, "Hi, Mom. I need you to sit down. It's bad news." The look on her face tore him up.

"Son, what's wrong? Is Dani okay?" He was walking back and forth nervously.

"No, Mom, she most certainly is not." He held his hands up and said, "Just let me say what I came here to tell you." She sat quietly with a concerned expression, eyes tearing up, still holding her hands in her lap.

"Dani and I broke up—for good, and nothing will bring us back together." His arms were flailing around erratically. "Nothing you say will change my mind."

His mom gasped as her hand covered her mouth, body straight, not moving.

How could he continue with his voice cracking and as tears slipped down his face? Since he couldn't remember the last time he cried before this happened, she was in complete distress, not knowing what to do.

"Right now isn't the time to try and explain to you what happened, because it will truly bring you emotional pain. When the time is right, there will be no choice but to tell you the whole, ugly truth. At the airport, I wanted so badly to spill the beans that I bought an engagement ring and was planning to propose when I got home. Surprising you by seeing a ring on her finger would mean much more than just telling you about it."

She smiled sympathetically.

Hagan surrendered without a choice to sobbing like a baby. His mom came over and put her arms around him, tears flowing down her face.

"Son, don't give up. It will all work out. She's a lovely girl. Your dad and I went through some tough times but look at us now."

His hands formed into fists and he squeezed his lips so tightly that he bit into them at how enraged he felt about his situation. How shameful to take it out on his mother. *Scream, just scream,* he yelled mentally to himself and tell her, *Well, did he sleep with your best friend*, but he couldn't do that to her. Thankfully, the ridiculousness of wanting to be mad at his mother ceased.

"Mom, I can't tell you right now what happened, and believe me you're not ready to hear it. You will not take it well. Nothing, and I mean nothing, will change that. Obviously, my true love is my job. I am not marriage material. It would require giving up too much. There isn't one woman out there that could change my mind or that would put up with this type of job, and I couldn't blame her."

His poor mother was at a loss for words. Heartbroken, concerned, and somewhat in denial.

"Can't believe I'm going to say this, but I don't think I'm capable of working right now. I am too emotionally unstable."

"Why don't you take some time off? We can find someone to

work in your place for a couple of weeks, or however long is needed."

"That's a really good conception." After he replied, he thought frustratingly, why is it I can't say something as simple as "that's a really good idea"? His mother was always getting onto him about his choice of words. He doesn't speak that way to make people think he's some intellectual; that's just him.

"I never take off time for myself. It's like our job is one big vacation traveling all over the world on one of our assignments, but never just me, myself and I. Besides, I don't want to endanger any of my teammates by not being able to focus."

Being an oceanographer requires a strong mental and physical attention to detail. That would be impossible to achieve at this point. Emotions were too unstable. It would not be safe for him nor the team.

"I just had a thought. Why don't you call up Fernando and see if he can get you on that cruise leaving out of Sanibel this coming weekend. How exciting it is that Sanibel was able to figure a way to bring a luxury cruise ship so close to us."

"You know, you may have something. Being in the water seventy-five percent of my life, it seems it would make sense to go to the mountains. Not me. I will never tire of being on the water or in it. Thanks, Mom. I'm going to give him a call. And finding someone to work until I return is indubitable?"

She shook her head and replied, "'Indubitable'. Maybe I'll check to see if Adam could help us."

"No!" he overreacted. His reaction startled her, and she almost jumped. The look on her face was confusion and incomprehension.

"No more Dani and now no Adam? What is going on?"

"No Adam, Mom. Please find someone else. Please. I need to call Fernando." He bent over, kissed her cheek, and walked out of the house. He hated to leave her like that, but she was not ready to hear the truth. There was no denying it would kill her.

"Fernando. Hey, I have a huge favor to ask of you."

"Well, hello to you, too," Fernando replied with a rushed tone to his voice.

"Sorry, good buddy. I need you to get me onto the cruise leaving this weekend."

"Do you know what you are asking?"

"I know it. You see, Dani and I broke up."

"What! Did you finally propose, and she declined?"

"No, and I need you to never tell anyone that was my intention to propose. No one can know. She doesn't deserve to find that out."

"Whoa. Hold on. I deserve an explanation, don't you think?"

"I guess you do. Look, I don't know if I can get through this without breaking down."

"Okay. I've never seen this side of you. I don't know how to handle it. Mr. Calm and Collected never loses it. I even started wondering if you have any tear ducts."

"Very funny, but you're right, my emotional state bothers the heck out of me."

"I mean, you're the one we all turn to when our emotions are out of whack or we can't deal with something difficult. You always have a way of calming us down. I don't know how to handle this."

"Thanks for the kind words. Well, here goes nothing. Our assignment was canceled, so we came home early. I stopped at the jewelry store and picked up the ring. Dani was supposed to be working on my computer at my apartment this week since hers is in the shop. She wouldn't take mine home and decided to use it at my place until her computer was reconditioned, so that is why she was there."

"You mean repaired, right?"

"Yes, you know what I mean."

"Sure, Einstein. I always know what you mean. I just happen to use everyday words like repair, fix, blah, blah, blah."

"Do you want to hear this or not?" He really wasn't in the

mood to talk about it nor be criticized for his choice of words. His face felt hot, and he knew it had turned red. Could he shoot fire out of his eyes? Watch out superheroes. He focused and tried. More idiocy.

"Yes, but please use words I'm familiar with. By the way, how come you and Dani never moved in together?"

Hagan rolled his eyes and decided to just get it over with.

"Our parents didn't believe in us living together without being married. Back to the story. So I quietly walked into my apartment, wanting to surprise Dani. There were candles lit, soft music playing, confirming the perfect time to propose. As I walked into the living room, she and Adam were on the couch so involved that they didn't notice me standing there."

He caused himself to cough because it was getting harder and harder to explain the situation. "It obviously was the most inopportune time."

"Wait! Wait! You can't be serious. I've known those two almost as long as I've known you, and that's a long time. You and Adam have been best friends since elementary school. Neither of them could do something like this to you. Are you absolutely positive of what you saw or what you think you saw?"

"Are you serious? I'm pretty sure I know how the birds and bees work, and believe me, they were working overtime."

"Wow, man. I'm so sorry. Really. Heading to the cruise ship now and will really try to get you on it. We have a lot of setup to do before Saturday. Keep your phone close, because I'll call you back soon."

"Thanks. I'll be waiting."

They hung up the phone.

~

He paced back and forth in the apartment, awaiting Fernando's call. While pacing, he became more and more intense and noticed the ornate box sitting on the nightstand. He threw it into his sock drawer like it was a bomb about to explode. When it hit the inside drawer, it sounded like an explosion as he threw it so hard. He didn't care and didn't even open it up to see if the ring was damaged. Who cares at this point?

Then he couldn't help but notice the necklace he bought at the jewelry store. It was as though a magnetic field pulled him over to it. It was shaped with a petite moon above what appeared to be a strip of ocean beneath it. The moon looked as though it was shining on the water and the most incredible colors swirled on the water part of it. Studying it with pure fascination, Hagan couldn't figure out how those colors appeared and, even more, how they swirled. *This is what I saw near the portal in the ocean that day. It's the exact same colors, too.* It hypnotized his mind, so that's why he'd purchased it. As he studied it, the phone rang.

"Good news. I got you on the cruise," Fernando exclaimed, excited.

"Thanks, man. Thanks so much. I hope it didn't take up too much of your time, being so busy and all with setup."

"Not at all. I was checking to see if I could get you a room when somebody called to cancel. It was like fate. Now, you need to call this number and give them your information when we hang up before someone else gets the room."

While talking on the phone, he couldn't help but notice the sun shining like diamonds on the water, looking through the window outside. The waves were gentle and teasing soft splashes on the children as they ran back and forth away from them. Music calms some people, but water calms him. Except, right now, there is a slight scent of vanilla still lingering from the candle that was lit last evening. That bothered him so, yup, in the garbage it went.

"Thanks again and I'll call you tomorrow on my way there. If you don't answer, I'll know it's because you were swamped with work."

"Sounds good. Talk to you then." Before hanging up, Fernando gave Hagan the phone number, and he called and gave all the necessary information to register. All he looked forward to was peace and quiet, so he didn't have to deal with his thoughts. He quickly packed his bags and threw the necklace in the luggage for an all-inclusive study of it later. There was too much to get done in order to make it for the cruise tomorrow morning. Weird, but it felt like something was vibrating in the luggage he was holding. Hagan zipped it open and felt around. Just clothes and that necklace. Since there was no time to waste, he chalked it up to psychosis. Obviously, his brain wasn't functioning right. Boy, would his friends have fun with that statement.

The couch was like looking at an electric chair. Staring at it caused more tears.

There was no doubt it would definitely electrocute him if he dared to sit on it. When he touched it, his body must have reacted to his thoughts, and it felt like a bolt shocked his body. He pulled his arm back fast and looked at it, wondering if he was heading for a nervous breakdown. Some would think that's an exaggeration—well, maybe a little. It was inevitable that his wonderful, so comfy couch would always invade his thoughts with crummy memories. He'd have to deal with getting it out of his apartment when he got back.

Trying to escape his thoughts, he started imagining himself as a fish swimming in an endless array of the beautiful ocean. While examining the ocean outside his window, trying to escape this emotional pain, he almost ran out onto the beach to jump into the gulf where he could be himself. That is the one place that always brought him back to who he was. But in order to make it onto the cruise, there was no time to waste and preparation was inescapable.

# Chapter Ten

Early the next morning, Fernando headed to the cruise ship, but for some strange reason, the traffic was horrendous. He ignored the e-mail regarding the grand openings happening today. His foot applied the brakes at the stoplight of Summerlin Road, and when it was clear to turn, he slammed on the brakes in the nick of time, literally just missing two women trying to run past. His tires screeched, terrifying himself and onlookers. He kept blowing air out of his mouth, shoulders drooping listlessly.

"Where the heck did they come from?" He bumped his head, pushing it into the windshield to watch them. Then he sat back and rubbed the temporal muscle of his head.

Still shook up, he opened the car door and stepped out to curse them out, but instead he watched as they tried running while vehicles slammed on their brakes and horns honked. It looked as though they were inebriated because they kept falling down. His anger turned to concern, and he yelled to them, wanting to find out if they needed help. The one lady looked back for a second with wide, fearful eyes, but kept running as she pulled along another woman. It was a confusing scene. All of a sudden, loud honking from behind caused him to jump and cover his ears, curse words flying left and right with anger all over the drivers' faces.

"Can't you see that I almost ran over those two women? Give me a break, man!"

The reaction from the people behind him was not what he expected. He looked back just in time to see a man jump out of his truck, body tight, jaw clenched, stomping his way with a look to say, "I'm going to knock you out, boy". Fernando jumped in his car and squealed out before the guy got to him, trying to spot the two women, but they were nowhere in sight.

The worried face and instability weren't the only things he thought about, but for a split second he remembered seeing an incredibly beautiful woman, and what else was it about her? He was too shook up to remember.

*Chapter Eleven*

Hagan woke up the next morning, listening to the alarm going off. The buzzing sound rattled his nerves, like his nerves weren't already in dire straits. It kept going *Bzzz, bzzz, bzzz* and his body made a cringing movement with each buzz. Then he noticed the time. How he slept through that annoyance for an hour was beyond him. Needless to say, the alarm clock went flying across the room, hitting the wall and pieces of it shattered to the floor. He was not himself one bit, and it bothered him greatly.

Always hearing how cool and calm his demeanor was in any situation, made him feel good about himself. When everyone overreacted to a situation, they could always count on him to think it through and come up with a successful solution. That credit goes to his parents, having learned this trait from experience in watching them handle any situation all of his life. A trait he'd earned honestly and was proud to have. Holding his head between his hands, he mumbled out loud, "Now look at me. I want to break something, hit someone, something to take my pain out on. I am so uncomfortable with myself right now." His fist pounded down on the dresser with a loud bam!

He finished showering in record time, worthy of being entered into *Ripley's Believe it or Not*. Exiting his apartment, a flier fell to the step. He picked it up, read it, and threw it back down in disgust.

"Now, I'll never make it to the ship on time," he muttered.

It occurred to him to give Fernando a call to see if he could keep the ship from departing until Hagan got there. He was speeding like an idiot, swerving in and out of traffic, so not himself. He chuckled about his current driving status. "Okay, truth serum time." He pretended to hold a syringe between his thumb and index finger and pretended to squeeze the needle into his neck. "Truth, it's so darn fun to drive his car like being on a racetrack."

Fernando picked up, thankfully.

"Hey, can you keep the ship from departing? I'm stuck in traffic." Hagan didn't have the nerve to tell him he'd overslept, for some reason, feeling as though that revelation would let him down since he'd helped him out.

"I think you'll be okay. With all the new establishments opening up today, we are behind schedule. Let me know when you're on the ship so that we don't hold it up for departure."

"Aye, aye, Captain...Porter. Just what the heck is your title?"

"I am a Gentleman Host."

"An escort?"

"You don't have to make it sound so dirty."

"I'm sorry. That's actually the perfect position for you. I have seen you charm the pants off the beautiful and not so beautiful; women of all ages, all sizes, rich or poor."

"Well, charming the pants off anyone is forbidden."

They both laughed. Ahh, that felt good.

"I meant to tell you, what is so exclusive about this cruise line is that each cruise is set up with a particular theme. This one is called *The Northerners Escape*, so pretty sure there will not be many single women on it."

"That is perfect. The last thing I want is to be involved with any women. I'm looking for peace and relaxation, nothing more."

"Good luck with that, man. Look, I gotta go. See you on the ship."

The boardwalk to the cruise terminal had so many new restaurants, hotels, shops, and other businesses opening up and today was the grand opening.

"Could anything else possibly go wrong?"

The next thing he knew, he was scrambling for the ship, dodging people left and right, bumping into people and they were bumping into him.

"Excuse me. I'm sorry. I need to get to the ship before it departs. Please, let me through."

Some people moved reluctantly, showing their disdain with sullen faces. He stopped and picked up a woman's purse that had fallen to the ground, not realizing he was to blame. "Here you go, Ma'am." She smiled sincerely, and he took off like a rocket. A child ran into his pathway and he screeched his foot brakes, looking behind to see if smoke lingered in a trail, and was inches from the child. Feeling delusional right now, he thought, let's face it, he was a mess.

The boy dropped his toy truck from the shock of him almost tripping over the boy. He picked it up and handed it to him. "There you go, little boy. You okay?" He smiled and nodded his head yes, while his mother thanked Hagan and pulled him back to her. Hagan's rocket ship feet took off again.

The boardwalk was blocked with luggage racks, people standing in line to get into one of the new establishments, food and beverage deliveries and every other kind of delivery blocking the pathway. The one thing he couldn't dismiss was the heavenly aroma from the baked pastries, sizzling bacon, and a variety of coffees. He hadn't eaten a bite for days and his stomach was reminding him of that fact. Drool started running down his mouth, so he licked it several times.

Standing in front of one of the new establishments, The Mystery of Coffee Café and, before he knew it, found himself lying on the ground on top of luggage bags that fell off the rack. Sprawled out, covered in bags and suitcases, he shook his head, trying to make sense of what had just happened and glanced over just in time to see who'd knocked him down from behind. It was a woman with the longest, dark, most beautiful hair he'd ever seen and she jumped up off the ground, but refused to look at him, nor did she apologize. That angered him. Enough was enough. He'd had it and was about to become everyone's worst nightmare, and his favorite comic book character, that angry green guy.

"If I were the good doctor right now, I'd be transforming into the coolest dude ever," He mumbled to myself. Lou Ferrigno made such a perfect *Hulk*, and Bill Bixby was perfect for his role as Dr. Bannister, he couldn't help but think about.

Hagan stood up and looked around for the woman who'd knocked him over and saw her stumble over boxes, carts and travel bags while she seemed to be struggling to pull along a woman with long, red hair. They kept falling. The younger woman was crying frantically. The woman who'd knocked him over looked back and their eyes met.

Her eyes were wild with fear. She looked away swiftly. He was bothered by the way they kept falling, even if nothing was in their way. Were they inebriated or was it some medical condition? He saw they were clutching onto the white, see-through fabric of a dress or gown that seemed to be five times too big for them.

"How is it they are barefoot?" he asked out loud. The scorching heat from the sun practically burned his hand on the walkway when he'd risen. Just as he said that, the women paused and ran their hands over those sizzling, hot feet, with eyes flickering and a look of pain in their faces.

He couldn't quit staring at the women. Not because they were beyond beautiful and captivating, which, they were, but because of the unusual way they ran and their facial expressions of fear.

Their eyes were so wide, and they pressed their lips together tightly. For some very odd reason, he felt like crying. Why? He didn't even know them, but there was something, like out-of-this-world something, odd and concerning.

Bystanders watched the women with curiosity and concern, but no one bothered to see if they needed help. Hagan was too far away to catch up to them, even though they tripped quite often.

By now they were out of sight, but something about them kept trying to surface in his mind. Everything happened so fast it just wouldn't register.

He walked up and got a coffee and something to eat. He stared at the sign. Something connected in his thoughts. Everyone he has ever known who has had a successful relationship met at the Mystery of Coffee Café. "Could there be magic connected to this café?" He couldn't help but wonder as he spoke softly out loud. His eyes had a twinkle to them, but he had to move like a racehorse to get to the ship before it departs so he couldn't dwell on that thought.

Time is running out, and he needed to get to the terminal, but once again found himself knocked down to the ground.

"What is the meaning of this?" he yelled in justified anger. He guessed his face was fire red.

A beast of a man glared down at him and didn't offer a helping hand, nor did he apologize.

He snorted in disgust as he ran off. Hagan couldn't place it at the time, but boy did he look familiar and P.U., his body reeked. His nose wrinkled and sniffed in disbelief. "Have some pride, man."

Some of the luggage had opened and clothing landed on top of Hagan's head. People giggled as they passed by.

"Yeah, real funny," he said, sneering as he pulled a bra off his head with a pair of undies wrapped around his wrist. Other clothing and tampons surrounded him. How embarrassing. In truth, he was pretty sure he would have laughed too, but the timing was off.

Now, this was getting ridiculous, so he jumped up in a fit of rage. The tension in his body was so tight and his jaw actually hurt from clenching his teeth so hard. Opening wide and closing his mouth several times didn't alleviate the pain.

Hagan spotted the men racing around and heard them yell, "Stop them! Stop them!" He didn't care about anything at that moment except confronting their rudeness. His body language must have been intimidating because people with wide eyes moved out of his pathway. In his mind, he felt like an outraged rhinoceros, snorting and scratching the ground with his hooves before charging. He was overthinking it, but hey, people were moving away for a reason. Not that he was very proud of it.

It was apparent these men were foreigners by the way they were dressed and by their accents. Hagan came to a screeching halt in front of them, waiting impatiently for them to quiet down so he could give them a piece of his mind, but a beast of a man spoke before he had a chance. The size of the man caused Hagan a little concern and to rethink his plan.

"Great. Just great. Where are they? We're as good as dead."

"Brutus! The squire is coming," another crew member added reluctantly.

Hagan began to speak, but the person they referred to as the squire walked up.

Quietly and clenching his teeth, the squire asked, "Did you see which way they escaped?"

With just mouth movement, he could hear Brutus reply, "Not really, Sir Aamin. There were too many people getting in our way. We can't find them."

*Who is this scrawny man causing this brute downright fear?* Hagan watched Brutus fearfully wipe sweat from his brow with a trembling hand and the squire's face was red with anger. His lips squeezed tightly together.

Teeth clenched, without opening his mouth, the squire replied, "For your own safety, I suggest you find them NOW."

If the scene in front of him wasn't so intimidating, he would have to come to the conclusion that the squire missed his calling in life. He undoubtedly could have become a world-renowned ventriloquist. With that remark and the intensity in the way the squire enunciated his words, Hagan's eyebrows raised and his mouth dropped wide open.

"Yes, Sir Aamin." Bad boy Brutus was nothing more than a timid pile of mush interacting with the squire and apologetically sprinted off.

After that exchange, Hagan decided it best not to say anything and continued onward to the ship, spotting Blue Peter on the masthead. The horns blasted, signaling passengers to board for departure. A whiff of diesel fuel was overpowering that caused a wicked cough as he ran.

As he ran, an older lady using a walker was trying to walk through the grass area to get to the sidewalk. He ran past her and put on the brakes. What kind of lousy person could ignore that sweet lady? His conscience was pounding inside, so he turned around. If he helped her, he most certainly would miss departure.

"Excuse me, Ma'am. Could I offer some help to get you to that restaurant?"

"That would be wonderful, young man." She smiled tenderly into his face, melting his heart.

At first he held his hand on her arm for support as they walked, but it was going to take way too long and he couldn't take advantage of his friendship with Fernando, so he did something unexpected. Really unexpected.

"Please don't think I'm being too forward, but I plan to pick you up and carry you to the restaurant. Is that okay?"

"Oh...well, why not let a handsome, strong man make my day? Let's do it."

He smiled and lifted her and the walker up into his arms. She was a tiny lady. He took her up the stairs to the host and explained that this sweet lady needed to get inside and be seated, that it was too hot outside for her to wait in line. Hagan's voice was a little demanding, but kind, at the same time. He didn't argue in the least and handled her with gentleness. He handed him a tip behind her back.

She pushed herself upward and kissed his cheek. "Thank you, young man. It is nice to see a real gentleman. May the good Lord bless you."

"Thank you. I'll take His blessing." He squeezed her hand and took off.

Looking ahead to the water, he saw the ship still there. "I can't believe I made it," he exclaimed with relief, but then ran straight into a porter pushing a luggage rack.

"Really!" Hagan yelled temperamentally, and shortly after realized it was all his fault not paying attention to where he was going.

"I'm sorry, sir. I really am."

The porter didn't reply, but his locution said it all and he began reloading the luggage that had fallen off the rack.

Hagan pulled out his cellphone and sent a text to Fernando informing him that he had made it onto the ship. As he looked over the railings on the ship, an announcement from the captain spread throughout the speakers. "Welcome to the Merry Mermaid. We look forward to a great cruise, the first of its kind, I'm happy to announce. You will be glad to know that the Beaufort scale is a marvelous 'o'. This will make for a most relaxing and pleasant cruise. All aboard and we will depart in two minutes. Good day to all."

Pondering in his mind the captain's remarks about a relaxing and pleasant cruise, he snorted in disgust. This cruise was a last-minute decision to help recover from a breakup of a relationship that lasted three years, with intentions of proposing. Now an engagement ring needs to be returned. So far, this has been anything but relaxing. *Let's just hope this isn't an omen of what lies ahead.*

As he glanced around at all the excited passengers standing by the rail waving farewell to the folks along the shoreline, it hit him hard that he was alone in the midst of all of these people. Stupidly, he held his hand over his head and glanced up at the sky to be sure rocks weren't falling, because of the pain in his head. Sheesh! Well, he was usually surrounded by family, friends or with Dani. That realization made him want to vomit, for real. He needed to move away before breaking down into tears. A distraction was needed and badly. *Who am I?* he had to ask himself.

The ship was now outward bound, and the horn blasted its final farewell. That helped to get his mind on something else, except the ship moved like a snail and almost to a stop. As he looked over the horizon, it would seem the captain didn't take into consideration the number of boats coming in to park along the piers because of the grand opening of all the new establishments. The put-put-put of boats sounded like they were making maritime music. He bet new departure regulations would go into effect for the rest of the cruises.

# Chapter Twelve

The two women that Fernando almost ran over were trying to run along the boardwalk and had been running for about six hours, trying to escape the abductors. Their bodies were dehydrated at serious levels. Not only did they need to drink water, they need to soak in it, but had to keep moving and run for their life or be caught. A wall was blocking the waterway or they would have dived in it.

There was only one way to escape the abductors, and that was to run away from the shoreline. They were aware that the abductors expected them to run toward it and were searching in that area. Regretfully, fear caused them to run maybe too far away. Bodies were close to collapsing. The waterway was their only route home that they knew of. They weren't from around this area and trusted no one. For good reason.

A strong, briny smell in the air led the women back toward the ocean. They struggled, bodies feeling limp, throats parched, licking their lips desperately needing hydration.

"Jorie, come. We need to run faster."

Chantara pulled Jorie out from a hiding spot and proceeded to run back toward the ship terminal, in the direction they just came from. She lifted her face up toward the sky and sniffed the air, smelling the repulsive body odor that was too familiar and for too long of a time in her life.

The abductors were close by. Their body odor of sweat, salt and a lack of cleanliness was a scent Chantara would never forget.

Could never forget.

When they brought Jorie to her just days ago, she was in no shape to escape, but now was determined. Thoughts of those horrible beasts doing things to her sister like they had done to her would be more than she could endure. Jorie was so distressed, protecting herself was unlikely. They formed a pact between each other to die rather than get caught and live out the rest of their lives abused by their disgusting captors.

They were prepared for that choice.

Chantara's thoughts kept popping up in remembrance of all the times they beat her when she was chained and too weak to fight back. She would never be able to endure watching Jorie be beaten, as the abductors had threatened to do in front of her. There were countless times they beat land and sea animals the same way they tried to beat her into submission. Remembering those times brought tears to her eyes. She glanced down for a minute because she felt the tears hit her arm. There was no way to protect the poor, defenseless creatures. Her heart pounded with serious anxiety and regret and her nose sniffled, trying to hold back tears.

Not only did this despicable group abduct women and children, but animals of all kinds to sell on the illegal market with no remorse for them or concern for local and international wildlife conservation rules and regulations. Other times, they were used in horrific ways. This illegal and cruel disregard for the lives of humans and animals brought huge monetary gain to their organization, which in turn benefited all involved in the operation. Life meant nothing to these monsters.

Because the sun's rays were fiery and blinding, they both felt their legs giving out, but the desire to escape pushed them forward. Using a hand to shield her eyes, Chantara glanced back and spotted the abductors.

Signs warning the customers not to enter or climb the walls were posted all over the boardwalk. Chantara and Jorie were too weak to climb over. Dehydration had claimed their bodies, making it almost impossible to go any further. The open water from where the ship had departed was their only hope now for escape. Being exceptional swimmers wouldn't matter until they rehydrated.

Finally.

Water.

If they were to survive, they needed to get into the water. Their bodies were shriveling up like raisins.

"Jorie, we need to be free. We swim to ship. The bad men are coming back. You ready?"

"I ready."

Like professional divers, they dove into the water and their oversized gowns slipped off, but that had no effect on them, whatsoever, and they were gone in a split second. The crisp, cool water provided instantaneous hydration. They caught up to the slow-going ship and clung onto a ladder that hung over the side. The area was clear of people since the ship had left the pier.

Chantara didn't understand nor could she speak the English language very well, but the little bit she was forced to learn was helpful. She was taught about ships and ocean life, clothing and food, and enough of the English language to help with communication.

Thankfully, the abductors were almost out of sight. They watched as the shoreline seemed to disappear way too slowly.

"Jorie, I think we safe."

~

Troubled, Brutus looked around. His expression revealed anxiety as blood pounded inside his head, veins bulging, penetrating eyes scrolling back and forth and his hands clenched into fists.

"Look out there. I can barely make out rippling near the starboard. That is not normal. It's them. It has to be. The name of that ship is called—man, I can't read that far away. 'Scuse me, sir. What is the name of that departing ship?" Brutus asked in a boisterous, uncouth mannerism.

"Why, that is the Merry Mermaid."

He lifted the left side of his mouth with a sneer, then blurted, "I never heard of such a name."

"That, sir, is because it is a new cruise line. Today is the very first cruise. The community of Sanibel is abundantly thrilled to introduce it. It is set up exclusively for themed cruises. This one is for Northerners to escape into the bright sunshine before the dreadful winter begins."

"Northerners. Whatever. Where is their first destination?"

"I believe the island of Barbados."

Brutus bolted back to the ship and informed the squire.

"Depart this ship immediately and stay on that course."

"Yes, Sir Aamin.

"I'll kill those tramps when I find them." He sighed, keeping that tidbit of information out of the squire's hearing range. His protruded lower lip quivered as he tapped his teeth together with rage.

Any crew person who deemed to be of no further use or any enemy of the crowned prince would be executed viciously in cold blood at the hands of Brutus. The escape of these two women was his sole responsibility. Failure to recapture them meant someone would pay dearly with his life. Brutus shook inside with fear, realizing that person who would pay with his life was himself. Sweat poured down his face. His clothes were soaked in it, causing his body odor to reek worse than the normal. Hygiene was noticeably not important to him or his crewmates. He used the back of his hand to wipe the sweat pouring down his forehead, snapping his hand forcefully that spread sweat droplets into the air.

# Chapter Thirteen

Hagan walked around the ship and was impressed with the craftsmanship. It had a Viking ship flavor to it. For a luxury cruise ship, their attempt to grab people's attention and imagine a voyage of adventure was quite successful, in his opinion. During his college years, he did a report on the building of Viking ships. The expert woodworkers used a broad ax to split oak trunks into planks. Using iron nails, they would overlap the planks.

Running his hand over the oak planks, he noticed they carved a spectacular mermaid figurehead. The Vikings usually carved dragons or snakes on the prow of the ship, but since this cruise line was called The Merry Mermaid, the exquisite mermaid figurehead was most fitting and quite captivating.

The creative workmanship in the design of the ship caught Hagan's interest, until he noticed the interior of the ship at each level was decorated in a winter wonderland theme. He busted out laughing because these Northerners took this cruise to escape thoughts of a cold winter, and now here it was mocking them. It certainly takes away from the tropical experience they had been promised according to the description in the brochure that probably drew their attention to it in the first place. It's not that it wasn't beautiful and tastefully decorated, but sheesh, he couldn't see this going over well with the passengers.

The cruise director was just feet away from him, so he thought he'd ask her a question.

Before he had the chance, he was pushed aside, unintentionally, by an exacerbated group of passengers. It was apparent to him that what was on their minds had placed him in their blind spot. Hagan took no offense.

"Excuse me, miss. I was told to express my concerns to you. This is my concern. Why is it we Northerners took this cruise to escape the cold weather, but instead we find ourselves tormented by a winter theme.

"Is this some type of joke?" one of the passengers commented.

"I don't know how to answer that except to say that the captain's wife felt the idea would match the theme for this cruise, since it is exclusively meant for Northerners."

Laughing hysterically, Hagan realized the passengers' remarks were exactly his thoughts. He laughed so hard over a remark that wasn't all that funny, and oddly then, he felt like crying.

"Get it together," he scolded himself.

His eyes darted back and forth with hopes no one was noticing this almost meltdown. Poor woman. He decided his question wasn't that important. All he wanted to ask was where the heck could he find peace and relaxation aboard this ship, the reason he came on the cruise in the first place. *How's that working out?*

In hot pursuit of his quiet location, he passed a club called the Mermaid Lounge. It caught his attention because it was the only spot on the whole ship—that he could see anyway—that wasn't decorated in a winter wonderland design. Curiosity pulled him in to discover the reason why. A striking, wooden, carved mermaid figure stood at the main entrance. The eyes were bewitching and gave an impression that they could look right through his soul.

He started to enter the club but turned back to look into the eyes of the mermaid version of Medusa, because the figurine was hypnotizing.

Irish folksongs played as he entered. Fabric hung down from the ceiling in various blue-green colors representing water. Various colors of green fabric hung down representing sea plants. Exquisitely painted mermaid portraits lined the walls. A sweet fragrance of melted barley with butter tones and subtle oak lingered, no doubt Irish whiskey. He remembered that scent from his college days.

"What can I get fer you?" the fubsy bartender asked, wiping a beer mug with a hand towel.

The barstool called his name. "Nothing, thanks. I'm not a drinker." For his profession, he needed to have complete control of his faculties, yet he couldn't resist coming in here. "How did you manage to avoid decorating the joint in a winter wonderland theme?"

"I simply refused. This is the Mermaid Lounge. People equate a mermaid with a tropical landscape." His accent was strong, but he spoke slowly and formed each word.

"I have to say, your décor is classy and eye catching." His eyes wandered.

"My original plan was to deck out the place with adult versions of a mermaid. It's not like children come in here." He snorted and mildly shook his head.

"Let's see, I beg to differ. This design is perfect for the shy of heart and classy enough for the artistic souls. You did well, my friend." Realizing he referenced this man as a friend, it hit him odd that he used that phrase. *Okay, so I didn't know him from Adam —why the heck would I have to use that name as a reference.* He called himself all sorts of names at that remark. His disturbing thoughts must have caught the bartender's attention, because he stopped wiping the mugs and stared at him. His phizog seemed to have a questionable, concerned look.

"From what I can see, your club will be bombarded with passengers who are dissatisfied with the rest of the ship's décor." He let out a hearty laugh. Hagan chuckled, remembering the dissatisfied passengers verbally attacking that poor cruise director.

"Well, in that case, should you be in need of earning some cash, I may need the help."

"You never know. I'll keep that offer in mind. I'm sure I'll see you later."

"Take er easy," was how the bartender replied.

As he left the bar, that mermaid figurine followed him with her eyes. A little freaky.

*Chapter Fourteen*

I t was dark out now, so Chantara pulled Jorie up the ladder and they hid in a lifeboat with a tarp of some sort covering it.

"I hungry," Jorie groaned. You would think a bear was growling, her stomach growled so loudly. She held a hand over her stomach, trying to quiet the roar. She couldn't speak much English at all.

"Maybe I sneak in to find food when people sleep."

Now that it was pitch dark outside, Chantara slipped out of the lifeboat.

"You want to come out?" Chantara had to constantly rephrase her speech into their language, because she had been forbidden to use it for all these years.

"No. I too scared."

The moon dazzled the ocean with mystifying beams of sparkling light. An ocean breeze tickled Chantara's nostrils with an appetizing, familiar scent. She bent over the side of the ship and the water sprayed a briny taste into her mouth. Her smile lit up her whole face. To her, it was nectar of the gods. With the mist of the ocean glimmering on her face, she tilted her head upward and closed her eyes, smiling as she breathed in the invigorating ocean fragrance. Then reality hit her. She crossed her arms and rubbed them gently, standing motionless and expressionless.

"Now I find home. How, though?" Her face contorted into sadness, biting down on her bottom lip to distract her thoughts from crying, hot tears forming in her eyes, but it was to no avail. The thoughts caused a deep, heart throbbing, unavoidable outburst of tears.

"How I find our family? I find! Please, moon above, shine a path to home." She looked at the moon with pleading eyes.

Jorie peeked out and felt sadness for her older sister. "Don't cry. We be okay." She always spoke in their native language.

Trying to be brave for her younger sister, she replied, "We be okay. You right. You try to sleep." Before the abduction, there seemed to be a built-in internal navigation system that gave her the ability to find directions to anywhere. That skill vanished and left her with a defeated and vulnerable outlook.

*Chapter Fifteen*

Hagan finally found a spot void of people on the fifth deck near the lifeboats. Staring out at the ocean, it was so quiet, peaceful and relaxing. He bent his head down and squeezed both sides of it with his hands, and whispered, "I never heard such quiet."

Then what he thought would help him recover from this megrim disposition was having the completely opposite reaction. Anger, bitterness, emotional pain seized his whole body. He felt his heart start throbbing, and he gripped the sides of the ship, rocking back and forth. Then he thought, maybe he was going about this all wrong.

Peace and quiet was obviously the wrong direction to help him get through his out-of-control emotions. Just maybe chaos and lots of noise was what he needed to work through all the clatter inside his head. He needed to get out of there. There was a heaviness in his chest. He pressed his right hand to his chest, hoping to alleviate the anxiety.

Before he walked away, something caught his attention from the corner of his eye. He turned his head in wonder and stared at a twirling of iridescent colors. It reminded him of the Aurora Borealis with milder colors, but this was the wrong location to Earth's position to be that. Mesmerized by the enchanting array of colors, a sudden need to get closer urged him slowly forward. Hagan gasped when he realized it was a woman that twirled in the breath of wind. She sang in a language so bewitching, but one he couldn't identify. He strained his eyes and leaned forward.

"Hello," was the only word he could produce.

Her naked silhouette was outlined by the colors that reflected from her skin and the moonlight. She finally saw him and froze, and the look of terror on her face tore at his heart. She didn't speak and stood statuesque. He took another step toward the most radiant and intriguing woman he'd ever seen.

"I didn't mean to frighten you," he said, extending his hand to greet her. She didn't budge. Surely, he hadn't thought this through. Talk about stupidity approaching a naked woman, trying to get her to shake his hand and talk to him was right out of *Ripley's Believe it or Not*, but his customized version he called, *Ripley's Believe it or Not* Idiot Edition.

"My name is Hagan Bennett." He felt uncomfortable for her, so he withdrew his hand and stood still for a moment.

"You don't have to be Sherlock Holmes to infer she's a stowaway," he mumbled.

"Are you a stowaway?" He mentally kicked himself for asking, as her nervousness transformed into franticness. He saw her breaths expanding, and her eyes darting back and forth as she scanned the ship wildly, giving the impression of searching for a way to escape, so he backed away. Even though it was pitch dark outside, the colors reflected off her skin and hair enough for him to see her.

*How, though? Strange.*

Before he could say another word, the ship began rocking back and forth violently, enormous waves crashing over the sides of the ship, winds howling ferociously. The rocking of the ship caused her to slide into him and they fell into a nook with Hagan holding onto her with all his might to protect her from harm.

As quickly as the raging storm began, it ceased just that fast. Almost like an invisible hand pushed them together. The moonlight burst out like a spotlight shining right over them. Hagan was finally able to focus, realizing he was holding onto the bare-naked buttocks of this incredible figment of his imagination. How he figured out that her breasts were uneven—but pleasantly firm— was almost comical to him. They were practically in his face, after all. As she loosened her grip, her breasts touched his upper chest area. He forced himself to swallow a few times and look away. There was an eerie green look in her eyes, which was odd and concerning to him. Then he quickly glanced around and saw neon lights reflecting off windows and metal.

He was experiencing a dizziness just touching her. Why? His body felt prickly, but in a pleasurable way. He doesn't even know how to describe this fervor, but he enjoyed it immensely. It's complicated; rather anomalous. He couldn't explain how bolts of electricity shot throughout his body. Wonderfully weird.

It was apparent the young woman just realized her predicament. Horrified, she jumped off him like a wild animal poised to pounce on its enemy. Hagan heard the sound of hissing and snarling. It was quite disconcerting. With a quickness, her nails tore through his flesh. He grabbed his arm in pain and felt the oozing of blood, looking up at her in shock and horror. He couldn't close his mouth and seemed to forget to breathe. He coughed, trying to inhale oxygen.

Hagan dazedly realized she was not a figment of his imagination. A figment wouldn't be painful.

"You not trap me. I not be captured again. I kill you." Her eyes looked murderous but sincere.

"Wait-wait-wait! I don't want to capture you. It's not my fault. The rocking of the ship back and forth caused you to slide into me. Please, I don't have any intentions to hurt you."

Still clutching onto the injured arm, wrinkling his face in pain, he asked, "Could I help you somehow? Do you need clothes or food or a place to sleep?" *She just attacked me. What am I saying?*

With apprehension, she spoke. "How I know you not trick me or hurt me?"

In his mind, he pondered what she said, and it broke his heart. Anyone could read between the lines. This poor woman has been mistreated terribly. Her expression of fear was real and intense. Tears came to his eyes at the innocence of her words in a tone begging for someone to trust.

"All I would like to do is help you in any way you need. I won't hurt you. What about this? I'll bring you back some clothes and food and set them down away from me. Okay?" That got a reaction, and her face lit up with anticipation.

"I love food. You set food down there." She pointed to a corner.

"Good. What would you like to eat?"

"No animal, please." He understood she meant to say no meat.

Through the speaker system, the captain spoke. "Passengers, we came upon some sort of freak of nature. The ship is not damaged. Staff will make their way across the ship levels to help assist with any injuries. My apologies. I feel confident that the rest of the cruise will be in perfect condition."

"So much for that Beaufort scale of a marvelous '0'. It's more like a catastrophic '10'," Hagan snapped.

"I'll be back," he said, walking off holding a hand over his bleeding arm walking to his stateroom. A painful moan escaped from his mouth.

Hagan replayed the attack in his mind. She had some serious, animalistic movements. There was not any movie or pictures of wild animals he could think of that would compare to her movements. Possibly a leopard, but no. He'd never seen a person react like she did. Research would be done at a later time. Right now, his injury needed medical attention, and he wanted to get back to her before she changed her mind and left or hid somewhere else. Very foolish of him, he knew.

"From having been all over the world because of my job, I can't for the life of me, determine what country she is from. Her accent has a unique timbre to it," he muttered while searching for clothing in his room.

First, he mused, he'd get treatment for his arm. No explanation was necessary to the cruise staff for the claw marks. It was mistaken for injuries from the chaotic results of the freak storm. The only complication was by the young lady administering treatment. She kept staring at him, forgetting what she was doing in treating his injury. Every time he glanced over, she was staring at him in a daze. Not meaning to sound arrogant, but Hagan was used to women going to extended means to flirt with him, but this poor, young lady was all out of sorts. Action needed to be taken before she needed medical treatment herself. He smiled at his reasoning, making more out of it than it should be.

"I think I'm good now. Thanks for your help," he said, eager to leave but didn't want to offend her in any way.

His genuine sweetness and kind mannerisms had charmed women of all ages. Not to mention those masculine, handsome features with a skin tone that looked as though the sun kissed it ample times.

Carrying platefuls of delectable food and pastries across the ship to the spot where he'd run into the young, frightened woman, he set them in the corner as he had suggested, noticing she remained hidden. Hagan stood far away and watched her walk out, reminding him of a scared mouse trying to reach a crumb of food while a cat slept just around the corner. She crept to the dish, flittering side to side like a bird, obviously on the lookout for a trap. After taking food to her hideout, she came back to the corner, still naked, and sat down and ate. It was a relief to see the change in her, feeling safe and all, because she ate cautiously but with much enthusiasm. She hadn't eaten in days and right now, that was first priority.

"Mmmm, what this I eat? It good."

She must be starved because he could hear her stomach growl from where he sat, opposite of her but a distance away, but she took dainty bites and ate everything on the plate. Observing the fizzy drink with curiosity, he had the impression she had just learned how to slurp through the straw. A full, wide smile covered her face and he could tell the bubbly carbonation tickled her nose as she rubbed it and giggled. The slurping was childlike and endearing.

Facing Hagan, she said, "Thank you, sir. That good food."

"You're very welcome. I brought those clothes for you to wear." He pointed to the clothes with thoughts of how beautiful her body was, but he felt guilty for those thoughts. His mother brought him up to respect women, and after her as a role model, of course it impacted him. He heard the sarcasm from guys all the time for his convictions. Not popular in today's world.

"Oh, thank you."

"I plan to sit right here all night. If you need any help, just let me know. After grabbing some blankets and pillows, I'll be right back." With no response, he walked off.

When he returned, the moon was so bright that he could see her clearly. That is when it became evident that her very long, dark hair and exposed skin had opalescent highlights that glistened. He stared with suspicion and with questions. His thoughts transported him right into a fairy-tale story. Something about her was beguiling, vibrant, and she possessed a fairy-tale beauty and demeanor.

There was a magical curiosity that teased his ideation. Even though he'd sworn off getting into a relationship, it felt like a love spell had been cast on him. Holding his forehead in his hand, arm propped up on the chair's armrest, he bent his head downward to break the spell. No woman was going to trick him ever again. But she wasn't trying to trick him. If anything, her body language made it perfectly clear to keep back. Sensibility restored his mind.

As she turned and looked into his eyes, he felt at that instant an ecstatic shock flow through his body with a quick shudder, like an ice cube went down the back of his neck. By the stunned expression on her face, he saw she'd felt the same way. Hagan realized these were the same eyes he'd looked into back at the dock. She was the person who'd knocked him into the luggage rack, and she realized it, too.

*The way her skin and hair glow, how does she plan to hide? That soft, effulgent aura of hers compliments the moonlight. It's like she stepped out of a child's storybook.* His thoughts ran wild with imagination, something that's always been limited in his mindset, but man, he was making up for all lost time.

Glancing here and there over the ocean, returning her eyes to him, she lifted her face up to the sky. He could tell she enjoyed the redolence generously provided by the ocean. It was cute how she laughed at the mist tickling her nose, giggling like a child trying to wipe the mist off. The black sky was shining like silk, with majestic stars twinkling happily.

Okay, *looney tunes* be gone. He swore the moon appeared to be smiling. He would have to say he was a little mentally and emotionally challenged right now. His head seemed to drop on its own in disgust, a feeling overwrought with wondering what was happening to his sensible reasoning. The most wonderful thing about meeting her, though, was that he hadn't once thought of Dani. Not once.

While she smiled at the moon, turning slowly in the breeze, a seagull landed on the edge of the ship.

"Flopper, is it you? Flopper!"

The seagull hopped up next to her. She picked it up and hugged it, then wept in earnest. Hagan was confounded at the scene and he saw how her teardrops sparkled in the moonlight like colorful diamonds. Then, a pelican flew down and snuggled up close to her.

"Shovel?" she whispered to the pelican.

Hagan didn't understand what he was watching, but it brought out emotions in him he never knew existed. She pulled them both close to her and cried like a baby. Pulling out hair strands and placing them in Flopper's beak, she spoke in a gentle, foreign language, then returned to using the English language, for whatever reason, he didn't know.

With teardrops and hiccups between each word, she pleaded, "Go. Go take this to Mother," ongoing sniffles, "and Father and tell them we escaped. We coming home."

They flew off immediately.

He couldn't dismiss the fact that she used the word *we*. Then he remembered seeing her pulling along a young lady back at the dock.

"I bet the other lady is hiding inside of the lifeboat," he said silently.

What he'd just attested produced a silent downpour of tears. She is pure as the first snowfall with the innocence of a child. How anyone could hurt something so precious didn't compute in his mind. So much for a tough and rugged exterior, because this scene was downright contemptible and cruel to feel the inhumane pain of this celestial creature.

Why couldn't he grasp in his mind what was so different, and bewitching about her? He wanted to admit to himself that she

couldn't be real, but that wouldn't work since he'd held her physical buttocks in his hands. This was just so bizarre. Of all people,
the one with no imagination, no thought to feelings, now was
riding the "whacko train" to psycho land. Maybe the breakup had
affected him at dangerous levels.

# Chapter Sixteen

Hagan woke up at approximately 2:00 a.m.. The unnatural way his head was bent caused a miserable, aching pain. The breeze caused golden and sun streaked white-blonde strands of hair to fall over his eyes. He removed them, running his fingers through his hair, and felt the pain in his neck from an uncomfortable position while sleeping. He placed his hands at different areas of his neck and twisted back and forth carefully. Then a mild crack resonated, and it appeared by his facial expression that he felt instantly better.

It was worth it.

He turned his head to search for Chantara, and it touched his heart to find this angelic creature sleeping next to him. Staring at her, his thoughts were unexplainable, and he resisted the impulse to touch her face, her hair, forgetting to catch his breath. He inhaled so quickly that he startled himself, grabbing the armrest for balance.

"As soundly as she is sleeping, how long had it been since she'd had a good night's sleep?" he whispered to himself, concerned.

He was too excited to try and sleep, overjoyed by the fact that she felt safe with him. The moon's rays shined over her, creating prismatic colors throughout her hair and vulnerable skin.

"Why can't I quit staring?" He was lost in some fantasy world. Then it hit him. Maybe her unusual beauty is a result of her inward beauty. There was something extra special about her, but he couldn't even try to explain why he felt that way, something with no rational explanation. An angelic innocence about her.

Daylight crept in discreetly. Pink cotton candy clouds covered the sky, giving an appearance of blushing from the flirtatious sun. She stirred and stretched her arms, moaning with satisfaction of a good night's sleep. Her eyes opened, and she stared straight into his. Not having her wits about her yet, with eyes that released worry and uncertainty, she jumped up and backed away.

"Everything's okay. I've been awake most of the night. I have no intentions of hurting you. Please don't be scared." He encouraged her by using a gentle, begging voice.

"You right. You don't hurt me, Ha...gan."

She wasn't certain how to pronounce his name, and her English skills lacked greatly, he couldn't help but notice.

"What can I do to help you? If you and your friend would like, you can take a shower in my cabin. I'm sure you would like to freshen up. It's not a trap. Please allow me to help you."

Thinking hard, she glanced toward the lifeboat, realizing he knew her sister was hiding and there was no attempt to abduct or hurt either of them. *Maybe he really help us. I see him before, but where?*

As she sat down nervously next to him, he remained still. There wasn't one woman that came to mind who could spellbind his thoughts as she did. He felt foolish, wondering if she was aware of his continual gawking at her.

"Why you nice? It a trap. No people nice."

He tilted his head and knitted his eyebrows together at that statement. There were a lot of really nice people that he has met. How could she characterize everyone as being bad?

"You don't really mean that, do you? There are many good people in this world. What happened to you?"

"Bad people trick me and act nice. It only a trick."

"It breaks my heart to know you feel that way, but I promise there are good people in the world. I'm sensing the tragedy of what you must have gone through is probably unforgivable. I'll keep my distance and protect you from any harm. Promise. Please give me a chance to prove myself."

"I scared, but I try." Her eyes dropped to the deck and caused angelic visions in his illusive mind.

"My name, again, is Hagan," he repeated because his nerves were out of whack and he was trying to engage in some form of conversation. "What is your name?"

"Chantara."

"That's a beautiful name."

"It means moon water."

"That's curious. My name means strong defense," he joked flaunting a silly smile, holding up his arms to make muscles. She stared at him, not amused but confused instead, so he responded. "I guess my parents expect me to be strong and a defender of all that is good."

Still not quite sure she understood, she produced an infinitesimal smile, wanting desperately to trust him; trust someone.

"So, what do you say? Do you want to take a shower in my stateroom? It's safe."

"Yes, I love. My Jorie love, too. We be strong to swim home in a day."

"Swim for home? Out here in the middle of the ocean with no islands close by? Not even Michael Phelps could swim that well."

"We good swimmers," was her only response.

"All right, then. I think you better take it easy with...your sister?"

"Sister, yes."

"Your sister must be really frightened, because I haven't heard a sound from her. If you feel threatened for any reason, I'll bring you right back here."

Somehow she managed to bring her younger sister out of hiding, but Jorie stood behind her and wouldn't come out into the open. She was sensational, gorgeous with mannerisms of a child. They both were childlike, he couldn't help but notice. Her hair had vibrant red colors with what looked to be various green highlights mixed all throughout, and it hung down past her knees. For some odd reason, he observed that colors didn't reflect off her as they did Chantara. She was wearing some of his oversized clothes he gave to Chantara.

"This is the key to my cabin." He held his hand out for her to accept.

"This no key," she remarked, scrunching up her face with questions.

"I'll show you how to use it."

They followed cautiously, clutching the pants in their hands so they didn't fall to the floor. At every door slam, every footstep, and every sound, they would jump. It was unsettling to watch them walk in sincere fear. What were they so afraid of or of whom? After demonstrating how to use the key card, he handed it to Chantara and backed away, not wanting them to feel ambuscaded.

"Now you try."

The tone of his words was just as important as the words used, he detected. She attempted a few times with frustration and finally opened the door, smiling widely, proud of herself. He smiled back.

"Wait to get in the shower until I return. I'm going to buy some bath products and clothes for you both and be right back."

In a short while, Hagan returned, holding several bags, and he knocked on the door.

Very slowly opening the door, her head poking out with caution, Chantara grabbed the bag. "What is these things?" she incorrectly expressed. To him, it didn't matter how wrong her grammar skills were. It all sounded adorable. *Don't worry*, he tried convincing himself, *you're just protecting them, but from what? From whom?* Oh yeah, he wasn't convincing to himself either.

With hesitation, he tipped his head with a look of confusion. "Well, the blue bottle is a fragrant liquid soap and the light blue bottle is lotion. There are toothbrushes, toothpaste, and shampoo for your hair, also."

She held up the loofah, studying it. "You pour the soap on that and wash your body with it," he explained while using hand movements showing how to use it. *How is it she doesn't know what these things are?*

"The fragrance is an ocean breeze, because you seem to like that smell."

A smile and a thank you, the door closed.

An hour later, he listened at the door and heard the shower streaming. He knocked. "Chantara, Jorie. Hello. Anybody there?"

"It feel so good. I love," Chantara's voice echoed from the shower.

In a few minutes, the door opened and she stepped out. He noticed how the hydrating water was invigorating and there was a serious change in her behavior. A drastic change.

"Would you like to take a walk around the ship?"

"I love."

"What about Jorie? Would she like to come?'

"No. She too scared."

"Okay. Maybe soon she'll feel safe enough to come out."

As we walked, without thinking, he grabbed her hand and started pulling her out of the way of people passing by. She pulled back fast and released her hand from his, jaw clenched. He assured her that it was innocent and nothing more.

What really bothered him was how she reacted, as if his touch was vulgar and she didn't seem the least bit interested in him other than someone to provide for her. He wasn't offended by her obvious disgust of him; he was annihilated—since he'd never had a woman dismiss him like that. On the contrary, they had bent over backwards to flirt with him. Man, that sounds arrogant. It's not how he intended it to sound. But the way she behaved, like he was the most grotesque person on earth when he touched her, could certainly ruin a man's ego.

To be fair, no matter how much he may disgust her, she needed help. He would do everything in his power to help, comfort and protect her. Trust, that's it. The way she looks at everyone like she needs to defend herself, it is clear something horrific had happened to her and she had nobody to trust; someone she could confide in and help her. When she didn't realize he watched her, he could see a very sad, broken-down angel. It made him want to burst out in tears to know she had been harmed probably mentally, physically, and emotionally. He was just guessing, but it was apparent he was right on the money.

Oh boy. She hadn't rubbed the lotion into her skin, and he needed to determine how to appropriately address it without hurting her feelings. It was uncanny, the lack of understanding she had for the simplest things. This had to be dealt with in a soft-hearted approach. He knew enough not to touch her. That could possibly send her into a state of panic, and he wasn't about to jeopardize an opportunity to spend time with her. He rubbed his arms and pointed to hers and she understood and rubbed the lotion into her skin, cheeks turning a rosy pink color.

Sniffing the fragrance after a few rubs, she affirmed, "I love."

Circumstances changed course significantly, since he was the one who felt trapped; trapped with desire, a body that feels like jello, accompanied by a thrilling, squeamish awareness in his stomach. *Love?* He had to be out of his cotton-pickin' mind. Way too soon and way too crazy. He was not marriage material. No, he would never fall for another woman. Nope. *Just help them, Hagan,* he said to himself unconvincingly. Another addition to *Ripley's Believe it or Not*, Idiot's edition, no doubt. It would read: world's stupidest man.

# Chapter Seventeen

As they walked around the ship, Hagan asked basic questions in an attempt to get to know and understand her better. "Where do you live?"

"Aquanica."

"Where is it located? What ocean?"

"No."

"Do you mean no answer?"

"No—yes."

"Fair enough."

All the passengers stared at Chantara, intrigued. She never realized that a rainbow of colors glimmered all over her body. He couldn't help but notice the people staring and then understood why.

"Let's go in that shop." He bought a garment for her to use as a cover in order to divert everyone's attentions away from her. The clothes he purchased were a little too big, but there was no way to know her size. She accepted the cover not really understanding why but wore it without hesitation. Now we could walk around without people staring, but he didn't know what made him think it would work. Her hair glistened as the sun reflected bursts of colors from her, not on her, and that fairy-tale beauty was too much of a distraction. The magical colors were in no way representative of some sort of skin product, because on her it looked totally natural, which was quite obscure to him.

He noticed how she watched everyone with discomposure, wondering why. Her eyes stared at each person, body slightly moving backward. He also saw her frustration at how she tripped so often, her mouth scrunched together in frustration.

He saw how she scanned the passengers with wide-opened eyes and nervously twiddling her fingertips. It just didn't feel like a good time to ask her about it. Building her trust into a relationship would be slow going. Trust is a biggie, and Hagan was learning a huge, but frustrating lesson in obtaining patience.

"I'm thirsty. Let's sit under that umbrella and order something to drink." *I have to get you out of the sun to keep people from staring.*

"I love."

While they sat by the pool talking, a server walked up and asked for their order.

"Would you like a cola, lemonade or what?" he asked.

"Lemon...ade?"

"You'll love it. We'll take two orders of lemonade, please."

The pretty server smiled and appeared to be flirting with Hagan. He saw how Chantara watched with confusion, not understanding why this girl bothered her. Hagan saw Chantara's pupils constrict when the server bent over and whispered something to him.

"I think it is some type of skin and hair product that she uses, but I don't think there is any such product that could look that natural. It's kind of mysterious," he remarked.

"If you could find out, I would be grateful," the server responded.

"She's sort of private about her life, so I wouldn't get your hopes up."

Chantara sat staring, he noticed. It had to be a misinterpreta tion on his part—or wishful thinking—because it looked suspiciously similar to jealousy. Not marriage material, he scolded himself—again.

Setting the drinks on the table, the server softly touched his shoulder as she walked off, constantly casting a look back at him with a deliberate, flirtatious smile. He debated if she was cognizant of how strongly her body language revealed she was flirting. But he couldn't help himself and smiled as she walked off.

"Chantara. Chantara. Hello."

"What? What wrong?"

"Are you okay? Try the lemonade."

"Mmmm. Good." Then her posture changed and she asked, "You know her?"

"Who?"

"The girl that brought this lemon."

"No. She's just being nice."

"Her want to be your mate, I think."

He busted out with a vigorous laugh. "You are just plain adorable." She cast an awkward look, wrinkling her nose and raising the left side of her mouth slowly.

"This lemon good."

"Yes, this lemonade does taste good," he chuckled.

An older gentleman in a Speedo swimsuit sat down on a chase lounge next to their table and next to Chantara.

"How do you do. My name is James," the man said, extending his hand for her to shake. She wasn't too keen on the idea of touching him, but Hagan encouraged her with confidence, so she placed a hand in his, just barely.

At first he was funny and engaging, making her laugh. Hagan watched her laugh, delighted by those darn charming attributes that spellbound his thoughts constantly. James started asking questions, making her squirm with a discomfort, so he had no choice but to refrain him from asking further questions.

"Is she your wife?"

"No, just a friend."

"What are you waiting for, or are you blind?"

"Never mind."

Hagan's reaction and their facial exchanges caused her to cower, while looking around for the closest escape, he noticed immediately.

"Everything is okay," he assured her, observing her concerned expression. She settled back down.

"Why people look funny? You and me don't."

"What do you mean?" he asked, confused and wondering why these people looked funny to her. They looked perfectly normal to him.

She touched her skin.

"Oh, you're referring to the people with a spectral look?" All the people were white as a ghost or sunburned. He and she were both quite tanned.

Her eyes and nose wrinkled up, indicating she didn't understand.

"Ghostly, white?"

Chantara nodded her head yes.

"You're right. Some of them do have a ghostly appearance," he said with amusement. "That's because they live up north where it gets cold and they don't get out in the sun nearly as much as you and I."

Several sunburned people walked around with their arms extended from their sides, walking in a funny manner. She shook with laughter. "They walk like me," realizing walking normal for her would take some practice.

He couldn't count the times she tripped over her own feet and seemed unstable and inexperienced in walking.

James ordered a chocolate mudslide and her eyes almost popped out of her head.

"What that?"

"A chocolate mudslide. Would you like a sip?"

"Yes," she expressed excitedly.

Hagan was quite concerned about her taking a sip of an alcoholic beverage because of her callow and sweet mannerisms. This could potentially be a bad idea, but he bit his tongue. He certainly didn't want to appear fatherly. Seriously, the feelings he has for her were anything but fatherly, but he felt responsible for her at the same time—and angry with himself for how his never-to-be-in-a-relationship pledge was heading in the wrong direction.

"Just take a sip." His reply was a little sterner than he'd rehearsed in his mind.

"Quit acting like her father. Lighten up and have some fun," James bellowed.

Hagan retorted back with a derisory stare, hoping to intimidate him so he would back off and do nothing to upset her.

"Here, honey, taste this." The look and moan of pure pleasure said it all. She inhaled the aroma, closed her eyes, smiled and let out a soft sigh. "It's delightful, isn't it?" James inquired.

She looked over at Hagan and repeated, "De...light...ful?"

"That means happy, pleasurable, good." She smiled with approval.

James kept encouraging her to take more sips. As Hagan expected, she almost immediately loosened up and started laughing at everything. To Hagan's surprise, she kissed his cheek and rubbed James' arm, becoming affectionate, completely opposite of her usual cautious behavior. Chattering and laughing was so unlike her, from what he could tell earlier, and he couldn't decipher the words that sounded like gobbledygook. Hagan started playing an "Oh, woe is me" tune biting his fingernails.

~

During the time they sat there—must have been hours—James would get up and talk to the server.

"Hello, young lady. My name is James. I've noticed your

interest in that fellow," he said, pointing at Hagan. "I have quite a bit of interest in his friend, so I've come up with a proposition for you."

He offered her a substantial amount of money to lure Hagan away from Chantara so he could trick her into coming to his stateroom with him. Desperately in need of money, she agreed.

"Pay close attention. When you see me casually shake my head yes, keep his attention so I can have some time to lure her away. She is simply titillating. My mouth waters for her."

"Make no mistake, that gorgeous man does the same thing to me."

While relaxing and relieved that James was still gone, Hagan glanced over at Chantara. She was curled up in the chair with hands covering her face, as though she was trying to hide. Was she trembling?

"Chantara, what's wrong?"

"Bad lady. She very bad." He looked around and saw people watching curiously.

"Where is she?"

With a quickness, she removed her hands from her face and pointed to the bar. Then she repositioned her hands over her face. He saw a mild shaking of her body. What could she be scared of?

"Are you talking about the lady with the white lab coat?"

"I think her wearing white clothes. I know not what lab coat is."

"It is like a white, long shirt or jacket."

"Yes, that the bad lady."

"No, no. She must be the ship's physician. She helps people who are sick or hurt."

"No!" she screamed at him, throwing her arms backward.

"People who wear white coat are bad. They hurt people and kill people!" She covered her face up again.

"Chantara. Please remove your hands and look at me." She slowly pulled her hands down but didn't move a muscle. "I don't know what happened to you or what you've seen, but I can tell it was traumatic. You are safe here with me. No one, and I mean no one, will touch you. You have my word." By that time, the woman wearing the lab coat walked back to her office and Chantara calmed down.

After finishing the lemonade, Chantara asked Hagan for a chocolate mudslide.

"It's probably not a good idea."

"Please," she begged tenderly.

He knew it was a bad idea, but she has some sort of supernatural power over him. What else could he do? By this time James had returned and lied back down on the chaise lounge.

He sulked about his decision and replied to Chantara's request. "Okay. I'll be right back, so don't go anywhere. Do you understand?" She nodded. Still on his mind was her reaction to the physician. What could she possibly mean by saying people with white lab coats are bad and kill people? What could have happened to this fairy princess?

"Well, young lady, now that your boring friend is gone," James said, "how about you and I have some fun? I suggest we head to my stateroom for some delightful fun. It will be a blast. Would you accompany me?" He winked with bad intentions plastered all over his face and hummed the song *Afternoon Delight*. Probably due to the alcohol, she was relaxed more than before and didn't notice his intent.

Remembering Hagan's definition of delightful, with broad open eyes and an epic smile, she answered. Yes, pleas...ure...able, good."

James looked over at the server and gave the signal. She quickly walked over to the bar and started engaging in conversation with Hagan. Then she pretended to want to show him something and tugged at his arm to get him to come with her. It was a sincere attempt on her part and the smile on her face revealed as such. Hagan, not wanting to offend her, stuttered in his words to make her understand he needed to return to Chantara. There is no way she would ever survive on her own and probably not be able to find her way back to the cabin. This was bad. Really bad. As he tried glancing in Chantara's direction, the server did everything in her power to keep his attention, even brushing up to him in a way too seductive approach.

Hagan was squiggling to get away from her when he noticed something. The server kept looking in a particular direction. He turned to see what she was looking at and realized it was all a setup for James to coax Chantara to go with him. He scowled. Fists clenched, there was no way he would hit a woman, so instead he offered her a distasteful interpretation of herself.

"You are a despicable human being."

"You're wrong. I want to get to know you—all of you. Come on. Let's go somewhere where we can be alone." The twinkle in her eyes had no influence over him except to be disgusted by her.

Hagan carefully pushed her away and took off running down the corridor to find Chantara.

James looked behind, hearing heavy footsteps, and gasped with fear. Hagan's face was bright red, and he was running way too fast for James to get away. Poor Chantara kept slipping because he was trying to make her run.

"Come on Honey. Let's move faster." James was becoming agitated with her slow movements.

Too late. Hagan ran like the wind. He would never be able to live with himself if she was put in another unsafe position. All the trust she was starting to feel toward him would vanish.

"Chantara, stop!" he yelled. She turned and smiled, clueless to what was about to happen.

"Just where do you think you're taking her?" Hagan growled, pausing beside them.

"For pleasure, delight," she said with a whimsical smile. "Happy. Fun." People in listening range stared with shocked and alarmed expressions.

"I don't think so." He gently took her hand, and she allowed him.

"Come on, man. You heard her. Pleasure. Delightful." Then James, who was white as a ghost, literally, and wrinkled enough to pass for a Shar Pei, waved his hand saying, "You need to get a life and learn how to have fun." Humming turned to grumbling. His evil plan had been discovered and defeated.

"And you need to tipple less." He dare not overreact for her sake. Without much luck he tried but was infuriated with the situation. Trying to hide the anxiousness in his voice so she would remain calm, it seemed to work. She could never know what James' intentions were all about. Distrust in people again was something that would hit her hard and he couldn't allow that to happen to her; not after what she'd been through. He hoped she would trust in him enough to confide very soon. He'd seen James scanning her up and down. It sickened him.

He looked at Chantara's confused face. "I have a better idea. Let me get you something better to drink."

"Yes, delightful."

"And the only delight you will experience." His remark confused her he could tell. Handing her a chocolate vanilla milkshake topped with swirls of whipped cream and chocolate curls, her lips curved up as far as possible.

"This delightful?" Cream around her mouth and smudge on the tip of her nose was so darn endearing.

Tickled by her statement, Hagan smiled affectionately in affirmation.

They walked over behind the ship near the lifeboats and sat in chairs. Seagulls were covering the sky squawking and chirping over the abundant school of fish passing by. Splashing, the ambient sound of waves crashing, were all the nostalgic things that spelled out *home* to Chantara.

Somehow, they managed to carry on a conversation, even though it was difficult for her. They laughed, talked about family and lighthearted subjects. It was so enjoyable for both of them. He realized Jorie had been left alone for an extended amount of time and escorted Chantara back to the stateroom. When they walked in, every snack that he provided to Jorie had been opened and devoured. Wrappers and crumbs were everywhere, blending in as décor. He just shook his head and laughed.

"Would you both accompany me to one of the ship's restaurants this evening?"

After speaking to Jorie, Chantara replied, "Jorie too scared, but I love."

"Well then, I'm going to give you two some alone time and go shopping for a gown and shoes for you to wear. Do you mind if I trace your foot so I get you the right size of shoes?"

"I no mind."

With a sweet romance movie playing on the television, he felt it was safe to leave.

# Chapter Eighteen

The temperature was perfect, with the right amount of a breeze. Hagan had been too caught up in taking care of Chantara to notice before. Taking advantage of some free time, he tried calling Fernando, but he didn't pick up, so he called his friend Kent instead.

"Hello", Hagan said cheerfully.

"Hey, I'm glad you called, but you seem more cheerful than I expected after finding out about the breakup."

"This cruise turned out to be exactly what I needed in order to work through my emotions, and unexpected, I might add."

"How could that happen so quickly? I mean, you and Dani have been together for three years. Are you sure you're okay?"

"Like I said, this is totally unexpected. I was in pretty bad shape when I got on the ship, but the way things are turning out, I couldn't be happier."

"Okay. I've seen enough movies to speculate that this change in you has to do with a woman."

"The last thing I wanted was to have to deal with any woman. I was on one of the upper decks when a storm hit out of nowhere, rocking the ship, and this fairy-tale woman physically slid into me. It was purely accidental—or an act of God. Dani hasn't entered my mind since.

"Kent, you wouldn't believe it. This woman named Chantara is a beautiful, mystical creature.

"Describing her could never be done, because she reminds me of an enchanted princess. She has luminous skin and the most tantalizing lips. There is a sensual aspect to her, but she is as innocent as a babe. Her scent is pure and sweet. When her angelic voice speaks, I get goosebumps. Something is fascinatingly different about her.

"Before you add your two cents, I know you think this is just a rebound reaction, and I have been carefully considering that, but it's not so. She is good, kind, and sweet as candy. I shamefully want to admit to falling in love with her.

"But what I learned from this breakup is that I can't even consider a relationship. This job takes up seventy-five percent of my day. That is unfair to any woman. I would have to find another type of work, and I can't ever imagine that happening. Dani didn't deserve that."

"Didn't you think you were in love with Dani?"

"Of course I did. I now realize I loved Dani but was never in love with her. Maybe that's why it was so difficult for me to work up the nerve to propose. Something just didn't feel right. You know me well enough to know I am way too sensible of a person to plunge into another relationship. I am deeply hurt by what she and Adam did to me, but it all happened for the good. Don't think less of her. I am as much to blame."

"When you're ready, the right relationship will automatically happen for you. Sounds to me like you are either infatuated or deeply in love with this woman. That is terrible how they decided to get into a relationship behind your back. Dani told me you caught them together."

"Is that all? Did she happen to tell you how I found them together?"

"Well, um, no, she didn't."

"I don't know how you would feel about walking in on your best friend and wife engaged in—I can't even say it. That betrayal of how far they went in their attempt to consummate their relationship is just too painful for me to discuss, and on my couch, of all places."

"Wow! She left those tidbits of information out. Gee, man, I am so sorry. I'm in denial. You and Adam—you and Dani—it's so wrong. This is devastating news. How can I help?"

"Thanks, but don't mention this to anybody. My mom doesn't know yet, and the only way to stop her from trying to keep us together will be to tell her all of it. Otherwise, she'll never let it go. You can see how difficult this will be and why I need time to do this right.

"Even though what was done to me is not reconcilable, I am just as much to blame, always putting my job before our relationship. I struggle with that because I ignored it knowingly.

"But, hey, is there any way I could get you to remove that couch out of my apartment? No matter what, memories of that scene will always haunt me."

"You have my word to keep quiet and I will get that couch out tomorrow morning. The key still up inside the piece of wooden plank where you always keep it?"

"Yes, it is. Thanks man. I need to get going."

They hung up the phone.

# Chapter Nineteen

After more than two hours of shopping and a brief nap on a lounger, Hagan walked up to the cabin door and listened. The shower was straining over excessive usage. He could hear a sound of the pipes screeching, like they were warning him that they needed a break. It seemed from the moment he left the cabin until the moment he came back the shower was in constant use. This isn't the first time, either. He knocked and knocked.

"Chantara, are you dressed?"

"No. I love. I love shower."

"I'll leave some bags of clothes on the door handle and be back shortly."

~

Cracking the door open, she grabbed the bags. Jorie wouldn't leave the room, so Hagan bought her a simply adorable pair of pajamas with a design of mermaids, and also a pair for Chantara. You would think they received a treasure chest of gold by the way they reacted. The retail shop had hired a designer to create a line of clothing as a means of advertising the ship's name, *The Merry Mermaid*.

Twirling in circles wearing the loveliest gown and jeweled low-heeled sandals, Chantara felt special and giddy. They laughed and were amazed by the soft, delicate fabric, squishing it between their fingers.

A knock at the door.

She opened it just enough to see who was there. With a smile, Chantara let him in. Every time he looked at her, she took his breath away.

Her cheeks turned a light pink at the way he stared at her. Jorie pulled the blanket over her head as she always did. When she saw it was he, surprisingly, she ran up and hugged him, but ran back quickly to the bed and covered her head. It made him feel good and a small, one-sided smile formed. He asked Chantara if she would allow him to braid her hair. She was fine with it. He had much experience in braiding his sister's hair...and ex.

Chantara sat on the comfortless couch as he dried her hair. "Do you color or highlight your hair?"

"No color."

"It must be the hair products you were using, but that still wouldn't explain all the colors reflecting off of your skin." Then he softly brushed her hair and shaped it into a braid, intertwining a ribbon he'd purchased at the shop throughout the braid that went all the way down past her back. Looking down at her, his eyes examined goosebumps on her skin. Confining her hair in a braid would hopefully detract attention away from the intrigue people had with her.

It's not as though she looked like a Christmas tree. The colors were soft and sparkled naturally, like the sun's reflection on rain-drops. But it was gorgeous and put fairy-tale thoughts into anyone's minds. All the many conversations with people around the ship revealed they held the same opinions.

She wore no makeup. Makeup would be an insult to her perfection.

"Take a look," he said, holding up a mirror.

She put a hand to her mouth and projected a quirky expression. "I love." Jorie had a widespread smile, showing her approval as she peeked out of the blanket.

The gown he bought for her was long sleeved, floor length, with a very low-cut back and fit snugly. The minuscule rhinestones covered every inch of the gown. With her natural glow, it was most fitting. The fabric was soft and had a luxurious feel. The braid hung down the center of the gown's low-cut back. She was the most mystical creature he has ever seen.

"Let me see what I can find for you both to watch while I take a shower." As Hagan flipped through the channels, a picture of *The Little Mermaid* popped up.

"Shellina. Shellina," they both yelled.

"Does that mean you want to watch it?"

"Yes, very much."

"Now that I think about it, a child's movie is perfect for you young-at-heart women." They didn't react to his statement, but watched the screen curiously. It's as though they didn't have television or any such thing in their country. Where could they be from? Outer space?

He turned around and took note of how they both sat back against the pillows with arms wrapped around their knees, chin resting on the knees, gobsmacked over a child's movie.

As he stepped down from the shower to grab a towel, the door opened and Chantara stood there, saying, "I see my friend Sparkles."

Facing an awkward situation, Hagan hurried and wrapped a towel around his body. A suspicion entered his thoughts at that very moment that she had been abducted and sexually abused. Without knowing the story, nobody could say for sure, but the signs were there and recognizable. She stopped and stared at him, slowly stepping backward, but when she saw that he wasn't moving toward her, or attempting some kind of sexual advancement, her demeanor changed to where she no longer seemed scared. Something about her brought out emotions he didn't know existed in himself. Where have they been hiding all these years?

Shockingly, she said, "You pretty," studying his body.

"Thank you. I'll be out in a minute." He rushed her out so he could recapture his control. His feelings for her extended far deeper than sexual desire. He truly cared about her. One wrong move could surely ruin any chance he had with her. What the heck was he thinking? Not marriage material, he kept trying to convince himself.

After the normal ritual, he dressed and walked out of the bathroom. Both women had the blanket pulled up to their terror-filled eyes. All he could see of them were curved brows and squinching eyes. "What's wrong? Chantara, what's wrong?" Him yelling released them from their fearful state of mind.

"Prince Raiatea. He bad. Very bad. He not pretty and nice like you."

"It's not real. You're safe here." He turned the TV off and caught sight of popcorn that covered the bed, sticking out of the inside of the sheets and covering the outside of the blanket. Very fond memories of years gone by came to his mind of his teenage sister having a sleepover. How they slept on top of and covered in popcorn, he couldn't believe. There were indentations from popcorn all over their skin. A smirk appeared on his face.

"Why you smile like that?" Chantara asked with confusion.

"Oh, it's nothing. I just can't get over how precious you two are." She smiled at the way he answered, whether or not she understood, but expressions and the tone in his voice was something she based a lot of her understanding by.

"Do you still feel like getting something to eat?"

She looked him up and down and smiled, not able to express

how handsome he looked in his tuxedo. "You pretty. Yes, we eat. I love."

He threw on his shoes and stood up, pulling some popcorn off her arms. "Jorie, we'll bring back some food for you." She smiled as Chantara used sign language to indicate eating.

"We are scheduled for first seating, so we should get going. Would you be okay with me holding your hand?"

Her charming smile and gentle bobbing of the head gave approval.

His hand grasped hers, and he swore electric shockwaves sizzled through his body. Her hand was flimsy and would fall out if he didn't have a grasp. But at least her expression didn't show she felt revolt at his touch.

As they walked to the restaurant, Hagan felt a sincere, over-powering desire to be alone with her and hold her tightly; shelter her from all harm. You would think all the outbursts would deter him, but he was caught up in some love-struck spell and proud to be escorting Miss Universe, Miss America or Miss somebody. The whole dang world couldn't take their eyes off her. And she's with him. His face beamed with pride.

"Well, hello stranger. Where have you been? I have called you many times. Are you avoiding me?"

"Fernando!" Hagan yelled while shaking his hand, truly happy to see him. "Must be bad reception out here because I've tried calling you, too, and then I got preoccupied."

"Oh! Before I forget, we are hosting our version of a Comic Con in April. Right up your alley, right? You better register quickly because it's already receiving a lot of interest. I'm quite certain of who you'll be coming as."

"Wow! You bet I'm signing up, and no doubt I'll be dressed or mostly undressed as my favorite comic book character, green paint and all." He tilted his head up in thought, resting his index finger on his lips. "For some odd reason, I think I'd rather dress up as my new favorite, since I spend all my time in water." How curious his statement hit him.

Many times in the past, he'd come to Comic Con without a shirt and his body painted green. Blond hair and all, he'd won first prize. That was so much fun.

"Fernando, please meet Chantara."

"She's with you?" His eyes bulged and his mouth dropped open. "Pleased to meet you," he said as he shook her hand. Then he snapped his hand back and produced a wicked expression of wonderment. "I just felt an unbelievable electric shock. It was strange, but seriously pleasurable. Hold on a minute. There is talk all over the ship about this woman who is too beautiful to be real. To put it into context: 'the fairest one of all'."

"There is definitely something magical about her," Hagan commented.

"I'm being paged, so I need to run. Great to meet you and good job, man," he said to Hagan with a thumbs up gesture.

"He look like yummy choc ice cream."

Hagan knew she meant to say *chocolate*. Stupidly jealous of her attraction to Fernando, he replied to the statement as a jealous schoolboy, ashamed about his reaction. "Yeah, that's the same thing everyone says about him."

*I wonder what she thinks of me. Not going to ask. That would be presumptuous of me.* They proceeded to the restaurant. After ordering dinner, she was preoccupied with the elegant decor. The chandeliers were exquisite and sparkled like the sunbeams on the blue ocean and the stars in the sky. Of course, and rightfully so, all eyes were on her. The server brought their meal, and she started eating before he could set the plate on the table. All the aromas in the room teased him, like they were swirling around his nose, edging him to follow. He was starved, obviously.

"Let me get out of your way. I can see you're quite hungry."

"Thanks, sir," Hagan said, watching her eagerness.

He didn't realize just how famished he was. *Please, let this dinner be relaxing. Please, please,* he pleaded to the invisible audience of pretend cruise guardians. He wanted everything to be perfect. It's a silly notion, but being such a comic book nerd, somehow he managed to include comic book characters in everything.

"I love."

She loves the food or me?

"You love what?"

"This food so good."

"Oh, I'm glad you like it," he lied through his teeth in an unenthusiastic reply. Then they resorted to small talk. He very much wanted to get to know her. Why everything she sees, eats, touches, and smells was all new to her. Believe it or not, he had gobbled up all of his food. Would anyone think him barbaric if he licked the plate? His fist automatically hit his head.

"Do you know how to get to your home?"

"Yes, I find home."

"Home for me is on Fort Myers Beach in Southwest Florida. My friend, Fernando, works with this new cruise line that leaves from Sanibel." He couldn't help but notice a smile form on her lips when he mentioned Fernando. He was disgusted with his reaction, and almost yelled out to himself to grow up.

A small boy and girl walked by. She waved and smiled at the children. "Splish and Splash," she remarked enthusiastically.

"Excuse me. I don't understand."

"My sister, Shellina, childs.

"Your sister has children?" She nodded yes, smiling with fond thoughts.

"Are you saying she named them Splish and Splash?"

"They love to splish and splash in water. They don't stop and my sister gets angry, but not much."

"Is that their real names?"

"No. Sereia and Taras."

"I get it. Splish and Splash are their nicknames." It was apparent by her expression that she didn't understand what nicknames meant, so she just nodded yes.

"Would you mind speaking in your language for me? How about say the words, I love you." *Come on, Hagan,* he scolded himself mentally.

The language was indiscernible, but eloquent and impassioned, and the tone in her voice was angelic and soothing. Why is it everything she does or says and her looks seem different from...well, from humans?

Another server walked up to the table next to us and placed the plates on the table in front of the guests. He couldn't help but observe how Chantara's eyes widened and a strange, black film glazed over her eyes. Her insouciant disposition changed immediately to a crazed, angry look.

"My friend Sparkles," she said, distraught. She bit her index finger nervously. She was becoming disturbed and unglued. He looked over and saw a full-size fish on the plate and remembered how she ran into the bathroom yelling the words, "I see my friend Sparkles." Realizing Sparkles was the name she gave a fish on *The Little Mermaid* movie, he carefully pulled her from the table and asked the server to send their food to the stateroom and to include the take-out order for Jorie that was ordered previously. They hurried out of the restaurant as the guests watched with concern and curiosity. By this time, she was sobbing uncontrollably.

*Gee, thanks for nothing, you good for nothing cruise guardians.*

She bent over, propping her hands on her knees and wept from the heart. Wet spots formed down her dress because she cried so hard.

Now back inside the stateroom, we ate in the cabin with episodes of *I Love Lucy* playing on the television set—a well needed distraction.

It was important to keep them safe, and they needed to understand that their safety always comes first with him.

Room service arrived again.

"What this?" Chantara asked, eager to taste, squirming in her seat. Jorie was hiding her head under the blanket. The porter stared at her with concern on his face while setting the sundaes on the table. Hagan explained that she is very shy.

"Hot fudge sundaes with marshmallow cream. Try it."

When the porter left the room, Jorie came out of hiding and swooned over the enticing look of the sundae.

They smiled and looked at each other with a face full of pleasure and satisfaction. I couldn't help but wonder, as I observed Chantara, how she was so deprived of everything. One would have to conclude she had been confined to a cage her whole life and has no knowledge about anything.

Still lost in thought: *She must have been so abused that it had affected her mentally. Her pets must have been the only source of affection. That's why she reacted so distraught at the sight of the fish on the plate. She reminds me somewhat of that woman, Sybil, with sixteen schizophrenic personalities, who had the same childlike qualities as Chantara and Jorie.*

That thought bothered him greatly. Just because they are from a different country that is probably very poor and doesn't have any of the spectacular foods, luxuries, and fun that we take for granted, doesn't make them ignorant. He refused to believe that and vowed to find out what had happened to them. Somebody has to stop those evil men who are hunting her.

While watching the television, reruns of *Hercules and the Legendary Journeys* came on the channel. Chantara and Jorie gasped, whispering back and forth and giggling.

"I take it you like Kevin Sorbo?" What's he got that I don't have, he wanted to say.

"He pretty and so strong. Good man. See how he help people and fight bad guys so they no hurt people. That man big and strong like my people."

"Well, you know this show isn't real. The monsters aren't real and the fighting isn't real." They both looked at him like he was off his rocker.

A battle broke out, and the scene shook the women up. In a meek manner, they screamed and held onto each other.

"Don't be scared. It's not real. Watch." He pretended to punch himself and fall on the floor. They looked at him like he was one marble short of being cuckoo. "See," he said. "I pretended to punch myself, just like they're doing on the show." *Do these two women not know the difference between television and reality?* "Look, I'll turn the TV off."

As he reached for the remote, they both screamed, "No!"

He dropped the remote and put his hands up in surrender. "Okay, have it your way."

As the show progressed, Iolaus came into the picture. They started laughing.

"What's so funny?" he asked.

"Why that boy fighting? He not big enough to fight. Boys don't fight until they grow up big and strong."

"Well, not everyone is big like Kevin Sorbo. He may be smaller, but he is strong and fearless. Size has nothing to do with being brave."

"Where I live, the men are all big and strong. No small men."

"How can that be? I have been all over the world and have never seen a country with one-size-fits all men." She scrunched up her nose and mouth, not able to comprehend what he said.

"You shouldn't make fun of a man's size. Size has nothing to do with a man's strength or courage, like this guy."

"I no make fun of him. He pretty, and very strong. I just not understand that you people have dif...ferent sizes of men. You big and strong like my people."

Well, that remark boosted his ego. "Really? You mean it?" His attitude perked right up.

"But, I have to ask, are you telling me that all the men in your country are huge and strong; no smaller-sized men?"

"No, none. They all big and strong, except for childs. That just the way it is in my people."

"My curiosity is piqued. Do you think I could visit your country?"

"Vis...it? What that?"

"Meet your people. Come to where you live."

"Oh, no! My people not let you vis...it."

"How would you and Jorie like to go and sit by the lifeboats, where we met? We could look at the ocean and just talk."

Chantara explained what he said to Jorie. Feeling a lot safer than she did previously, Jorie smiled widely with a shake of her head to mean yes. "We love," Chantara replied with enthusiasm.

# Chapter Twenty

They all took turns changing into leisurely clothing, except Jorie, who was already in her PJ's, and then walked to their spot. It never failed. Men would surround the women, making them very uncomfortable, almost to the point of panicking. They weren't used to all of the attention or they received the wrong kind of attention. Except for him, he realized, they were skeptical of all men. That thought put a smile on his face. He needed to get them out of here and fast. They made it to their spot and sat down.

As they stood at the rail, giggles and excitement traveled from their direction. Then splashing from below could be heard, and they both waved to the ocean. He got up to see what was going on and Chantara made a very, very, unusual sound. There was no way to describe it. No more splashing and giggling. Whatever was going on had disappeared, like she sent a message to whatever it was to leave. They were acting funny, looking at me like they hoped I didn't see what was going on. Chantara kept dropping her head downward trying to avoid eye contact.

Comfy and relaxed in our chaise lounges, a child screamed nearby. He could tell by the screaming and crying that the child was unhappy about something; most certainly not getting his or her way. Chantara covered her ears and squeezed her eyes tight together.

"Save child. Don't let them kill child. Please, save child. No bad people hurt anymore childs." Her ears were covered and eyes were closed so tight that you'd swear they were glued together. Hagan saw a noticeable trembling, and her arms were wrapped around herself, almost in a fetal position, and the crying was uncontrollable. The child stirred up some type of bad memory; something undoubtedly horrific. She bent over in more tormented, agonizing sobs. It confounded him, broke his spirit, and a trail of tears streamed down his face. What had this poor thing seen?

Not expecting it, she jumped up in rage and started to run toward the crying child.

"Chantara, stop. I'll check it out. You stay here. Everything's going to be fine. Please sit and wait for me. I promise nothing bad is happening to the child."

She sat down, but gut-wrenching tears and sobs kept coming. In a few minutes, he returned, purposely walking up calmly to her.

"The child is fine. He was upset with his parents because they wouldn't let him have candy. Candy is not good for children, but good for us," he expressed with a wide smile. Hagan unfolded his hands that revealed a variety of chocolate candies. They each took a bite and chewed, trying to identify the taste. It appeared their thoughts floated to a heavenly realm of pure bliss. As happy as the chocolate seemed to make the women feel, Chantara still had a serious case of the sniffles. It broke his heart. What could have happened to this poor angel?

"You've had chocolate before, right?"

They both shook their heads no and Chantara answered. "No, never. It the yummiest thing I ever eat." It seemed like Jorie was understanding our language a little more. They ate every piece of candy and held each other's hands, gently bopping up and down in flavortopia, my invented word for a utopia of divine-inspired flavors. Maybe now would be a good time to confront her about the tears; there were so many tears she shed that surely her tear ducts had to be dried up.

And that's another thing. It is just simply weird, but her tears were a work of art. There is a swirl of color in her tears. It is so beautiful, even though it is sad, but how is there color in her tears? He has no logical explanation. As "Spock" would say, "Fascinating."

"Is there any way you could tell me why it upset you so much to hear that child cry?"

"No. No talk." She covered her mouth with her hands and cried again, almost violently, gasping for breath between the sobs, as though she couldn't catch her breath before the next round of sobs began.

Hagan gently pulled her into his arms, slowly and as carefully as possible, while she cried. This scene was just too much for even a tough and rugged, macho man. He cried with her and Jorie held her hand in emotional despair. To be honest, he was second guessing if he wanted to find out what happened to them and to the children. He felt no one could come up with a word to describe what was causing her emotional distress. That overpowering feeling, again.

To be honest, he wasn't a fan of *feeling*. It was just too nerve-wracking and hit below the belt.

Everyone finally relaxed, and he needed to change his thoughts before transforming into, you guessed it, his one and only angry, green friend and search for those monsters. They decided to head back to the stateroom and figure out what they could do. Hagan had some brochures that would provide information of all the activities.

On their way, a man walked past them, then stopped dead in his tracks like he'd been shot with a freeze gun. Hagan saw everything through the eyes of a comic book character, his only source of imagination—until now. Hagan stopped to make sure he was all right. It looked like another one of his comic-book heroes shot him with paralyzing rays. He slowly walked up to us with his eyes glued to Jorie.

"How...how...how do you do?" He could barely formulate into words. He extended his hand for her to shake. She, of course, hid behind Chantara. This guy was determined to meet her and approached her again. Hagan had to step in.

"Hey, you need to step back. These women aren't from around here and have had very bad experiences with people. They trust no one. If you go near her, I'm sorry to say I will have to take action, and I don't wish to do that. This isn't a joke or a threat. I'm serious."

"I'm so sorry. I would never do anything improper. It just struck me hard that I have never seen women as beautiful and enchanting as these two are. Are force fields real? Because I swear it feels as though I am physically being pulled by some magnetic force to her. It is the most bizarre and perplexing thing that has ever happened to me in my life." His head shook as he gazed downward.

"Look, I get it more than you think," Hagan replied. "I have ended up as their personal bodyguard, it seems, but I love spending all my time with them. They're not up to meeting people, so please don't make this worse than it already is for them."

"I understand," he said and walked off, glancing back at Jorie now and then. It was like finding a treasure chest but not able to open nor get near it.

# Chapter Twenty-One

They relaxed in the stateroom before heading out to what most likely would be the next disaster. Talk about being an optimist, but that's a failure he is proud to admit to at this point. He pulled out some brochures, and they searched for something that would seem fun to do. They changed into some casual clothes and passed a club. The band was playing the song "Wild Thing." The two women stopped and watched with amazement at the people dancing. Their bodies started swaying. Hagan decided to demonstrate a salsa dance for them, thinking it was his forte when it came to dancing. Not the reaction he had hoped for. They busted up laughing, covering their mouths with their hands and even had tears forming in their eyes from laughing so hard. Talk about giving someone a complex, so obviously he stopped. Now that his feelings were officially hurt, he let it pass. At least he got them to laugh.

"Nice moves," a beautiful woman commented to him on her way into the club. Shoo, that changed his expression and he felt better about his moves.

"Let's go in and dance," he suggested.

They both crumpled up their faces, not understanding what dance meant.

"Come on. I'll show you. Just move your bodies to the music."

It was hysterical at first. Still finding it difficult to keep their balance, they slipped a few times, but he was able to catch them. And then it was as though they started dancing in such rhythm, that it actually felt as though they were the rhythm. Very, very weird and almost sensual to watch. The laughing and fun was therapeutic for them, and for Hagan.

Next they walked further and a child's game room with tire gliders, slides, bounce houses, video games, obstacle courses and you name it came into view. Needless to say, they played for hours. Not just them, but the gentleman enamored by Jorie joined in on the fun. It wasn't easy getting Jorie to feel comfortable around anyone but Hagan, but she finally did as long as he didn't get too close.

Hagan introduced himself. "I guess we should be on first-name basis," he said, extending his hand.

"My name is Drake Evans. I can't quit thinking about her. Do they have magical powers? This is just nuts the effect she has had on me with just one look at her."

"You noticed that, too, huh? I have no answer. Zilch. Absolutely none," he said while shaking his hand.

"Nice to meet the man who has everything. Am I right or am I right?"

"No, you're not right. I'm just helping to take care of them, protect them. You know, I'm really glad to have someone who understands the magnitude of my situation."

He laughed casually at the remark while his eyes were glued to Jorie.

Jorie's reaction to Drake was still on the timid side. That was obvious, as she kept hiding behind Chantara and looking at him with wide, untrusting eyes. He looked like some lovesick puppy, and when she accidentally touched his hand, electric sensations erupted throughout his body as he shuddered. He looked at Hagan with questions, searching for answers. Hagan knew those questions very well and couldn't begin to explain any of it.

After total exhaustion—well, for Hagan and Drake anyway—they went to the buffet bar and filled their plates with pasta, fruit, veggies, and a ton of desserts and sat down to a well-deserved pig out. Before entering the buffet line, he whispered to Drake to dare not take any kind of meat. He purposely kept the women away from any of it. Even though Jorie could not communicate, just being near her and seeing that childlike smile was all Drake needed. We said our goodbyes to Drake, grabbed some cups of hot chocolate with gobs of whipped cream and chocolate curls, just the way these two angels like it, and headed to the stateroom.

"I have another idea. Let's take some blankets and pillows and sit out near the lifeboats."

"Yes, I love," Chantara said.

Hagan proceeded with small talk. "I don't know if I told you this but I'm an oceanographer and work a lot in these waters. That means I study the ocean and help take care of it and all the sea animals in it. I care about them."

Eyes and mouth revealed her shock as she pushed herself upward, as though a memory came into her mind, and she replied, "I know you."

"What you mean is you have seen me working?"

"You save my seal friend, Slickers."

"I have saved some seals, yes."

He sat back and watched her. It was amazing how this grown woman had all the traits of a child. Even the names she chose for her pets seemed simple, a name his nieces would have given to their pets. His heart and mind were teasing him with the perception that he was deeply in love with her—head over heels in love—and he couldn't suppress those thoughts.

They couldn't get enough of the smells and sounds of the

ocean. Hagan watched as they appeared to be surveying the water intently for someone; something. They were always doing this.

"We'll dock at Barbados tomorrow. What are your plans?" he asked while staring out over the ocean.

"We go home."

"Is your home near that island?"

She thought about how to answer, forming a befuddled look that indicated she was trying to explain that it is not her home. "Not much."

"Will I ever see you again?"

"I no think so."

"Please think about it. I don't want our time together to end."

"I think."

"Do you believe in love at first sight?"

"No. I no think so."

"Why not?"

"A mate is given to my people.

"Arranged marriages, you mean?"

"Yes—no—I know not." She didn't understand or didn't know how to explain.

"Do you have someone at home?"

"Marin, but no more," she replied with sadness as her eyes teared up and her head drooped. "Jorie has Tydal," she commented quietly with a sadness to her voice.

"Will your mother and father make you marry someone?"

"No. No. We love our mates. Jorie almost ready to be Tydal's mate."

"Could you love me?"

"Yes—no. You not my people."

"Did you love Marin? What happened to him?"

"Yes, I love." She was hesitant to answer any more questions. "No more questions."

He went too far, asking too many personal questions, and she withdrew from conversation. "Let's go back to the room and I'll find something for you to watch while I run some errands."

Hagan needed some time to himself to think things through. Frustration of not being able to break through her emotional wall and get her to fall in love with him—he didn't even know where that came from. He is not marriage material! It all was ruining his mood, especially since he was in denial about his true feelings toward her and this would be their last night together. They need to depart in the best of terms, even if she decides not to see him ever again. That is a heartbreaking thought. He practically ran out of the room.

His melancholy and angry mood was in a battle to claim his soul. There was no way to know which was winning, but he felt his green friend tugging at his nerves, dying to make an appearance. Maybe he'd seek psychiatric help when he got home—or better yet, make an appointment with his pastor. He always had a way of helping him work through tough and emotional problems.

So he walked into a shop and noticed immediately some bath products. Mentally, he thought, he was looking for a fight and this poor clerk was right in his destructive path. His mind replayed these commercials that claimed soaking in a tub using bath products would make all our troubles go away. He wondered if this false advertising ever resulted in a lawsuit. He was being stupid just looking for someone to take his frustration out on.

"I think I'll just give the clerk a piece of my mind for assisting these filthy, rich monopolies in stealing our money under false pretenses," he mumbled under his breath. As his feet swished heavily back and forth on the way to the register, a display of comic books caught his attention. He had to stop and check it out.

"No way *Jose*. How did I miss these two issues?" He grabbed some and threw them into his basket. "Now this is what will relieve tension and stress in our lives." He was glad for the distraction because this clerk didn't deserve Hagan's intention of going off on him. Shaking his head at himself, he approached the clerk in a cheerful manner instead.

"Unbelievable," the clerk remarked with explosive interest while looking back and forth to the comic books and then to Hagan.

"I was thinking the same thing. How is it I never saw these issues before?"

"No. That's not what I was thinking. I was thinking how crazy it is that you look just like him. The spitting image." He was pointing to *Aquaman*.

"Let me look at that," he said, feeling mighty good about himself at the moment. "Wow! He really does look like me or me him. *Aquaman* belongs to *DC Comics,* created by Paul Norris and Mort Weisinger, some valuable trivia information. Geniuses," he couldn't resist sharing.

"You could have been the model they drew him from."

"It would seem so. Thanks, man." This perked up his mood.

When he returned to the stateroom, he could hear the shower running again. What is their obsession with the shower? Maybe it's some kind of cleansing therapy to help deal with the past abuse.

After knocking on the door fifty times—total exaggeration—Chantara opened the door. Her whole demeanor had changed and the charming smile welcomed him inside. That's all it took to feel happy—well and looking like this merman. Looks never played a role in his mind before, but at this point, he was looking for anything to grab her interest.

Since they were in their pajamas, he asked, "How about we grab some blankets and pillows and go sit on the deck in our favorite spot?

"I love," she replied happily. "What that?"

"Comic books." She looked carefully at them and let out a meek gasp as she snapped a hand to her mouth. "That you?"

"No, but I was told it looks like me." His smile was so wide, all his teeth appeared.

"Who is this man if he not you?"

"He was just made up for a comic book series. It's not me, really."

"I like him." He smiled again as his ego was being stroked mentally.

"Sometimes I feel like him the way I love being in the water. Maybe he'll become my new comic book hero." She didn't know how to respond, obviously, and looked at him curiously.

*Off unto another disaster*, he couldn't help but think, and what's strange about that is he didn't even care.

# Chapter Twenty-Two

They listened to the calming waves of the ocean splash gently against the ship, making an oceanic melody. The stars sparkled brilliantly and those magnificent array of colors still reflected from her. He could sit here forever watching her. She hummed a tune he was not familiar with, and it sounded like she should be in a heavenly choir. He broke the silence by telling her a joke.

"I have a joke."

"What joke?"

"It will make you laugh."

Her countenance lifted. "I like to laugh."

"Here goes. Why did the fish blush?"

A shrug of the shoulders signified she didn't know the answer.

"Because it saw the ocean's bottom."

The continuous laughter was therapeutic to where she almost cried. It's been a really long time since she laughed like she was doing after hearing a dippy joke and in the way she did on the child's playground area. It felt good to see her laugh. The laugh had a joyful, mild, but curious connotation to it. Sort of like a dolphin, but much sweeter and so much more adorable.

"That make me laugh. I like you."

"I like you, too." *More than you'll ever know*. "It's getting late. We should get some sleep. You and Jorie can sleep in my bed, and I'll sleep on the couch."

"No, sleep here."

"Why not? We already have pillows and blankets and we're dressed in loungewear, plus Jorie is already sleeping in the lifeboat. I peeked in to check on her."

Thinking back to last night, rubbing his neck from the pain he woke up with, he realized the discomforting couch wouldn't be any better.

The song, *Feelings*, that had started his whole new adventure in life, played throughout the sound system. It has such a soft and alluring melody, he couldn't resist, so he extended his hand to her. "Would you please dance with me?"

At first, her face appeared to have a pinkish tint and her eyes looked down to the floor. Then she raised her eyes and looked into his, extending her hand slowly and taking his hand while smiling in an adorable, shy manner. He carefully pulled her up close and they swirled back and forth to the song. Her scent was naturally alluring and calming, both at the same time. As they swayed and swirled to the music, they ended up in an area where the moonbeams shined on them like sun rays. Her eyes sparkled and the moonlight naturally captured her glow. The moment was magical. They gazed into each other's eyes. Staring at each other, it was undeniable, he thought, positive that flutters captured her mind, body and soul just like his.

He couldn't resist any longer and softly brushed her hair away from her cheek, and electric shock waves traveled throughout his body. As he lovingly stared into her eyes and with the softest touch possible, he very tenderly caressed her exotic skin and luscious lips. In a whisper, he begged her, "Please, may I kiss you? I won't do anything but kiss you. Please," he pleaded. The invisible force trying to unite them in passion was enigmatic.

She melted in his arms. "Yes, I love."

Their lips touched and sensations burst out like a volcanic eruption. He begged her to allow him to kiss her longer. She accepted without any qualms with a welcoming, almost begging warmth. He kissed her delicately, parting her mouth open with his tongue. The kiss was gentle but desire built, soon seeking some sort of release. They both felt the heat and connection. Hagan wasn't referring to lust or sexual attraction, but mind, body, and soul attraction. He had never felt this kind of passion kissing any woman—a kiss that would follow him throughout eternity. It felt so right and so powerful between them.

The song ended, and he knew for her sake to pull away before she felt uncomfortable. For some reason, they continued to twirl to the sounds of the ocean. She was, no doubt, a world-class twirler. He led her back to the chairs, and she held onto that dreamy look in her eyes, claiming his hands.

Wouldn't you just know it? Horrifying screams traveled to us from the other end of the ship. He jumped up and told Chantara to check on Jorie while he went to see what was going on. A woman was leaning over the ship's rail screaming with a look as though she was about to pass out.

"What happened?" he yelled.

Sliding down to the deck floor, staring in a daze, she could barely say the words. "My son fell into the ocean. I turned to look at something, and I heard him yell as he fell over. My husband ran to find someone to stop the ship. I'll never see him again."

She appeared to be going into shock. Hagan scoured the ocean for the boy. "How old is he?" he asked, like that question would matter at this point, but he needed to distract her.

"He's thirteen. I don't guess it matters that he is a good swimmer."

Chantara came up behind him and put her hand on the woman's shoulder and amazingly calmed her instantly, but more screams were yelled.

"Sharks. There are sharks all around."

"I help you, son," Chantara said nimbly. "I swim good."

"But the sharks will kill you. They...they probably kil"—and she couldn't force herself to finish the sentence.

"Sharks no hurt me. I be fine. I go now."

She stood up on the ledge and Hagan panicked.

"Chantara, don't jump. You'll never find him and you'll never be found. Please don't do it," he begged, almost hyperventilating.

With the sweetest, most angelic smile, she said, "I be fine. No worries," and she dived into the ocean.

Hagan couldn't think. His chest was heavy and he began to perspire. "What do I do? What do I do?" Silently, he prayed to God to not take her from him and to save the boy. Should he jump in the water or what? Taking his shoes off, and leaving his cellphone on a chair, he started to climb up onto the rail when someone grabbed his wrist. His eyes looked wildly to see who held him and was shocked to see Jorie standing there.

"No worries. She be fine." She actually spoke in English, but shattered English.

"Chantara is down there...with sharks!" he exclaimed with a crazed expression. He felt such fear at that moment, but Jorie continued to gently tug at his wrist, trying to coax him down.

"She be fine. No worry."

A woman yelled, "Look! Someone is down there with the boy."

The ship had shined a spotlight down onto the water and he could see Chantara swimming with the boy who appeared unconscious; or worse, dead. Right in the middle of all of those sharks. Like, right out of some Sci-Fi film, the sharks turned and swam off, as though they were given orders to retreat.

By this time, news had traveled throughout the ship, and passengers and crew staff alike were watching the rescue; gasps and applauds roared through the air. Picture after picture was snapped.

The lifeboat had been lowered and on course to pick up Chantara and the boy. The crew pulled the boy into the lifeboat, and once in it, the crew proceeded to revive the boy. The lifeboat was rocking back and forth over the waves. Chantara gently moved the staff out of the way and conducted the lifesaving technique herself.

Hagan couldn't move a muscle and stood frozen and baffled at what he saw. "Who is this woman?" he couldn't help but whisper to himself. Those same words were heard throughout the ship. Her techniques were different from what he had learned. He looked over at Jorie and her adoring smile lifted his spirits. He became emotional and hugged her in gratitude; shockingly, like someone performed CPR on him. She wasn't the least bit uncomfortable with his gesture. At this point, he took advantage and softly kissed her cheek.

The next thing he heard was the crowd applauding and he saw the boy coughing. Chantara looked up at him and he blew her a kiss and propped his elbow on the railing to support his heavy head filled with relief. And frustratingly, he felt like sobbing. What was wrong with him?

"What is going on—really?" Hagan struggled with his mental capacity. Everything he ever believed in and trusted, being around Chantara, had thrown that rule book right out the window. Now, he was a firm believer in *having a feeling about something*. How would he ever redeem himself with the team? Passengers would have videos of the whole scene to back up these feelings. Facts.

Now on deck, the mother ran to her son and squeezed him tightly. He pleaded with her to let go of him so he could breathe. Then the mother and son came over to Chantara, tearfully thanking and hugging her with a wholehearted gratitude. "How can I thank you? What can I do to show my gratitude to you for saving my son?" Tears poured down the woman's face while holding onto Chantara's hands. The scene was downright heartwarming.

Hagan heard a lot of commotion and looked in the direction where it came from. Someone was pushing through the crowd. Of all the people he didn't want to run into, Curious Christine and her band of merry cameramen and women forcefully pushed their way to the mother and boy. This was bad—really bad. She won't stop at anything to get a story. People like that suck the life out of something so intimate and personal. He knew her enough to realize this wasn't some humanitarian feel-good story. Fame and fortune were the underlying factors; that much he discovered through experience being interviewed by her more times than he cared to admit.

"Chantara, take Jorie and hide in a lifeboat until I come and get you. Hurry!" he whispered adamantly. She couldn't discern the urgency in his voice, it was evident. "I'll meet up with you soon. These people are going to surround you and take pictures and question you unmercifully. Please go to the lifeboats and hide."

He changed his tone to keep from upsetting them. The mob was headed their way and they ran for their lives, uncomfortable with the attention they would receive. There was no way they could withstand a mob of people pushing into them, cackling like chickens because of the excitement in witnessing the most incredible rescue of their lifetime or in person, anyway.

"Christine, how nice to see you again," Hagan lied through his teeth, but she was well aware of that.

"Hagan Bennett, I should have known you'd be involved in something like this."

"I have no idea what you're talking about."

"Please, we both know I'll find out the truth. My sources tell me this woman was with you. Girlfriend? Acquaintance? Bystander?" Her face with a shaking of her head, shrugged shoulders and extended hands said, without speaking a word, *well, what's the story?*

"Speak or forever hold your peace."

"I'm not getting the connection, and sorry to say, I have no story for you. Do not follow me, or I will ask the captain to restrain you and your crew. Do not, and I repeat, do not follow me."

"Do you really think it's fair to not give this woman the opportunity to tell her story and be honored by the public for her courageous act? Who the heck is she and how could she survive those shark-infested waters? Now, that's a mystery and a true humanitarian story. By the way, how is it you look even more scrumptious than you did before? I could eat you right up, you hunk of man, you."

"I'm quite certain you are aware of the phrase, 'Flattery will get you nowhere'."

"As you wish, my love."

He cringed at that remark. She just didn't do it for him. She was very pretty, but selfish and pushy.

"Okay team, 'divide and conquer'. Someone always knows something." She winked and turned around heading back in the direction of the crowd.

Talk about no shame; she made it clear many times that she wanted them to connect physically, no matter how repulsed he acted to her seductive gestures. Ugh! The thought was incomprehensible, but he guessed some guys fell for that stratagem.

Passengers were getting replies and phone calls regarding their social media downloads with photos of the rescue event. News reporters, scientists, you name it, were all urgent to get the first interview. Major news outlets were negotiating for the hugest story of the year.

Hagan took off in a different direction and to different levels of the ship to steer people away from Chantara and Jorie. He would turn around just in time to spot some people secretly following him, like they were on some type of spy mission shadowing their suspect.

He was dumbfounded in their amateur attempt.

"Tom Cruise, you're not folks." They blushed and returned in the direction from where they came. In about fifteen minutes, after dressing in all black to blend into the dark of night, he headed back to find Chantara and Jorie.

They sat for a few minutes when an announcement blasted through the speakers: "Ladies and gentlemen, please help yourselves to our very own ship's creation cocktail called *The Merry Mermaid* in honor of the woman who courageously dived into the ocean to save the boy. I would be pleased if this woman would join me at the captain's table for a toast. By the way, the flavor of this cocktail is unlike anything you've ever tasted and is as enchanting as the name given to it. Please, everyone, join us if you can."

"Can we taste?" Chantara asked.

"I'm sorry, but that mob of people will never leave you alone. They will follow you wherever you go. Your safety will be compromised. You don't want the abductors to find you, do you?"

She fought for breath at the terror of the possibility and grabbed his arm for protection.

"It's okay. No one knows where you are or who you are. You're safe. But I have questions. Just how did you survive in that water? I know how destructive water density currents can be and how they can drag you under for miles. In all our deep dives, we begin the dive with a safety line hooked to our dive suits. We would never attempt to dive without it until we are certain it is safe. You were not in safe conditions. How did you find that boy and how did you survive the currents and sharks? It's not humanly possible."

Her defense wall was up. "I swim good."

"That's not a good enough answer. How and what made those sharks leave?" His voice was restrained.

"I know not."

"You said when you are stronger, you will swim for your home. From what I just saw, you should be able to swim that far now. Am I correct?"

"Almost. Jorie too weak yet, plus my family is searching for us. When they find us, we will swim home."

"Are they coming by boat?"

Like his statement was silly, she shook her head. "No. They swim."

"Of course they do."

He rubbed his forehead in frustration. Of course, he knew from past experience not to push her into answering a question she wasn't comfortable with. "I'll drop the questions for now, but I need you to provide me some answers soon." As if this wasn't enough excitement...

# Chapter Twenty-Three

A lone again. They bathed in the serene beauty and atmospheric sounds combined with ocean waves smashing softly against the ship—an orchestra of God's creation conducted by His own hands. That moment was cut short, as normal, the way things seem to happen sporadically on this cruise. An emergency alert message from the captain blasted through the sound system with an urgency. Hagan couldn't help but wonder. *If you happened to be sleeping like a baby—and why is it we refer to a good sleep as 'I slept like a baby'? We all know that babies wake up every three to four hours. Anyway, too bad for you lucky people sleeping soundly. Prepare yourself for what lies ahead. Leviathan arises from the depths of the sea to devour your children and destroy the ship. Man your battle stations and prepare your weapons.*

All kidding aside, his mind needed some form of distraction before undertaking an earth-shattering disaster like a voyage with *The Chronicles of Narnia: Prince Caspian.*

"Passengers, embrace yourselves and take cover—quickly! It seems we are heading straight into another storm that arose out of nowhere. Take shelter immediately!"

The winds began to pick up and now howling a war cry, it

seemed, to surrender the ship or die. Waves picked up strength and the king of the sea was showing his fury because they entered into his restricted waters, his personal space, no doubt. The waves splashed over the side of the ship, and it caused a chill to flow through his veins. Hagen embraced himself, shivering. The ship rocked back and forth violently. Could they be in a hurricane? His chair flipped and he found himself grasping for something to hold onto.

"Chantara, Jorie, we need to find shelter. Now!"

He admitted to being terrified. The wind tore planks of wood off the ship.

"Chantara," he screamed because he couldn't see through the torrential rain and hear because of the howling winds. He pondered with fearful eyes. *All we need now are rogue waves, meaning that sarcastically.* She put her hand on his wrist, and he tried to focus on what she was saying.

"I be right back. No worry. We be safe."

"No! Do not leave me! We need to seek shelter immediately. We cannot survive this rampaging storm."

"No worry. I be back."

She grabbed Jorie and headed down to the other side of the ship. He pulled himself up, holding onto the railing but found it hard to keep his balance because of the hurricane-force winds—at least that's the way it felt to him—and imagining how difficult it must be for them with the problem they already have losing their balance. He was overwrought with complete and unequivocal terror. As strong as he was, how could those two women force their way through this storm and where were they going? His hair was completely standing out straight away from his face, being windblown.

There was only one choice: be a man and find them or wallow in patheticness. He remembered his Uncle David always saying, "You put the 'ic' in 'pathetic.'" If he hadn't been frightened, that memory certainly would have made him chuckle. He had his own dictionary of made-up words, like "patheticness".

Time for one of his comic book characters to emerge and send the imaginary flashing help signal. His personal favorite: Hero Hagan came to mind, cape and all. "This is it.

Bring out your good ole friend, Mr. Courageous." He made his appearance and Hagan courageously moved with great difficulty in the direction Chantara and Jorie had gone. The rain caused the deck to be slippery, so he had to proceed with caution. "How in the heck could those two manage to walk the way they trip in normal conditions?" In about three minutes, the storm died down to a complete, mind-boggling halt. He'd never seen such outrageous acts in his whole life.

The next thing he heard was a voice that should not be from this world. It was so lovely and bewitching. His thoughts were scrambled like eggs. The wind stopped; the waves were calm; no more rain and the moon and stars came out. Hagan was just waiting to wake up from this ongoing dream. It had to be.

In the near distance, he could make out two figures coming his way. It was easy to identify Chantara because of the soft array of colors that reflect from her. He grabbed her and held on with all his might, pulling Jorie into his embrace.

"You two are going to be the death of me. Don't ever do that again. No diving into the ocean, no walking around in a typhoon, nothing dangerous again. My heart can't take it and I'm a healthy, strong man. Where did you go?"

"We went to look at storm."

"What do you mean by that?"

"We go down to see the storm better."

He was bumfuzzled and righteous anger crept in. "Why?" was all he could manage to ask.

"I know not." She shrugged her shoulders and had a skewed frown.

"Someone was singing and then the storm stopped. Was it you singing?"

"Yes," she answered, uncertain why it was important, softly scratching at her pajamas, not knowing how to react. He rubbed his head and ran a hand through his hair. That monster Leviathan took the form of a pounding headache beginning. He kept rubbing his head, squinting his eyes in pain. His response would be irrational since he couldn't make any sense out of her, so he asked, "Weren't you afraid of the storm? It was terrifying."

"No, we not scared."

"This is going to sound stupid, but do you have some kind of superpowers where you can stop a storm?" That question sounded pretty stupid to even himself, so he imagined they must be thinking the same thing.

"I know not." Either she didn't understand his question—which is the most likely explanation—or she didn't want to answer and give away her secret powers. Maybe he should give up on comic books for a while.

"Hagan okay?"

"No. Hagan is getting a big, killer of a headache. My head is pounding."

"I help you. Sit."

So he sat, because he needed to catch his breath before the next catastrophic event hit. She ran her satin hands over his head, gently massaging his temples. Her touch instantly put him to sleep.

# Chapter Twenty-Four

When he finally awoke, Chantara and Jorie were standing by the rail, giggling and talking. Their hair was flying in the breeze and he couldn't take his eyes off of them. His head automatically leaned to hear their conversation.

"Do you think Hagan could be my mate? I like being with him. When he touches me, it feels so good. I do not want to leave him. Could he come and live with us and our people? What do you think?"

They were speaking in their language, and the only word he could identify was his name. Everything else was mumble jumble.

"How could he live with us? He is not our people. I don't think our people will let him live with us. But I really like him and he really likes you, too."

Chantara placed a hand on her heart and smiled, lost in a world of dreams. While they carried on their conversation, he pulled out his cellphone and searched the Internet for their country, but all that came up was some fantasy kingdoms of the underwater world. Then he swore he saw fish jumping out of the water like they were performing at a sea themed park. Whistles and clicks traveled through the air. Then a high-pitched squeak, trills and grunts echoed through the air.

On all decks, oohs and awes were shouted. He had to see what was going on. Chantara and Jorie were making some indescribable sounds. Applause, and flashes of light from pictures being snapped were coming from all decks. As Hagan walked up quietly, his eyes had to be deceiving him. The sea animals actually looked like they were performing.

That couldn't be it. Wake up, Hagan.

"Way to keep under the radar."

They both gasped, startled by his unsuspected appearance.

"Are you talking to the sea animals?"

"I know not."

"You do know. I need some answers. How are you doing that?"

"I know not." She really didn't know how to answer his question.

"Can you speak to the sea animals?"

"We just talk to them."

"And they understand you, don't they?"

"I think. I know not."

"Are you trainers for some sea-themed park?"

She looked at him like he was a lunatic. "I know not."

"From my experience and work with sea animals, there has never been one person who could communicate with them like you do. They understand what you're saying. How can that be?"

"I know not," she replied in surrender, fidgeting.

"There is something so mysterious about you two. Your beauty, your angelic voices, movements, stopping a raging storm, that you deny doing—just everything takes my imagination to worlds unknown. Can you make them leave?"

She looked at him like why would he want to do that?

"Please," he said sincerely.

What happened next confirmed his suspicion. He was clinically out of his mind. *Commit me now.* She made some unique melodies and all the sea animals retreated. He glanced back and Chantara and Jorie were hugging each other and crying, hopping up and down in genuine happiness. What was making them so happy? Could they have received some subliminal message from the sea animals? What had he gotten himself into? Needless to say, he wasn't unhappy about his situation.

He gave up on trying to be sensible and figuring anything out. Just gave up.

They cuddled up in their chairs and Jorie was already asleep in the lifeboat. Just before they fell asleep, Chantara gazed into his eyes. "I like Hagan. You pretty man. I like you so much."

Blushing, he closed his eyes.

# Chapter Twenty-Five

The next morning, they both awoke at the same time.

"Good morning, my angel," he said, smiling, aches, misery and all, rubbing his neck.

With a sunshine of a smile, she touched his cheek and her eyes lingered on his. Then she whispered like the sound of a soft breeze rattling leaves, "Good morning;" so quietly that he could barely hear it. Flopper was snuggled in her lap. There was an innocence about her, even in the way she pronounced her words. Charming was too mild of a word to describe her.

"Why don't you and Jorie take a shower while I get us some breakfast?"

"We love."

He knew enough to give them the space they needed, and that they would be taking an extensive amount of time showering, then he would come back with breakfast and clothes. Hagan sat down and drank a really fantastic cup of coffee, inhaling the aroma that seemed to calm his nerves. Then he pondered sadly that this was their last day together. His thoughts shifted to all the extremely long showers these two angels took. He'd never known anyone to take such long showers and as frequently as they did.

"They're going to turn into fish, if they aren't careful," he said, snickering at his own satire.

The waiter poured him some more coffee and he sniffed the aroma and took sips, enjoying the flavor and peacefulness for a moment. How ironic. The reason for this cruise was to find some peace and quiet, but he found nothing but disaster, one after the other. He giggled because he wouldn't change anything. It felt like he was the protagonist of a fantasy novel.

"Pictures. I can't let them leave without pictures."

"Hey. I've been looking for you everywhere. Did you see the headline in the paper?"

"No. I was just getting ready to check my phone and news updates. What's up, anyway?" he asked Drake.

"Here's a picture of Chantara saving the boy who fell into the ocean. The title of the article is 'Mermaid Saves Boy'."

"Well, that's just silly. Mermaid? Ridiculous."

"I don't think the intention was to make the article about mermaids. It's just a clever hook the reporter used to draw in attention, and boy did it ever."

"How can you tell that is Chantara?"

"There's sort of a resemblance."

"You didn't happen to mention her to anyone, I hope?"

Drake looked cautiously at Hagan, trying to piece together his thoughts of what he unintentionally wasn't saying. "No, why?"

"I'm going to tell you something about them that you can never divulge to anyone. Promise me."

He pushed himself up in the seat, face bright with anticipation. "They are mermaids?"

"No. They escaped an abduction, but Chantara is too scared to talk about it. Many times something happened to bring back memories and she cried uncontrollably. I'm pretty sure it involved adult and child sex trafficking, and maybe more horrible things. I just can't get her to talk. Jorie does not speak our language nor understand it. She relies on Chantara to translate, which is tough enough because she doesn't understand or speak much of it herself."

"That is terrifying to hear."

"I think I ran into their abductors on the way to the ship. A mean group of smelly seamen. I fear they will stop at nothing to find them, including murdering anyone who gets in their way. No facts to back that up but there is a real gut feeling about it."

"Hagan, over here."

"I'll be back in a minute, Drake. Don't go anywhere. I may need your help." That statement cheered him up. Hagan guessed he wanted nothing more than to see Jorie again.

"What's up, Fernando?"

"The captain is asking to meet the woman who saved the boy from drowning. I hear rumors that it was Chantara. Would you mind bringing her to the bridge to receive a medal for bravery?"

"No one can know about her. It could endanger her life. I'll tell you more about it later, but I have too much to do right now. Don't you tell anyone, including the captain. I mean it." His facial expression was aggressive, but his remark caught Hagan off guard, and he was worried for their safety.

"Hey, don't shoot the messenger. I'll tell him I was misinformed. I almost forgot. It bugged me when I met her because I felt I knew her from somewhere. Then I remembered. When I was driving to work, she and another woman ran right out in front of my car. I barely missed running them over. They kept falling, almost staggering, like they were drunk or something. I know it was her. I'm glad she's okay, and the other woman, is she okay?"

"Yes, they are both fine. You're right, though, I can't figure out if they have some sort of medical condition or what because they both seem to trip over their own feet. Look, for your safety and theirs, don't breathe a word."

"Say what?"

"They're victims and someone wants to capture them so badly, I feel they will do anything to find them. Anything!"

"Okay, you've got my word. I'll not speak a word of it."

"Oh, Fernando, we're going to be late," a beautiful woman dressed in very expensive clothing yelled. Fernando tipped his head and raised his left side of the mouth with a whimsical smile. "Duty calls. Catch you later."

All Hagan could do was shake his head and smile. "Man, I love that guy."

"Thanks for waiting, Drake. Here's my proposal. Everyone on the ship is looking for Chantara and Jorie. Right now they're taking super long showers. I swear they would live in the shower if they could. We have a secret spot on the fifth deck that is usually abandoned of people because of the lifeboats getting in the way of their view, so we claimed the spot. If you would bring us some breakfast, that would be a big, huge help. Nobody relates you to them, so they won't be suspicious of the breakfast order. Give us about an hour and then come up there without bringing attention to yourself. Just make sure nobody sees them."

"You have yourself a deal. I can't wait to see Jorie again, but I can't help but feel sad for what they've been through."

"You and me both. Thanks."

Hagan gave him the order, reminding him not to bring any meat, and took off. Wouldn't you know it, James and that server were sitting at a table absorbed in a serious conversation. He handed her something underneath the table and she went to the bar, but her back was facing him so he couldn't tell what she was doing. She delivered the drinks to an older couple and went back to the table by James and gave him a nod to say *yes*. Not sure what that nod was about, but his suspicions were sky high at this point.

He moseyed on over to them, and the server looked at him with a guilty grimace.

"If I didn't know better, I'd swear you two are scheming up

something bad. I think it's time to speak to the captain. I'll not stand by and let you two ruin any passenger's vacation."

They looked at each other with an "uh-oh" kind of look. Then James sneered at him. He found a cruise attendant quickly.

"Sir, I would like to speak with the captain. It's an urgent matter."

"Please, could I help you? The captain does not wish to be interrupted unless it is an emergency."

"It could very well turn into an emergency. It is quite important."

"Follow me then. Please wait here until I return. What is your name, sir?"

"Hagan Bennett."

"Please come in, Mr. Bennett. Captain Blackbeard, please meet Mr. Bennett."

"Blackbeard, for real?" Hagan said humorously, hoping he didn't offend him.

"I get that all the time, as you might suspect. Beard is spelled with two 'E's'. Now, how may I help you Mr. Bennet—wait, that name sounds very familiar. It'll come to me."

"I better attend to my other duties, captain. Will you need me for anything else?"

"No thank you. Hold up, porter. Did anyone find that woman who dived into the ocean to save the boy yet?"

"No, sir, not yet."

"Drat. That will be all. Thank you. Now, what is your concern, Mr. Bennett?"

"Well, sir, I believe you have a couple of con artists on the ship. A server on the upper deck, but I don't know her name. I can point her out to you. The other older gentleman's first name is James. They teamed up together to separate me and my friend until I caught them at it. I caught James slipping the server something under the table and then she delivered drinks to an older couple just before coming in here."

He continued on with his suspicions. "We both know of unfortunate circumstances where a person is slipped some drug into their drink and then the person who drugged them takes them to their stateroom and robs or seduces them. I'm not certain, but I am sure something like that is going on. This could give your cruise line a bad reputation if you don't get a handle on it."

"That most certainly is concerning. You have my word I will investigate. Let me make a phone call and get someone on it right now. I will have you point these two suspects out to my attendant and we will take it from there. Thank you, sir, for bringing this to my attention. I owe you my gratitude and, if it proves to be a real situation, I will reimburse you for the cruise fare."

"Thank you, sir, but would you give me the fare for the comic com version of your cruise coming up in April instead? I just have to come on that cruise."

He shook his hand and said, "That's a deal. I'm sort of a comic book nut myself. Hey, I just realized something. You look just like *Aquaman*. Amazing."

"Thanks and I am hearing a lot of that lately." His chest puffed up with pride.

Shortly after, he pointed out the server and James to the captain's attendant secretly.

# Chapter Twenty-Six

On the way back to the stateroom, Hagan passed a chapel and felt an urging to stop in. He sat in a pew but just stared at the cross. The emotional turmoil of everything he'd been through almost made him break down and cry. Sob. Melt down. Turn into a monsoon. Take your pick. He lowered his head, and he poured it all out to the Lord. "Please give me clear direction, Lord. I feel like I'm drowning."

Next thing he knew, a hand touched his shoulder and the pastor's gentle voice said, "'Trust in the Lord with all your might...' Son, follow your heart, even if love takes you to the stars in the heavens or down into the depths of the sea."

He looked over at him. His head had been bowed in prayer when he spoke. He smiled warmly and patted Hagan's shoulder, then walked off.

Then he got up and returned to his stateroom. Believe it or not, the shower had just turned off. They were going to grow fins if they weren't careful. He tended to laugh at his own wit, and he knocked on the door. Chantara opened the door barely covered up with a towel. Jorie always remained out of sight. As he handed over the bag of clothes he purchased, because he realized they must be out of clean clothes by now, and walking toward the bathroom she stepped on a piece of the towel hanging down and it fell to the floor. Hagan froze. After picking it up, she smiled shyly, but yet didn't seem overly concerned. She was beyond a ten, however you calculate that, *even with uneven breasts*. It's not as though her breasts were grotesquely structured; quite the contrary. They were as amazing as the rest of her features. Her complete backside was uncovered as she walked into the bathroom.

Not only had he noticed her sensual, ravishing body, but something was odd. Barely noticeable lines were all over her skin. It was concerning and confusing, wondering if it had anything to do with the awkward way of walking.

She walked out and looked adorable and sensual, all rolled up into one package. He'd bought jumpsuits with a cover-up shirt, a floppy hat and oversized sunglasses. Chantara would be too easy to identify because of the natural array of colors that illuminate her being, so the disguise needed to cover them up completely. Then he helped fashion two low-hanging pigtails for both of them. The look suited their innocence. They danced around with excitement over the glittery sandals, and then they proceeded to the deck to eat breakfast.

Just as they arrived at their personal spot, Drake walked up with breakfast, staring at Jorie like he was under a spell. He had a silly, animated expression on his face. Hagan shook him slightly to get his attention.

"You got it bad, man." He removed the hand from his shoulder.

"Huh? What?"

"I fear I may need to perform CPR on you if you hang around too long. Will you be okay?"

"That bad, huh?"

"Oh yeah, pretty bad, but I can relate. Come on everyone. Time to eat."

Drake sat next to Jorie, making her a little uncomfortable, but once he handed her the food, she trusted him like a puppy does his new owner. She smiled charmingly at him, and he dissolved into a pile of mush.

Hagan removed hair strands from Chantara's face in a romantic gesture, soaking in her beauty and charm, hypnotized by the color of her eyes. They were the color of the ocean. Sometimes it looked as though the ocean, itself, swirled in them and they would change back and forth from ocean blue to a turquoise color or something like that. And there were times it looked like a clear film dragged over her sclera. She put her hands around his face and said in a dreamy tone, "I like Hagan. I like you much."

That statement made him happy, but sad. Drake took pictures and he managed to get some pictures of Jorie and him.

"Before I leave, here is my cellphone number," Drake said and handed it to Jorie. She held it with a look of confusion, not knowing what she was supposed to do with it.

"She doesn't understand," Hagan said. "Put your number in my phone and I'll put mine in yours. That way, we can stay in touch. That's all I got for you, buddy—at this time, anyway."

After they exchanged numbers, Drake said to Jorie, "Don't go anywhere. I want to give you something and I'll be right back."

Chantara was getting much better with understanding our language and translated the request to Jorie.

He came back with a bouquet of flowers and a cuddly stuffed dolphin animal with a necklace around it that could hold a picture, Hagan assumed he hoped would be of him and Jorie. She squeezed the dolphin and hugged it. Her face lit up with a waggish feature and she was excited by the necklace and how it sparkled. The breeze built up and her hair blew out and covered the sky before settling back down and some falling innocently in her eyes. Without thinking, he gently removed the hair from her eyes. She flinched a little, but then relaxed as though she was getting comfortable with him. He smiled with eyes reflecting a dumbfounded look, permanently affixed to her, until Hagan nudged him back to sanity.

Then the oddest thing happened: Jorie took a bite of the flower and munched on a few of the other flowers. Her cherubic face smiled, looking back and forth at each of them. "Mmmm," she kept moaning.

"What just happened?" Drake asked, not understanding Jorie's actions.

Hagan spoke to Chantara, and she whispered to Jorie. She stopped eating the flowers and sniffed them with closed eyes and inhaled the glorious fragrance.

"In their country, it's a delicacy," he answered halfheartedly, not sure he bought it.

"We'll be docking shortly, so I would like to say my goodbyes and be on my way. My friends are waiting for me."

Drake shook Hagan's hand and hesitantly hugged Chantara and Jorie goodbye. It's never certain how they may react. Finding it hard to let go of Jorie, he stood back and stared at her like he was trying to physically transplant her face into his memory. He looked sad as he walked off.

# Chapter Twenty-Seven

Eyes popped open wide, as his mouth fell open, and Brutus wiped his nose using the back of a hand and then wiped it on his pants, sniffling like allergies were bothering him. He grabbed the newspaper and ran to find the squire.

"Squire Aamin, take a look at this article," he said, clearing his throat from the allergy problem at the same time. The squire was a lanky man with thin, almost shoulder length scraggly hair, wearing very expensive, designed royal clothing. If it wasn't for his personal guards, he wouldn't be intimidating in the least.

Brutus's face was prideful and he stood tall as the squire read the article, "Mermaid Saves Boy".

The squire's overly-smug disposition was meant to intimidate anyone in range of him. There were always big, burly guards following him around. Even though Brutus was a good four feet taller and probably one hundred pounds heavier, the guard's weapons were always in their hands. If it wasn't for that, Brutus would have broken the squire's scrawny neck in two a long time ago. He glared at them with a spiteful hate.

The squire smiled as he read the article and looked at the

picture. He raised his head away from the article, and with an evil expression, stood deep in thought.

Brutus was such a twisted human being that human life meant nothing to him. Taking someone's life had no remorse or effect on him, whatsoever. He watched the squire, anticipating for him to break out with some maniacal, evil laugh. Instead, the squire just breathed some heavy sighs in the form of laughter. Brutus was very disappointed, like watching a horror film done wrong. His facial interpretation of that moment was of discontent.

Then, to his surprise, the squire looked back at the article and broke out in an iconic, dastardly laugh. Brutus stood up straight, his eyes lighted up and his smile became uncomfortably wicked. He exhaled his sick relief, folding his arms over his chest.

"For your sake, this is good. Once the cruise ship docks, we'll hide in the background and grab them at my command."

"Yes, Squire Aamin," he replied, with beads of sweat dripping down his face. The guards gave him a scornful look and pointed their weapons at him as he walked away from the squire.

# Chapter Twenty-Eight

"This is our last day together. We will be docking in about two hours. I need information. Please tell me what happened to you, so I can help you," Hagan asked sincerely. These wicked abductors will always be on the lookout for them and their lives will never be safe. Who in their right mind could live with themselves knowing that without doing anything about it?

The mild breeze caused her sweet, pure scent to flow in his direction. He turned his face up to the sky and sniffed, inhaling the scent into his secret chamber of Chantara memories.

She was apprehensive, fiddling with a piece of thread on her clothing, but began the story. "I was playing with Sereia and Taras. They got caught in trap and I got them out but trap closed before I get out. Then I send alert to my people, but they not get to me before bad men pull me into ship."

"Wait. Are you saying you were in the water? Do you know where you were? By an island, off the coast, where?"

Scouring the ocean, she drew in a breath, pointing. "By that island. I know where home is now. Jorie, look, home!"

They both became quite emotional, trying to fight back tears, and it looked as though they were going to jump over the side of the ship.

"Stop! Don't you dare jump off the ship!" He had to catch his breath, and the women watched him cautiously, questioning what could make him so frazzled.

"In order to help you, I will need to find this prince. Once we dock, I'll see to it you get home. Please continue. I need to figure out how to end this eldritch plan of theirs." Clearly, she didn't understand what he said, and yes, he could envision his mother rolling her eyes at him. *Will I ever learn? Probably not.* That's just who he was. He decided to speak as simply as possible to help her understand what he was trying to find out.

She gave him an appreciative look, followed by sadness at what would be exposed, tearing at her clothes unintentionally from the mixture of anger and painful emotions.

"The people hold me prisoner at a place they called *All Your Fantasies Come True*. The bad lady make me say that name over and over. She said is what I have to say to cli...ents. She act kind of funny when she tell me to say it. The other building was called the *"New World."*

"Okay, good. Now, who is this Prince Raiatea? He abducted you, right?"

"I think, but I know not. They hide me in cage on ship and sail far, far away. Men try to touch me and cut me."

"Why would they do that?" His thoughts went back to the moment she stepped on the towel and it fell to the floor exposing her nakedness. That is when Hagan acknowledged the lines. Could those lines be from cuts? His thoughts filled him with horror. The lines were only noticeable if you were close enough to stare at her body.

"They lock me in giant cage in the prince's house—big, big house. I not escape. Sereia and Taras cry and be scared, so I have to save them."

"Did the prince capture you because he wanted to marry you?"

"No. He want to touch me and do bad things to me and take off his clothes, but he not pretty. He scare me so much. I scare him, too, because I get angry for what he was doing to me. I could bite him, but the rest of me was chained and I couldn't get out of them. Then he yell to men that they need to find a way to keep me from thrash...ing a...rou...nd. I not know if I say words right. It stop him and he leave me alone, but then he send man to do bad things to me, but I kill man. It was scary and I not even know I kill him. It just happen."

It was quite disturbing to hear the prince's intent and that she could kill someone. Hagan realized she must have been out of her mind and didn't realize she killed him. "But how could she and by what means did she kill him?" he mumbled quietly, disturbed by her confession, and then forced himself to hear the rest of the story.

His words were a fumbled mess, trying to envision the scene in his head while wondering how she could kill a man. What strong man couldn't overpower her? Now is not the time to stop. As hard as it is to hear, he had to know everything there was to know about this place and these demons. "What happened next?" he asked a little hesitantly.

Being uncomfortable talking about it, she continued for his sake, constantly adjusting her seating, looking down in what appeared to be shame and regret. "Men and women put me in chains and I not move. I too weak. The prince tell them to leave and he come and start touching me and making bad sounds. He smell bad; he look bad and was dripping water." He knew she meant to say dripping sweat. "His mouth kiss my body and his hands touch me in wrong places. The touch make me sick and I get angry."

She held her stomach as though she could still feel how nauseous it made her feel, rocking back and forth, swallowing over and over to prevent herself from throwing up. You don't have to be a psychologist to figure that out.

"I bite him and he slap me and beat me with a thing he called a whip." Her words were forceful now. "Then he go away. Later, men come in room and he tell them that he will get good money for men to touch me. He will be rich, very rich because of me. Men think bad things. Women mean, too. They no like me. Woman try to teach me to talk, but she get angry and say I not talk good and I not smart. She keep teaching me. I try, but I no like her. She hit me a lot."

"When I first met you, you were naked. Why?"

"Because bad men wanted us to wear clothes that would fall down fast. They always look scared when they come to me. I not understand. The gown fell off as we went in the water."

"Did your mother and father look for you?"

"Men take me far, far away. They not know how to find me."

"Not all people are bad. Do you think I'm bad?"

"No! You good man. Nice man. You don't try to touch me or do bad things."

"Were you always kept in chains?"

"Yes and no, because I so weak from not eating. If I too weak, they take chains off for a little time. They not know how to help me or give me good food. Nobody want to be nice to me."

"Was there anyone that was decent to you?"

"Yes. Sparkles, Glitter and Pokey nice."

"These are your fish, right?"

"Yes, and turtles—oh, and cook. She sneak in and talk to me and bring me good food. Her nice, de...cent."

"I understand."

He felt this large lump in his throat and it was parched. Would it be wrong to stop this conversation now that she trusted him enough to explain what she had been through? If he didn't change the subject momentarily, he feared he wouldn't pretend to turn into one of his favorite comic book characters. There was some form of him that needed to be released and find these beasts. These poor, naïve, and such precious angels. Even after all she had been through, just look how kind, sweet and loving she was. He would be a horrible, rotten person after an experience like that. He wondered how long she was held captive before she and Jorie escaped. How many more innocent women were in chains right now? The time was now, temporarily, to change this discussion.

"Let me show you my pictures. This is a picture of you and Jorie and one of you and me." She touched the display window out of curiosity and commented: "We pretty. You and me."

"Agreed. We sure are pretty together. This is a picture of my mother and father." Tears filled her eyes and she held the phone to her heart. "Aw, love, yes?" He didn't know how long she had been kept away from her family, and he couldn't begin to imagine all the loneliness and pain she felt.

"Yes, love. Here is a picture of my sister."

"Very pretty. She nice?"

"So nice. I love her very much. She has two little girls like Sereia."

A smile formed as she stared into the sky.

"This is my ex-girlfriend."

"Ex-girlfriend! What that mean?"

"We are no longer together. She didn't like me."

"What!" she expressed with an animated expression. "She no like Hagan! Is she bad? She very pretty. What her name?"

"Her name is Danielle but we call her Dani. No, she isn't bad. She is in love with my best friend. Well, he's not my best friend anymore."

"That wrong. Dani hurt you?"

"Not as much as it will hurt to leave you. Now, that hurts."

"No! I not hurt you." She became flustered.

"I meant that I will miss you terribly when you leave."

His words melted her heart. "I miss you, too."

"Here is a picture of my German Shepherd dog, Adamaris, and his little, brown, short-haired, shelter buddy, Aerwyna. Since we work in the oceans, my mother gave them merman names."

"What merman?"

"It is a pretend being that is part fish and part human."

"Yes, I know now."

Putting her hand over her heart, she expounded softly: "I love. Dogs cute."

"They are with my parents on one of those islands," he said, pointing. "Hey, please meet my parents before you leave. Just for a few minutes."

"Okay, but we go home soon."

"That's a deal. We'll walk through town and I'll buy you and Jorie some delightful treats." That always got their attention. They loved experimenting with new flavors and everything they ate was a new flavor.

"Delightful?" she said, smiling with verve.

"Sure, we'll call it that."

He wanted to find out more, but if he was being honest with myself, it was a scary thought to find out what graves of past abuse would be unburied from her subconscious if he pressed her to keep talking about it all.

The moment came when they would dock, and they all felt the solemnness of that moment.

# Chapter Twenty-Nine

As passengers prepared to disembark for the day, Hagan picked up on the hesitancy in Chantara's face. Her eyes flashed around the area. She felt it. That internal gut feeling was sending warning signals.

"Chantara! Chantara!" Finally she snapped back to attention. "What's wrong?"

"The bad men are here. I know it. I feel it. I smell them."

I pulled some scarves out of the luggage and wrapped them around their heads and placed floppy hats on their heads and oversized sunglasses around their eyes. They squinted and looked around curiously. Then witty smiles sculpted their faces.

Scarves are necessary as a disguise to cover up every part of Chantara, especially since she had that enchanting, fairy-tale glow. I wondered why Jorie didn't have it, but that really wasn't important.

"This should keep you safe for now."

Standing in line to go ashore, an aggravating voice sounded from behind him. "Well, hello, Hagan," Curious Christine commented, expecting a sarcastic response from him. That was normally how he responded to her, but it was always justified.

He pulled Chantara and Jorie behind him. "What do you want?" Like he didn't already know. The other passengers watched their reactions back and forth.

"Any chance you changed your mind and are anxious to let your friend tell her story?" Her camera crew was moving around, trying to film Chantara's and Jorie's faces, but he held them closely behind him out of their view.

Chantara and Jorie were grasping onto his shirt, worry growing in their faces from his tone of voice. He looked back for a second and noticed their knuckles were white because they were holding onto his shirt like it was a life or death situation. He needed to end this quickly.

By this time, she had pushed her way through the crowd holding a microphone with the camera crew following right up close now. Invisible steam was spouting out of his head, or at least it sure looked that way. "I told you to leave them alone. You are putting their lives in danger."

"How," she answered briskly, holding the microphone to his mouth.

"You don't get it, do you? Actually, I think you do get it, but putting someone's life at risk to write your story doesn't bother you in the least; does it?"

"Oh, come on, Hagan," she replied in a pouting voice, puckering up her lips like he was supposed to think it was an adorable addition to her next deceptive attempt of tricking him into talking.

"Look, just get back or I will use force. I don't believe in hitting a woman, but I am struggling with that perception of you."

The bystanders were appalled by her behavior and began pushing her back behind them in line where she should have been in the first place. Then they formed a barrier to keep her away from them. He thanked them. Maybe not so much Jorie, but they started to get to know Chantara and were mesmerized by her gentleness and kind heart, just something special about her. Jorie was too shy to be around any people.

"Make no mistake, I'll get the story," she whispered to her crew.

*This is a woman used to getting her way, but not today*, he thought in a prideful manner. Everyone was walking down the pier and Chantara was slightly trembling, combing the area for the abductors.

He squeezed her hand tightly to encourage her. She looked up at him, attempting to work a smile on her beautiful, enticing, lovable face. They were here. She knew it and he felt it, but the disguise paid off and they were momentarily safe. He still couldn't get over how he referred to "I felt it," because he was new to the world of being in tune with his inner senses.

Hagan glanced back at the ship and James and the server were being escorted down the plank in handcuffs. He smirked, because their intentions were unkind.

Feeling unsure, he pulled his angels behind a food stand so he could look for the abductors. From Chantara's description, Brutus would be easy to spot as huge and intimidating of a beast as he was, but they weren't around. Frankly, he would rather know where they were to avoid running into them. With more caution than ever, they proceeded on to tasting some marvelous foods and desserts. It never failed. Chocolate was always the winner. They ate french-fries, rice and peas, salt bread, Tiki pies, crepes, you name it. They were in heaven, and being such angels were easy to relate to.

They came upon a park with playground equipment. He chased them and they played a good ole child's game of tag. It even got a little bit physical as they accidentally shoved each other down and they, of course, still tripped over nothing, to be honest. It was to the point where they could joke around with each other, play fight, and enjoy the heck out of each other's company. Hagan nicknamed her Chantara *Hanna-Barbera*. He just loved those cartoons. Good times.

Some cats started coming toward them. At first they brushed up to Chantara and Jorie, rubbing, being affectionate. Then they started licking their feet. Next thing he knew: "Owe! Hey, what are you animals doing?" Chantara asked. Jorie scooted away and she stood behind him with hands holding onto his shirt.

"What's wrong?"

"These animals bite us." She ran behind him, too. He saw the cats nibbling on them, but he thought it was a friendly gesture, not trying to eat their skin. Oh my, that didn't sound appealing.

"When you say animals, you are referring to these cats, right?"

"Cats? What cats?"

"These animals here. You've seen cats before; right?"

"No, not see. I no think we like...cats. They hurt when they bite." Her eyes blinked continuously, and she tilted her head with shame in her eyes. All animals loved her, but now she found one that she wasn't comfortable with. It was apparent these thoughts were making her feel ashamed that she felt that way, so he scooted the cats away and they continued to explore what other flavors awaited them ahead. And how in the heck was it she never saw a cat before? Now he was convinced she was from another planet.

He was stuffed, but they were just beginning, it seemed, and begging for more scrumptious foods, until he talked them into taking a break.

Passing a jewelry store, Chantara looked in the window with excitement. "Treasure."

"It's called jewelry." Maybe from where she's from it is called treasure. Who knows?

"It pretty jewel...ry."

"I have something for you, but hold on. Stay right here and don't move. If anything goes wrong, run in this store and find me." She shook her head yes. When he came out of the store, they watched him intently, wondering what he had in the bag, wiggling around like they were playing with hula hoops. Not wanting to keep them in suspense, he handed Jorie a bracelet with a diamond-studded seahorse. She responded so joyfully, *cute as a button*. He smirked because he didn't get that saying. Since when is a button cute? He clasped it around her wrist. She absolutely loved it.

Next, he pulled the necklace out of his pocket that he'd been carrying around, waiting for the right moment, and this finally was the perfect moment. He then handed Chantara *Hanna-Barbera* the necklace.

"This for me?"

"I'm pretty certain this necklace was made just for you. Yes, it is for you. See the glittery moon and beneath it, what I am calling moon water. See the dazzling colors on the water. It's like looking at you. Since your name means moon water, I can only conclude this necklace was made specifically for you."

"Thank you, Hagan. I love. I love." Her face was genuine. A woman with her beauty should be used to being showered with gifts and attention, but she seriously hated attention and giving her a simple gift like chocolate makes her happier than the most expensive gift; he just knew that.

"I don't ever want you to forget me."

"Hagan. I not forget you." She kissed his cheek, and her eyes watered. "I love." Once again, she loves the necklace or him? Let's face it. He felt doomed with love as badly as he wanted to deny it. Now all he wanted to do was convince her to stay with him and maybe soon, marry him. He realized it sounded foolish, but his heart broke with more pain than what he'd witnessed in his apartment with Dani. It's confusing, what he felt for Chantara *Hanna-Barbera* was completely real, strong and powerful; unexplainable.

After fastening the necklace, he turned and there he was, Leviathan, that beastly man. Before the man saw them, Hagan managed to escort the women behind the store, searching for a place to hide without them knowing what he was up to. It would only cause them unease. Wouldn't you just know it? There was a secluded spot with a bench to sit on and the area surrounding it covered in trees, vines, flowers and whatnot—a most romantic spot.

"Let's sit down for a minute in that beautiful spot?" he said, pointing, constantly checking over his shoulder for you know who.

"No, we not sit. We go home now," Chantara protested. Her face reminded him of a child about to throw a temper tantrum from not getting his or her way.

"Just for a minute, please. After all that food, I need to sit down. Just for a minute.

"Okay."

They inspected each other's jewelry and jabbered endlessly at the designs, especially the glitter, watching it sparkle as they moved it around in the sunlight. He pretended to bend down and smell some flowers as he peeked through an opening to see what he could see. A group of men stood in a circle, and Brutus stood high above them, scanning the area for his two angels. Brutus looked his way, so he lowered himself down further toward the ground. Hagan glanced over at Chantara and she was sniffing the air. Something told him she had some sort of enhanced olfactory senses. Her face turned fearful.

"It's okay. That's why I brought you here to hide," he said softly, then looked back over toward Brutus and he and his shipmates as they began walking off in the opposite direction from them.

"Brutus and his shipmates left. We can go now."

Just the sound of his name gave Chantara shivers.

"We'll head over to the shore and rent a boat; then go visit my parents for a moment before I take you two home." They both smiled in anticipation.

"Hagan, I bring back treasure for you from my home," Chantara commented.

"There is only a few hours before the ship leaves. You can't get back by then."

"Stay with your mother and father, okay?" she said.

"Yeah. That sounds good. I'll do that," he replied.

Hagan called his parents and planned to rent a boat but stopped momentarily before leaving for the island. "Hold it a minute. You will just love this. Don't look and don't go anywhere. I'll be back in a jiffy."

Sniffing the air, they just knew whatever that smell was would be sensational. As he walked back to them, a terrifying shriek came from Jorie like nothing anyone had ever heard. It was ear piercing, incomprehensible, abnormal and uncharacteristically loud. He dropped the surprise on the ground. The squire was holding onto Jorie, and another sorry excuse of a man had grabbed Chantara. She was holding her scarf in her hand. It must have blown off of her head and they spotted her.

You would think he'd be used to all the strange happenings that went on around Chantara, but oh, no, it still shocked the heck out of him. She struck that animalistic pose, snarled like some predator, and hissed before she tore her nails through both of the men's arms. Hagan pulled her back, and both men grabbed their arms with blood gushing out. She wasn't done and Hagan struggled with getting control of her. Her strength was uncanny, and the contortion in her face scared him. He had to get control and keep them safe somehow.

Cautiously holding her arm and Jorie's, he examined the injury she caused. To his horrific surprise, she'd torn through their skin all the way to the bone. These men needed medical assistance quickly. Some bystanders ran up and he asked them to call for medical and police authorities. After he quickly explained what had happened and informed everyone surrounding us of the urgency to get these women to safety, we turned and ran, but he stopped and said, "One second. I'll be right back."

The way these two love food surprises, he could not keep this snack from them. It was fun to eat, and they needed fun. What he bought them was wrapped up anyways, so he rushed in, picked it up off the ground and saw Brutus and his evil, hairy band of human waste closing in on the area of commotion, and then they ran for their lives.

# Chapter Thirty

A t the location of the injured abductors, Brutus and his team ran up and helped the squire and the other injured man to safety. None of the bystanders had any intention of trying to keep them there until the authorities came. Nobody was stupid enough to try and battle Goliath, or commonly referred to as Brutus. Hagan glanced back as they ran and saw the bystanders run off. He couldn't blame them.

Hagan's angels tripped a few times, but he managed to get a good grasp on their arms and kept the pace going. They passed a ship with a foreign flag that looked out of place. He recognized the ship from the day at sea where they were capsized. Safe and sound, they made it to the boat shack where he could rent a boat. He had them sit down on the bench so they could catch their breath while he went inside the shack.

Within moments, he hurried back over to them, sat down on the bench and said, "Look what I've got."

"Pretty colors. Can we eat?"

"Yes." He pulled off a piece of cotton candy and handed it to them. They shared it and stuffed it in their mouths and were enlightened to a whole new world of flavors.

"This is the best," Chantara exclaimed with so much excitement she kissed his cheek and grabbed the bag. They gobbled it up in a couple of minutes.

"More, please."

"How do you two keep your weight down the way you eat?"

"I know not," was her reply, because she didn't understand what he meant. He almost—almost made the "oink-oink" sound, laughing at himself.

In the store, some chips and colas got his attention, so he ran back in and bought them. He didn't know why, but it fascinated him to see their reaction. Everything we take for granted is enthralling to them.

As they sat there looking out at sea, he handed them some potato chips with sea salt. "What do you think?"

The crunching sound was fun to them. *Crrrr...unch* echoed over the area. They laughed. "I love this, too. It taste like ocean."

"Oh, I get it. You are referring to the salty flavor." She shook her head yes.

"Now try these." He watched their faces as they tried figuring out what they thought about the flavor. "This is salt and vinegar chips. Do you like?"

"It taste like ocean and seaweed. I like."

"Seaweed? That makes sense. You always seem to relate everything to the ocean. Why is that?"

"I know not."

Truth is, he decided she didn't understand what he meant.

Brutus was probably getting close, so Hagan requested they head over to see his parents. They both were relieved to be getting out of there. He had informed his mother that he was bringing two women for them to meet. She became silent at that statement. He mentioned that Jorie was painfully shy and to not approach her, which was significant information they needed to know before arrival. He'd also informed his mother that he needed to tell her everything that had happened between Dani and him. It just had to be done, more so for his mother now than himself. His heart belonged to Chantara forever, and it would never again belong to Dani. She reluctantly accepted his request. Very reluctantly.

After taking their hands and helping them into the boat, they drove to the island where his parents were staying.

"Here we are." He saw his parents sitting on the beach with their dogs.

His parents ran up and embraced him in a loving hug while the dogs ran around, brushing up against him waiting for some attention. Hagan bent down and cuddled them as they licked his face. Grinning, the women watched happily about the exchanges between them.

"Mom and Dad, please meet Chantara and Jorie."

They embraced Chantara in a light-hearted hug. Jorie backed away, so they just smiled at her. "It's a pleasure to meet you," his mom said.

"Happy to meet you," Chantara offered sweetly. The dogs ran over and wiggled up against them. They fell to the ground with the dogs licking and crawling on top of them. There were giggles and playful dog noises. Then the scarf blew off Chantara and his parents saw the iridescent colors, looking at him with questions in their eyes. All he could do was shrug his shoulders. He was just as in the dark as they were.

Sitting at the umbrella table, Chantara looked puzzled at his parents. "I know you. I see you, too."

Thomas and Melana turned and looked into each other's eyes. A look of confusion revealed they were not able to make sense from what she tried to relay.

"Do you mean you have seen my parents working?"

"Yes!" There was excitement in her voice.

Melana had baked some chocolate chip cookies and offered Chantara and Jorie some. They accepted with much, much gratitude. By now, it was obvious that all it took was some yummy food to ease any doubts or worries they may have.

"Mmmm, this so good. What is it?"

In total confusion, Melana tilted her head. "You seriously have never tasted chocolate chip cookies?"

"Mom, they aren't from around this area or, I think, any civilization from my best estimation. Every food I give them to taste is a new flavor to them."

"Not even chocolate chip cookies?"

"I'm afraid not. Anyway, I think now is as good of time as any for us to have a talk."

"Let's go sit at the next table. Dad, you'll need to entertain these two women."

"My pleasure."

Melana gave him the evil eye that translated in all universes.

"It's okay, Mom. These two are not the flirtatious types. You have nothing to worry about."

"Maybe not with them, but your father..."

"Mom, he only has eyes for you."

"I'm being just silly, aren't I?"

"Yes, but it's sort of cute."

I pulled the chair out for her and we sat. I stuttered at first, because this was not going to be an easy thing to tell her. "I'm just getting right to the point. Dani and I are NEVER getting back together EVER."

"Son, you're being too hasty. Three years is a long time and you can't throw all those years away over some squabble. I love her like a daughter."

"Some squabble. Is that what you think?"

"Well, yes. I mean, what else could there be?"

"Okay, Mom. Put on your seat belt and hang on. This is going to be difficult for you to hear and very painful. There is no way to avoid this conversation, because you have to let it go and this is the only way that can be done." The look on her face was tearing him apart, but he had no choice in the matter. This needed to end now. Thomas glanced over at Melana and a concerned expression developed on his face, but the giggles of Chantara and Jorie brought him out of it.

As you may suspect, after he filled in all the dirty little details of the breakup, she wanted to be in denial.

"Son, are you certain that is what you saw or thought you saw?"

"Oh, Mother, you certainly don't want me to describe to you what I saw in detail. It will embarrass and upset you more than you are now. Trust me, you don't want to hear the details."

"This breaks my heart. For them to hurt you like this, they have hurt me. I don't think I care to ever see them again."

"Now it's my turn to tell you not to make a hasty judgment. Just because Dani and I...and Adam...are through, doesn't mean you have to end your relationship with them. I know how much they mean to you and how much you mean to them. Just don't invite them to your house or any family gathering or anywhere I will be.

One more thing, I realize I am just as much to blame as Dani for this breakup." His mom raised a curious eyebrow.

"You see, Dani tried to make me see that we were drifting apart. She called my job the other woman. I ignored her willfully because my job was more important to me. Taking all of this into consideration, I realized that I am not in love with Dani. We love each other, but we're not in love. There's no spark. I don't long to see her. You're not going to believe this—"

"You're in love with Chantara."

"How did you know?"

"I have never seen you look at Dani the way you look at her. I think Chantara loves you, too. Her eyes glow when she looks at you. Not only are you an incredibly handsome man, but you are good and caring, very intellectual, easygoing, and you will help out anyone who needs it: strangers, family or friends. You talk to anyone. Besides your father, you're the best man I know. I'm so proud of you.

"Hagan, what is it? There is sadness in your eyes." She placed her hand over his and offered a sympathetic look.

Glancing over at his dad and his angels laughing, his heart cried out in despair. "I fear this may be the last day I will ever see them again. You see, they were victims of some real evil crimes, but for their safety, yours and Dad's, I can't tell you anymore. The people after them are killers. We barely escaped with our lives. They aren't from around here. Actually, I've never heard of their country and if I'm honest, sometimes I don't think they are of this world."

"That's funny, because I feel the same way, like they stepped out of some fairy tale. Everything about them causes me to question just who are they. As much as it hurts me to lose Dani, I can't help but feel fond of her already. Something is so special about them. They're unworldly and perfection.

"Wait a minute. I read an article yesterday about a mermaid saving a drowning boy from your cruise ship. I started to call you but then got interrupted. That article is about her; isn't it?"

His mom was salivating to find out, not that she's a busybody, but who wouldn't want to know the truth about that article? "I have no earthly idea how she survived saving that boy. It's a mystery to me, too."

"The article calls her a mermaid."

"Did you happen to notice who wrote the article? Do you see a fishtail and fins on them? Come on, Mom, who has no imagination, whatsoever."

"Wow! That felt good to use my imagination for a change. Look, I don't have answers for you, but I will pray about it."

"What if I'm wrong about how I hope she feels about me? What if she doesn't feel about me the way I do her? I mean, wouldn't she want to stay with me if she did?"

"The poor thing is fearful for her life. I'm sure when she is safe and secure, you will be the only thing on her mind. You must remember: 'To the world you may be one person; but to one person you may be the world.' —Dr. Seuss, of course."

"That quote helped me through many challenging times in my life. Thanks Mom." She patted his leg, and they went back to the table and engaged in conversation for a moment.

"Mom and Dad, I'll be back soon. These women need to go home."

"Where is that?" she asked. Then she remembered not to ask too many questions and corrected herself by saying, "That's not important. I hope we get to see you again."

"I love Hagan's mother and father and dogs. I love," Chantara confirmed with sentiment.

Everyone smiled and waved goodbye as they walked down to the pier where the boat was located. His parents couldn't explain why they were so drawn to the women, especially Chantara. They could see the love in Hagan's face, and it hurt deeply. She had no intentions of hurting him, they knew. It was just an unfortunate situation.

## Chapter Thirty-One

Hagan sat on the pier with the women.

"May I drive you and Jorie to your home?"

"No, we swim. We strong enough to swim now." She was aware of the confusion in his face.

"I tell you, but you not understand."

"I'll try my best to understand."

"But this is not like you and people." It was difficult for her to explain. "When those bad men catch me that was because one of my people, Cetus, turned bad. He made deal with prince for me and told him about me, and that is why he make so much money." Her eyes dropped down to the bench as she timorously rubbed it with her fingers.

He sat patiently not wanting to distract her. "Go ahead," he spoke softly with encouragement.

"Wait! I see Mother and Father and Tydal, way out there!" Both women became sentimental and exhibited an eagerness to jump into the water. He had to find out the whole story before they left in order to save Chantara and Jorie from those horrible monsters.

"Where are they? There are no boats anywhere."

"They in water."

His eyes rolled. Not again. What was she about to unveil? He mentally gripped himself for another mental TKO. "You're not going to tell me that they are swimming, are you?" *Please don't*, he begged silently.

She shook her head yes, smiling like he understood.

"It's just not possible for anyone to swim that far."

"My people swim that far. You people, no."

"I'm trying to understand. How can someone swim that far without drowning?"

"We no drown. We live way down there." She pointed down to the water. "Way, way down there. No man come down that far."

"I still don't understand. You can't live in water."

The shaking of her head signified yes, over and over to be sure he understood.

"So, you live in some secret underwater city? Is it like a secret government experiment?"

She leaned her head back and wrinkled her nose. "No. I not understand."

"How about this?" he said in jesting. "You're like a mermaid?" He chuckled.

"I forget what mer...maid is."

His handy dandy cellphone pulled up pictures of mermaids on the Internet. He showed her the pictures. She smiled and her face lighted up like sunshine.

"Yes, yes."

She was sincere. He was baffled. "No tail or scales?" he said with sarcasm.

"We fish and human. Out of water, our tail change to legs. In water, our legs turn back to tail. It doesn't happen right away. Takes time to turn, because it a very hard thing to do. If we not strong enough, we could die. There is not scales. That picture make it look that way, but our body have a look like scales.

Mother and Father way, way far away in water. It take time for them to get here. We can see and smell things very, very far."

A heavy weight of despair covered him, knowing the abuse she received had affected her mentally. He sat silently for a moment, trying to analyze what she said. *That's why she believes what she is saying. He didn't see any signs of mermaids. Maybe the abductors made them wear mermaid costumes. Something still didn't fit, though. That unexplainable beauty and colors that were a part of her and out of the ordinary. They're not like the rest of us. The language is riveting and enchanting.*

"See, Cetus is my uncle. We were very close. He lost his mate and it change him. He tell prince, that what you call us, mermaids and merman, have one mate for life. I tell you what he tell prince. We live about three hundred years. Marin and I ready to be together but the prince kill him before it happen." She lowered her head and began to cry, then sob, then a dam of tears broke out. He held her hand and gave her the time she needed to recover. It was severe emotional pain for her.

"What happens is—I try tell you what Cetus say. It hard for me, but a fragrance starts se...creting from our bodies and it starts like a fren...zy between merman and mermaid. I use your word for us. There is a magical ceremony and when the internal mating begins, we go into our home and come together. The passion and love is exploding—what Cetus call it—and nothing like you people know. If the prince keep me when it starts and I not be with Marin, he would experience—I think that the word Cetus tell him—love...making that no people ever feel. It is way beyond your thinking. With Marin gone, I not be able to be with or want another mate. But I feel funny around you. I know not what I am feeling."

It felt like a handful of feathers tickled through her body and her heart pounded as she stared at him.

"One day, Cetus help prince catch one of my sisters during her breeding time. He make a man try to do things with her and all men and women watch, but something bad happen. My sister come out of the mating mind but she not know what was going on and she get very angry and kill man. We can only mate with our merman. She not even know she kill him. He not have her fragrance and it cause her mind to not be right.

Another man go to her and they watch. She kill him, too. We strong, especially during our mating time. The prince want to keep me in chains and do those things to me, but we escape when they put us on ship to go to his secret home."

I sat in utter shock. Speechless.

"You see, Chantara and Marin made for each other. I have him fragrance and he have mine. I love him so much, but now he gone." She was emotional now and trying hard to fight back tears, gently wiping them from her face. "A merman finds man that take away his mermaid when mating time begins. He find her. You not stop him. My sister's mate find her and killed men and women to help her escape. He not help it. Please, tell no people this."

A tear dropped from his eye. "I can't help but believe you." He lowered his head and pondered what she said. What she told him was devastating, and how could anyone come up with a story like that? For anyone exhibiting signs of an over imaginative mind, this story was too surreal to be fictional.

Why he couldn't quash his thoughts at this particular time of being deeply in love with her was plain out ridiculous. After what he just heard, these thoughts made him angry at himself. His mind brought back that exploding revelation and nausea claimed his body, realizing he wouldn't be able to spend the rest of his life with her. Falling in love with her was at warp speed, not a healthy start to a relationship. Of course, the whole idea sounded completely irresponsible and irrational. She showed no signs of having feelings for him other than gratitude.

"Hagan, there more bad, bad, very bad things that happen."

Before he could reply, he noticed Chantara and Jorie begin to tremble and scan the area in distress. "What's wrong?"

"Jorie go, now!" Chantara ordered.

Brutus and the crew strutted toward them with dart guns filled with an anesthetic, except Brutus loaded his gun with bullets. The near-death experiences he dealt with over their escape incited hatred toward the women. This man, with a personality of a tyrant, justified throwing his own crew members down on the ground to get to Chantara.

"Go, Chantara," Hagan warned. "I'll meet you tomorrow at the cay, the one with the enormous volcano. Go!"

They dove into the water. Darts started flying through the air —and bullets. Brutus means to kill them and anyone who got in his way. At the moment, Hagan had no way of knowing what kind of ammunition was being used, but there were two distinctive sounds from the firing of their guns. He shielded his eyes from the sun scouring the ocean before he ran off. Checking to be sure the women swam away, he saw what looked like fish swerving with extreme quickness and agility. Hagan started to turn around and run, knowing these men would try to capture him to use as a bargaining tool to get his angels back. "Oh no!"

# Chapter Thirty-Two

Jorie floated up to the surface.

There wasn't time to think, so Hagan dove into the water, threw Jorie into the boat, and started the engine. Darts and bullets buzzed past him, just barely missing his head. If you're familiar with the firing of a gun, then you know the difference between a dart and a bullet flying past your head. Finally, he was out far enough to idle the boat and check on Jorie. Thankfully, Chantara picked up on their scent far enough away to give them a head start, but not by much. He had stashed a gun in the boat out of their sight for safety reasons but didn't have time to pull it out and insert bullets. He wouldn't make that mistake ever again.

Chantara stuck her head above the water and screamed. Relieved, Hagan realized it was a dart and it didn't go in deep enough to keep Jorie down too long. The dart just went barely beneath the epidermis, on top of the dermis and missing the subcutaneous tissue all together. He silently thanked the Lord with a quick bow of the head.

"Chantara," he yelled loudly. "She's going to be just fine. Meet me over at that island." He pointed to it. Chantara was not in good shape, fearful for their lives, worried about Jorie.

"I'm going to kill you," Brutus spit out of his mouth roaring like a lion and using other vulgar words.

Hagan wasn't quite sure what Brutus was yelling, but it wouldn't take much of an imagination to figure it out. He kept right on driving the boat to a secret location. He hoped. While driving, he couldn't help but ponder about where Chantara's parents could be, because they must be way out there and not close enough to see what happened. He threw in the anchor and waited for Chantara.

"My Jorie. Is she——"

"She's going to be just fine."

Chantara pulled herself up and held onto the handrail of the boat with a face deeply tormented by the sight of Jorie being unconscious. Hagan explained her condition and that she would wake up soon. After about fifteen minutes, Chantara's face turned pale and she screamed. He looked behind to see Brutus and some men heading their way from the island. One of the men aimed a gun at them, so Hagan quickly pulled out his gun and shot, luckily hitting Brutus in the arm, causing him to drop the gun. It was pure luck, honestly, or maybe God was watching out for them.

The anchor was pulled up in record time. There should be some competition of strength to see how fast someone could pull an anchor up into the boat. Having to do it this fast was not an easy task. Hagan yelled for Chantara to follow him. The boat sped off like it was well aware of the need to speed. Where he lacked imagination in the past, he surely made up for it on this trip.

Hagan saw Brutus running toward them, shoving the injured crewman out of his way. Except, he couldn't help but notice it looked like every step he took caused unmeasurable pain and suffering. There were bruises all over his exposed skin area and his face was swollen like a grapefruit. They were well on their way and safe now. Searching for a location to stop, Hagan remembered this one little island that was hidden behind another island, so he turned off the engine and carefully paddled the boat in a disclosed area of mangroves out of anyone's view.

Chantara popped her head out of the water and took him by surprise.

"You scared me for a moment. How did you get here so fast?"

"What I tell you? I swim good."

"Right, mermaid."

She stared at him for a minute like she forgot the definition of a mermaid. Then he could see the light bulb come on and she replied with a feistiness, "Yes, mermaid." It sounded so seductive the way she said it and a chill of intrigue ran down his spine.

"How we help Jorie?"

Jorie started slowly stirring. "I brought along a lot of water, because I thought the way things were going, I better be prepared. Once she wakes up, I'll get her to drink a lot of water and also soak her body in the ocean."

Jorie's eyes opened and not knowing what had happened or what is going on, she gasped in fear. "I here. No worry. You okay," Chantara assured her.

She sat up and sat still, trying to figure things out. Hagan explained to Chantara what had happened and how they need to resolve it. She translated it all to Jorie. Jorie tried standing up, but slipped back down. He steadied her, and like he was playing a game of charades, got her to start drinking water. Another bottle and another bottle. He and Chantara held onto her and lowered her into the water to complete the hydration.

Something popped into his mind. "Speaking of hydrating, shouldn't you be transforming into a mermaid by now?" He pushed his head around to see her legs but, nope, they were still there, however, her eyes had more of a defined aquatic look to them. "Well?" he said in jesting.

"It take time," she replied almost frustrated.

"Okay, Chantara *Hanna-Barbera*. I believe you." For some reason, his nickname for her always made her giggle and she smiled at him affectionately.

"We ready to go. I send alert to my parents where we are and they sent back message. I so happy to get to see my parents. It been so long." She cried softly for a moment. He rubbed her hand.

"So...you sent out a source signal and then they replied and you heard the backscatter?"

"I know not," she replied with a face full of questions.

"You called them and they answered?"

"Yes. Hagan, I need to tell you more about bad peoples."

"Can you meet me at that cay over there with the volcanic ash beds tomorrow morning? It is too unsafe for us to talk right now." He pointed to it to make sure she understood.

"Yes, I do that."

"Please be safe."

"I will. No worries." Before they took off, she placed her hand on his face and looked into his eyes. Hagan thought he would lose it right there and then. Their eyes teared up, and she gave him the impression she was trying to remember his face. Then she whispered so low that he had to strain to hear, "Thank you, Hagan. Thank you." She kissed him softly on the cheek and looked hard, but softly into his eyes.

*A person she could finally trust* sunk in her mind, but Hagan just wasn't certain what her thoughts were saying.

As they swam off, he wanted to beg her to stay with him. Never leave. But how selfish would that be. He knows how sad he would feel never able to see his parents again. What a happy reunion for Chantara and Jorie.

Knowing how to maneuver through these waters was easy for him since he worked in these waters so much. Taking a different direction back to the island where his parents were staying was the only safe means, even if it meant an extra hour or two. Passing by him was a stream of glittery colors. The water oscillated in a rapid thunniform but whatever it was it was too quick to identify, even though his thoughts were spinning as to what he suspected it to be.

Finally, able to relax and feel safe and secure, he couldn't help but notice the beauty flying past him. Usually, he was so busy, he took it all for granted. What a terrible realization on his part. From now on he would "stop and smell the roses", or ocean and so on. Look what he'd been missing. His serene moment was ended by his cellphone ringing. Reception was hit or miss out here, so he guessed it was meant to be.

"Hello," he almost answered in anger.

"It's Drake. I couldn't wait to speak to you. Any new developments?"

"Yes, but you better sit down; you're not going to like what I have to say."

"This is not at all how I envisioned this phone call going. Go ahead, ruin my life."

"Hey, now, calm down. You had to expect this could happen."

"You're right. I hesitated twice before calling you. That little voice inside already was tormenting my soul. It's a denial thing."

"I'm going to get right to the point. Jorie is engaged and I just left the spot where she was going to meet up with her fiancé. It's hard to explain how much influence they have over us from just the short period of time we have spent with them. It's kind of like living in a dream world. Their world is nothing like ours, is the observation I concluded. We come from two different worlds. Their mate is determined at birth, so there is no getting around that. Are you okay?"

"No. What do you think? I mean, it's like Jorie cast a love spell over me, because I can't quit thinking about her. I'm not referring to her physically—well, that's a complete lie. When I touched her, I felt sensations in places I didn't know I had."

We both laughed at that revelation.

"No matter what happens, you can never tell anyone about them. Any attention drawn to them could risk their lives. Promise me you will never betray them. Sometimes I think I've imagined them in my mind. It's like they walked right out of a child's story-book. They are so completely different from anyone I've ever met."

"That's because they're not from our world; right?"

"How silly is that statement, but if anyone has the right to believe that way, it is us."

"And I will tell no one about them. Trapped in some love spell, I would never compromise their safety. You can count on me. Please keep me updated with any news of them."

"You can count on it. I'm so glad I have someone to confide in regarding how Chantara makes me feel, because it's just abnormal —*Twilight Zone* strange. Look how consumed with Jorie you are."

"There's truth in that statement, good friend. I suspect you and I will become good friends."

"I beg to differ." There was complete silence from him. "We are already good friends."

"Hey, man, you had me going there for a minute. I need to go, but I'll get in touch with you soon."

"Take care." We hung up the phones as I pulled into the docking area to my parent's place.

# Chapter Thirty-Three

His parents ran down to the dock, waiting for him in anticipation.

"Did everything go okay, Hagan?" his mom asked earnestly. She gently laid her hand on his shoulder.

"Yes, but not without difficulty. I'm so exhausted. If you don't mind, we'll talk in the morning. I need to get some sleep." *Fat chance*, he couldn't help but think. There is so much to think about with all the new developments, past and present.

That night, Hagan sat in his bedroom in a sullen mood, but at the same time it was like being in an out-of-body encounter, or in ambedo, because his mind drifted to images all around the areas from the first day he met Chantara until this very moment.

*Maybe I do need to check myself into an asylum.*

*Mermaid?*

This breakup must hurt him so much, he couldn't face the reality of it. *Have I been creating some sort of magical realm in my head?*

He pulled his phone out and scrolled through the pictures, and there she was—no figment of his imagination, not a hallucination. *She's real*, He exhaled a sigh of relief.

Now that he thought about it, he better not wait until

tomorrow to drive over to that island. Those men will be searching for them. He better forward this picture of Brutus to his dad so he could be on the lookout for him tomorrow. It's a little blurry, but who wouldn't notice the size of that Brobdingnag. He couldn't let these guys get away. The wickedness of what their trafficking plan was doing to these poor victims needed to be exposed. If it took the rest of his life, he would find the prince and all participants in this evil, ungodly organization. It would be an insult to the animal kingdom or to us to refer to them as animals or human; they're nothing but monsters, he couldn't help but think with disgust.

He grabbed some comic books before walking downstairs to find his dad. He poked his head in the study and his dad looked up from reading some newspaper article.

"Dad, I need your help."

"Sure, but did you hear about this story?" he asked, holding the newspaper article for him to look at. Hagan recognized the description of the murdered man. It was one of the crewmen on Brutus's ship who'd attempted to grab Jorie. The one Chantara tore her nails through all the way to the bone. Hagan guaranteed the squire made Brutus kill him—or maybe his guards. He really didn't know.

"I know who the victim is, and trust me, he probably deserved what he got coming to him, as horrible as that is to say." His dad looked disappointed in his statement.

"Just let me explain before you jump into any misguided perceptions. Chantara escaped a trafficking ring. She has endured cruel and inhumane things. I forwarded a picture to you of a man named Brutus. He and his crew will be watching for her and me. You need to follow them to the ship and get any information on them you can. They will kill anyone that stands in their way. I suspect that is what happened to this monster. I caught him trying to abduct Jorie before Chantara clawed him with her fingernails.

"Dad, these men are violent and evil. Don't let yourself feel pity for this creep. What he has most likely done to women is horrendous and unthinkable. I know what I'm talking about. Find out the facts before you make a conclusion, you always tell me. Now, I'm telling you."

"How can I dispute that? Using my own words against me."

"I'm leaving for one of the islands this evening where I will meet up with her tomorrow." Choking on his attempt not to cry, he managed to say, "Tomorrow may be the last time I will ever see her. She can't risk anyone finding her."

"We will be on the lookout. You can count on us. Son, we recognize something different about her and Jorie. What is it?"

"Sorry. I promised her I wouldn't tell a soul. I can never break that trust."

"Don't be sorry. We raised you right. Be careful. We'll get them, Son."

"Thanks, Dad, but don't let on in any way that you're following them. They will kill you." He patted Hagan's shoulder and gave him a supporting smile. He changed clothes and put on a baseball cap, and grabbing fishing gear and comic books took off, with hopes the fishing disguise would throw the abductors off.

It worked.

# Chapter Thirty-Four

Leaving his parents' apartment heading to the island to see his Chantara *Hanna-Barbera*, he was stunned, not expecting to see this person walking up to him in the parking lot.

"Dani, what are you doing here and how did you find me?"

"Hello, Hagan. Finding you was the easy part but getting up my nerve to speak to you is the hard part."

"Let's hear it then. I'm in kind of a hurry."

"Wow! After the ending of a three-year relationship, you want me to hurry up with what I have to say?"

"I'm sorry, but time isn't on my side."

"Well, excuse me for interrupting your—what? Fishing or a trip to the store to buy some silly comic books," she said, her eyes resting on the ones in his hand. "You act as though whatever you're up to is a life or death situation. I mean, come on. For the sake of three years, can we at least take a few minutes to be civil and just talk?"

"You lost that privilege when you destroyed my couch, which, by the way, was the most comfortable couch in the universe. I had it removed from my apartment. The memory it brings to my mind will never go away."

"Hold on. It is more upsetting to you that you had to get rid of the couch instead of getting rid of a three-year relationship?" She was acting childish and unjustifiably offended.

"Sure, we'll go with that." He shook his head and frowned at the absurdity of her remark.

"Let's start over. I'm sorry. Now that I've had time to think about things, I am deeply sorry for what I've done to you. There is no justification. I don't know if this will make any of it feel better to you, but what you saw that day was not planned and it was the first time anything like that came near to happening. It literally just happened."

"You're right about one thing, it doesn't make me feel better. Dani, if you only knew the thousands of opportunities I have had to be unfaithful to you. I was raised to have good morals and control."

"I appreciate that. Truly, I do. And that is what I came to talk with you about. I still love you, Hagan. Couldn't we give this relationship another try? I will never let anything like this happen again." Her eyes were pleading and tender.

"That's good to hear, but you forgot about the other woman you always referred to in our relationship, and rightfully so. You are not the only one to blame in this breakup. I take full responsibility for being so involved in my work that I ignored you. You were lonely and I knew it, and nothing was going to change with regard to the other woman—my job, so I apologize sincerely for making you feel alone."

"Thank you for admitting that. Could we give this another try?"

"The one thing I came to realize is that we're not in love with each other. We will always love each other but will never be in love with each other. I'm sorry, but you will find out that this breakup was the best thing that happened for both of our sakes. You never did answer how you found me. I would like to know."

Dani was a little shocked to hear his statement about not being in love with her. That was totally unexpected and she wasn't convinced that she felt the same way. What was even worse was that the way he explained it was in such a cool and calm matter-of-fact manner, it scared her. Three years is a long time to come to a conclusion that fast. "Your mother called me."

"When did she call you?"

"Yesterday morning."

"I see now. That makes sense. I really hate to tell you this, but yesterday I had to tell Mom the whole ugly truth of what happened between us. There was no choice, because she was never going to stop trying to get us back together. What about you and not my best friend?"

"He isn't you, I realized too late, and your friendship seems to mean more to him than me. Back to your mother. I can never face her now. This confession had to kill her. Your family has always been closer to me than my own family. I can't imagine never seeing them again."

"Dani, I'm sorry, but that's the way it has to be. I think a reconciliation should be the goal with your own family. Even though I accept as much responsibility for this breakup, you and Adam betrayed something so sacred in everything I believe about friendship and love; for Mom, too."

"Don't you think we can still work this all out? Come on, Hagan."

"No, because we're not in love. Here is why it will never work out." He scrolled through his pictures on the phone and showed her Chantara's picture and one of Chantara and himself. The anger and hurt in her facial expression was almost devastating.

"Well, that didn't take you long, now did it?" Her fists slammed into her hips and she gritted her teeth, holding back an eruption of angry tears.

The jealousy of looking at this beautiful, enchanting woman was too much to bear; not just that, but the look of love in Hagan's face.

"Have a good life, because you've ruined mine!" she belted out and vanished into the dark. She climbed into the car and drove away.

"Dani," he yelled as she drove off. He didn't really want it to end this way, but there was nowhere else for the conversation to go and time wasn't on his side. He has to get to that island, because unbeknownst to Dani, this was a life and death situation, but she didn't know that. Nevertheless, he took off for the boat and his disguise seemed to work.

He packed the boat with snacks, and peanut butter sandwiches— "Oh, she hasn't tried this yet. She'll go wild over peanut butter."

On the way to the island, he figured he better call Fernando and have him collect and store his things left in the stateroom. At the island, Hagan lay back in the seat of the boat and popped open a fizzy drink that brought Chantara to his mind toot sweet. He smiled, rethinking about the first time she opened a fizzy drink and how cute it was to see the excitement in her face, the adorable giggling, and he was caught up in some love spell again. And that's not all, the sound of opening the can must have been heard and he received some guests.

"Well, well, well, look who is here. Hello Flopper and hello Shovel." He was able to brush his hand over their feathers and found how enjoyable it was to be trusted by them.

"Look, you two. I'll see what I can find for you to eat, but it won't be much, because you are supposed to be on a strict seagull and pelican diet, but I won't tell if you don't."

Shovel gobbled up the snacks in one swallow and Flopper flapped his wings in a silly manner. "I see why she named you Shovel, mister, and how you flap your silly wings is proof that your name fits you to a *T*, Flopper."

After laughing over the asinine commotion they made, he gave them some more snacks and returned to his seat to try and catch some sleep. Fat chance of that. He pulled out a comic book but couldn't focus. Fear started to come over him; a fear that maybe he'd never see Chantara again. If she doesn't love him, why attempt another abduction by coming back here today, or worse, what if her father won't allow her to come back? The thought came upon him suddenly and caused a great deal of inner turmoil. He had to try and take his mind off of this worrisome disposition or he'd be on edge when she arrived. His stomach was in knots, his brain frazzled beyond repair.

With very little sleep, he sat up, looking around for Chantara. Flopper and Shovel stood guard—well, stood guard over the snacks.

"Whoa! What was that splash?"

Skimming the water, he saw what looked like huge whale flukes that caused a spectrum of colors as they smacked the surface of the water. It was fascinating and spectacular to watch.

Now that it was safe, his name was called. "Hagan, I here."

With a quick gasp, his heart skipped a beat. He ran around the boat looking for her and stared in disbelief. "You're okay. I was so worried. Could I pull you up into the boat?"

"I think it better to sit on rocks. No people; right?"

"Right. No people."

Something was different about her eyes, he couldn't help but notice. They were more defined and had the look of ocean water, as though the ocean swirled in them. Hagan jumped out of the boat and ran to the rocky beach area while keeping his eyes on her. "Ouch!" He stubbed his hallux on a rock, so he had to watch where he walked. Soon, he found the perfect spot and waited. As she approached, he saw everything and froze like his cold-as-ice comic book friend had just zapped him with his ice gun. She told him, but he didn't want to believe her. Pulling herself up onto the beach, she smiled brilliantly, extending her hand for him to grab.

His face revealed complete shock and he couldn't comprehend in his mind the magnificent, physical transformation in her and was unable to physically move.

"Hagan okay?"

Finally, he came out of this trance. She was astounding, compelling, better than any fable could produce. He worried if he closed his eyes she would be gone when he reopened them.

"You not like?"

"Sorry. Like, no; love, yes. I just can't believe my eyes."

She didn't compare to a children's story description of a mermaid. The perfectly colored scales covered all the way up to her neck and then the skin was exposed all the way down her back to the buttocks. They looked like scales, anyway. When the sun shined over her—and even when it didn't—it was a sight to behold.

"You're wearing the necklace I gave you."

"Yes, I love. I have treasure for you, too."

"The only treasure I want is you. You are more valuable than any treasure chest of gold and silver."

"Don't move. Mother and Father want to meet man who save Jorie and me."

She made some unique, melodic sound and heads popped above the water. His heart raced, and he felt vulnerable and uncertain what to do next. Boy, did he feel out of place. Chantara felt like the misfit in his world, but now he was the misfit in this script.

"Please meet my father, Galon. He have treasure for you. Go to him."

He stood up but still could not move his foot forward. Galon was intimidating to look at. His size and strong physique were obvious as his tail swerved back and forth on the water. The ripples on the water from the movement looked more like waves and his expression was kind but confident, demanding attention but in a humbling way.

Chantara noticed his fear. "He not hurt you. Go."

As he walked down into the water, Galon approached and patted his shoulder with a droll smile. Hagan smiled in return. Was he staring into the eyes of royalty? There was no way to know. Galon shook his head in a gesture of approval and handed him a large scallop shell filled with gold and silver coins.

"I'm speechless," Hagan remarked.

The blinding refection of the sun flashing off the coins caused his eyes to squint.

"Thank you, sir," and he bowed to show respect.

Next, her mother moved forward. She was breathtaking like Chantara. The smile was sweet, innocent and welcoming. She also demanded attention but in a very charming, who-could-refuse-or-want-to manner. She handed him another shell filled with jewels, but with astounding stones he had never seen in his life. There were even some very mysterious ornamental keys mixed in with the jewels. *No wonder Chantara was confused by the stateroom key card.* He stared in disbelief. The sound of a very distinct resonance that was indescribable echoed before she slipped away. He bowed as she disappeared behind him.

Jorie and Tydal came forward. Chantara slid into the water and came to his side. "Please meet Jorie's Tydal."

Hagan's thoughts were everywhere and he couldn't quit thinking how good it is that they weren't human, because compared to human men, there was just no scintilla of a comparison. Women would never look at men again. They were huge, with very unfair, toned muscles. Handsome wasn't a good enough word to describe them. Mermen reminded him of a combination of his comic book hero, *Thor*, and his new favorite comic book hero, *Aquaman*. Shocker there. Tydal patted his shoulder and he almost fell over from what appeared to be a gentle pat. Shockingly, sweet, angelic Jorie hugged him and handed him something weird.

"I'm taken aback. Do you have any idea what this is?" He

referred his question to Chantara, knowing Jorie would have no way of understanding it. She wasn't able to respond, because to them, it was meaningless. He opened the oak slipcase that was magnificently preserved with high hopes it held a treasure that people all over the world had been searching for since the Titanic sank. Placing a hand over his overly-excited heart, he was at a loss for words. "How did you find this? This is the lost Rubaiyat, a book of medieval quotes and poetry. It is jewel encrusted. You have no idea how valuable this is; do you?"

"We know not," Chantara responded.

"There are more than one thousand small and delicate emeralds, rubies, amethysts and topazes, each set separately in gold. Would it be all right for me to turn this over to the appropriate authorities? I would never let anyone know where I obtained it. This will be quite the unveiling. By the way, you are nowhere around the area of where the Titanic sunk. How did you get a hold of this?"

"We go all over the waterways of the world to explore, but we always come back to our home. You see, our world is unseen to man. You could never enter into our kingdom. It is like a world of its own and filled with majestic treasure and adventures. It so beautiful and so much to discover and see. So much more fun than your world."

Tydal handed him a shell filled with some liquid substance that appeared thick like mercury and had magical colors that sparkled and glowed. The colors resembled the colors that reflect from Chantara, which was quite an easy observation to make. He looked at Chantara with questions.

"This is moon water. Feel it. In my world is a pond and waterfall of moon water."

It felt like silk and had a mild, vibrating sensation. "I've never seen anything like this before. What do I do with it?"

"You show no people! A tiny taste make you feel good, feel love, want love, exploding love. All my people taste it, but only I get the magic to my body and hair. Mother said when I was born the moon shined down on me and made a pool of moon water in adoration of me. I know not why."

"I know why. You are a treasure unlike anything else in the world and the definition of love. God saw something very special in you. Being with you fills my heart with explosion. I don't need moon water to capture that awareness."

She didn't understand.

Something behind him made a whale of a splash. "What is that?"

Chantara had a scolding face, and Sereia and Taras jumped up next to them. She introduced them. They were fun, kind and mischievous, and he fell in love with them instantly.

"Hagan, can we talk? I need to tell you more things about bad people. It so bad. I meet up with my family after we talk. They go now."

They all waved and smiled affectionately to him. Hagan did the same. There was a bond of love they had that all people of the world could recognize.

Remembering, a thought came to his mind how the Bible tells us that *love* is the greatest gift of all and the love they shown for each other was a precious sight to behold. He watched the water ripple as they swam off.

# Chapter Thirty-Five

Of course Hagan wanted to find out everything so he could help stop this human trafficking ring but hearing the anguish and inhumane things Chantara had been subjected to was seriously, without any doubt in his mind, going to permanently turn him into Mr. angry green man, and rightfully so. He would love her forever and always with a love so deep that it hurt physically as well as mentally. He could be completely honest with himself now.

"As much as I dread hearing these horror stories, I must. Please, tell me."

She reached over and placed her hand on his, causing every wonderful sensation UNKNOWN to man. No way to describe it, but it also had a calming effect that he was grateful for.

"These bad people want to feel exploding love with me. The prince said I was his but made other men come to me because he afraid what I do to him. He watch men try and he get excited and it make me sick to watch him. He laugh when I kill men, but I not help it. I have strong, sharp and long fingernails and teeth that you can't see, but it like a weapon my people use, plus we strong. We protect ourselves and our people and can't help it when you people die. We don't know it happen or feel it happen.

"When they capture my sister, sweet, sweet, Jorie, prince know I upset. He tell me I do what he want or I watch them kill her. He mean it and I not let them hurt my Jorie. He do things to me and scream like he crazy from what he feel. His kiss and touch make me so sick."

She held a hand over her mouth and puffed out her cheeks like she was about to vomit. She was sniffling and trembling at the remembrance. He pulled her gently into an embrace and softly brushed his hand over her silky hair and tears slid down his face. He could never explain how heartbreaking it is to watch her reveal such pain.

She positioned herself up straight. "I tell him I not do those things with Jorie watching, and if they touch Jorie, I not do those yucky things." She took a deep breath before going on.

"That not all the bad things, Hagan. I hear childs crying and screaming." She placed her hands over her ears like she could still hear, and then she sobbed with such an intensity that she almost became listless. If anyone witnessed this degree of suffering, then they would know what it feels like to have your heart torn in two. He pressed a hand on his heart. It physically felt like it was tearing.

"Let me try to tell you more. I hear women and boys and girls, but I too weak and chained up to help them. They not feed me and help me. Prince take me to place and tell me if I don't co... op...er...ate, Jorie end up like these people.

"In this place was shiny tables and so bright, it look like the sun was there. Jars of sea animals, and other things I not know what they are were all over the room. We keep walking"— She stopped talking and breathed in and out.

*This was going to be bad and I think I know where she's going with this,* he thought in terror. He kept swallowing and forgetting to breathe until he coughed.

"On tables were many people, animals, and my people, dead, cut open. Some looked like animal and peoples put together; even childs. Then I see him."

She dropped her head in her hands, swallowed hard and cried so hard that she gasped for air. But she is strong and determined, he could see, and wants to help him find them and end their hellish experimentation practices and sex trafficking, so she pulled herself together.

"Marin dead and parts cut out of him. There was many peoples in white coats, like lady on ship. Then one lady brought food to me and asked if I would like to taste mermaid fish. I not know what mermaid meant then. She said it yummy. They all laughed. It not funny, but I think she just being funny. How they laugh with hurting and making peoples and animals dead?"

There is not a human alive that could laugh at such evil. These aren't people; they're not human. "Please continue."

"Next they take me to this place that had hot, hot fire and it smell like dead. So many dead peoples and animals. It smell so bad. I get sick." She held her stomach feeling nausea developing and the other hand covered her nose as though the odor followed her.

Like any compassionate person, he held onto her for about thirty minutes, and they cried together. *God only knows what you've been through, my poor* angel. When they were able to pull themselves back to the present, she said something even more bewildering.

"Hagan, stay with me. I think I have you fragrance. Do you have my fragrance?"

Her colorful, tear-stained face was warm and sincere. He was naturally caught off guard by her proclamation.

"I—you—what?" His mind went blank for a moment. "I need to think about what you just said. There are no boundaries to how much I love you, more than I can express, but I can't live in the water and what about my mother, father and sister; my job? Would you stay with me?"

"I not be able to live away from my people. I not like your peoples."

"You're right. After the horrific experience you had with my people, I understand. But please be aware that there are good people in my world. Just like Cetus turned bad, so does some of our people. Regardless, everywhere we went, people stared in wonder at you. You could never survive in my world. You are like a magnet that attracts the looks of everyone we pass."

"You right, some of my people turn bad, too. If you stay with me, you be first human to be accepted. Your mother and father can come, too. My father can make you all mermaid and mermen, what you call us. You can become a people anytime, but you can't stay out of water for five days."

"Are you saying I can look like that?" He pointed to Tydal and Galon with high hopes. They had bopped back on top of the water at that moment.

"Yes, you would, but you pretty just like you are now."

"Chantara, I have to think about this. It's a cumbersome decision. Sorry, but I need to go and give this some thought." Clearly, he didn't expect to be placed in this situation, but the thought is intriguing, frightening and exciting. Holding her hands, Hagan genuinely stared into those mesmerizing eyes and softly whispered, "I love you. Don't ever forget it."

"Hagan, don't forget me." I could see she was torn, disappointed. Her fingers moved slowly from his as she entered the water with hesitancy. His face was so intense not wanting to leave her, and his love for her was so passionate and so hard to describe. He was truly close with his family and leaving them would be devastating to all of them. Now he saw how she must have felt being away from her family.

Before she almost disappeared, he yelled to her to wait. He couldn't let her leave yet. When he looked into her sparkling eyes, it felt like his heart stopped beating. He could never be happy with anyone else, and he didn't want anyone else.

"Chantara, let me explain my love for you by this movie I just watched, so you will have no doubts. It really captures just how deeply I love you. In this movie, a man and woman were deeply in love. The man was a soldier and called to duty at the front line of a battleground. After meeting you, I actually wanted to watch a movie with passionate romance whereas, before you, it would have bored me to tears.

"The woman said to him, you will return to me, won't you? Her face ached with the thought of losing him. I couldn't believe how special it felt to hear him call her his beloved. Normally, it would be way too mushy for me. I connected the passion between them with the passion between us."

Hagan tenderly lifted her face into his hands, not certain if she understood what he had said. They stared into each other's eyes and their love for each other almost felt like fireworks would explode, it was so genuine and electrifying. He placed her hand on his heart and said, "You are my beloved. No matter how long it takes or how complicated it gets, I will return for you."

They kissed long and passionately with a warmth that could melt snow.

He slowly slipped away, keeping his eyes on hers. But something changed in her face. Almost a knowing sadness; perhaps unrequited love in her mind. His heart skipped a beat. Did she know something he didn't? At that moment, his stomach felt sick with thoughts that this may be the last time he may ever see her. He walked away with his hands on his stomach, given in to defeat, not even trying to stop the tears from flowing.

"I love Hagan. I love." Her words echoed through the air.

Hagan glanced back and blew a kiss to her as she lowered into the water, waving, perhaps, a final goodbye. The loving solicitude between them was tragic, because the outcome of their love was undetermined at this point.

# Chapter Thirty-Six

Hagan arrived back at his parent's apartment and walked inside depleted of energy and the ability to reason with his thoughts. It was all too much and if he had to talk about everything, we all know where you could visit him. Yup, *One Flew Over the Cuckoo's Nest*. "I think I'll do you proud, Jack Nicholson," he said in a joking manner with a tiny bit of seriousness.

His parents ran to him, so he held up his hands and gently said, "I am so exhausted that I have to go straight to bed. I promise, I'll tell you everything." *Well, maybe not everything; maybe leave out the part that Chantara is a mermaid and wants me to become one.* His eyes almost rolled back into his skull, thinking how psychotic it sounded. He closed hard and opened his eyes twice to relieve the oncoming tension. Nope, did not work. He rubbed his fingers back and forth over his forehead. Nope. That didn't work either.

"We'll talk about it tomorrow. I promise, and Chantara is fine. Good night."

"Go ahead, son. I pray you get a good night's sleep," Dad said sincerely. His mother kissed his cheek. Thoughts of his parents were overwhelming at the moment. *I can't even begin to acknowledge the love I have for my parents. It is precious to me. Now, even more so.*

Shuffling his feet, he went to the bathroom and rummaged through the medicine cabinet. He grabbed a couple of pain reliever tablets and chugged them down with a large glass of water. His swallows were so hard and loud, he wondered if his parents heard the "gluc-gluc-gluc" sound.

The next morning, his parents asked if he wanted to go get some breakfast. They must have heard the bear growling in his stomach. "Yes, please."

He was putting up a front for his parents. They love so strongly and unconditionally that he could see what his fears were doing to them, and he just had to find a way to ease their worries. They walked down the boardwalk and stopped at a diner. After eating like a pig—he was starved, he hoped he didn't embarrass his parents—he opened up about all the disturbing and gruesome facts Chantara provided. They were quite upset, even bringing his mother to tears. Now they were adamant about helping him find these monsters. He knew a lot of long hours would go into researching their location.

His father placed a hand on his shoulder and he held a serious look. "Son, I found the information about that ship. The authorities are checking into it, and we should hear something soon."

"That's great news. Did you see that man named Brutus?"

"Oh, my world! Are you sure he isn't Goliath reincarnated?"

"Right? He's terrifying to look at."

Strolling down the boardwalk, people were out enjoying the crisp, ocean air. The aroma of pretzels, popcorn and cotton candy floated through the breeze. Chantara and Jorie would have their noses lifted up to the sky sniffing like a dog on the trail to find the scents. He giggled affectionately, even wanting to break down and cry. Sheesh! Children were running around, folks laughing, all oblivious to what lay beneath and what was happening in the criminal world. It sort of bothered him, but before he was privi-leged—sarcastically he pondered to himself—to this new hagridden information, he was a happy-go-lucky fellow. His mom would be exasperated with his choice of words if he spoke them out loud. What he meant to say is tormenting information.

As he looked around, he accidentally bumped into this man and child walking by. The man snarled at him when Hagan apolo-gized. The little girl, around eight years old, had this fearful look on her face and a few tears dropped down her face. The man held her up way too closely to himself and uncommonly tight for a comfortable distance between two people—even for family members. He stopped and stared. It was like the little girl was begging him to intervene. She kept looking back at Hagan with pleading, scared eyes. The man aggressively kept tugging at her.

"Hold on a minute," he said to his parents. "I may be paranoid and a little on the looney side right now, but I have to check something out or it will eat away at me. I may be making a blun-dering idiot of myself, but I have to at least find out."

"Find out what, son?" Dad asked worried.

"Stay close and come to my help if I need it."

"Wai—Come back here, Hagan," Melana demanded.

It was too late. As he approached the man and girl, with a quickness, getting his plot together of what to say, carefully and in a friendly manner, he said, "Excuse me, sir. I recognize this child, but I forget your name. What is it?"

He became nervous and started looking around furtively. "I don't have time for this."

Then he pulled the girl away from Hagan and she started to cry. "Shut up!" he yelled at her. That was Hagan's cue. He jumped in front of him and told the man to stop.

"I'm not moving until this little girl tells me her name." He took his hands off of her and came in close to Hagan with an intimidating look. He's twice his size in height and weight. What he didn't expect was that terrifying, sharp knife to come out of the man's belt strap. Hagan pulled back, and he started thrusting the knife at him. Needless to say, his eyes were the size of grapefruit, exaggerating, but they were wide.

"Get the little girl to safety," he yelled to his mother. His mom ran to his side, gulped and grabbed the little girl, then ran for cover while dialing 911. Thankfully, this was the emergency number in Barbados. He turned back to this psychotic man.

"You were abducting that little angel, weren't you?" He spit the words out, dodging the knife.

"Wouldn't you like to know?" the man snarled using a few choice words.

All of what Chantara confided in him came back to mind, and you guessed it, hello angry green man. All of his strength training and fighting skills were present and accounted for. He was preparing to use the techniques he had learned over the years, hoping they weren't too rusty. Like a striking snake, he kicked the dagger out of the man's hand and kicked him right in the face, and he tumbled to the ground. So, Hagan jumped on top of him and punched his face.

Those innocent faces kept popping into his mind, children and young women being abused by disgusting men like this guy. Angry tears slid down his face as he continued to punch him. The guy was now unresponsive, but Hagan couldn't quit hitting him. There was so much rage and hate inside his head. This was the first time he ever felt genuine hate, and it was consuming him. His eyes teared up with each punch.

In the back of his mind, he thought he heard his father yelling at him to stop, but he couldn't think clearly, until his dad managed to grab a hold of his wrist. It discombobulated Hagan's thinking, and he looked up at him as a lunatic. Anger had taken hold of Hagan's mind. This was not the type of person he was. His last scuffle was as a boy.

"Son, stop before you kill him. He's unconscious and the police are on the way."

Lifting his head, he could hear sirens in the near distance. "I'm sorry. I don't know what came over me. In my mind, envisioning the evil intentions of this man and the abuse this little girl would receive was easy to determine. If you hadn't stopped me, I could have killed him and not even feel any remorse about it."

"After what you have found out about sex trafficking, I would have probably done the same thing, especially in your circumstances, with it being real and personal to you. This is not who you are, though. You have to get control of yourself and not allow anger to rule your emotions."

"That makes sense, except if I didn't move on my assumption at that time, what would have happened to this little girl? Timing was just wrong."

His dad patted his shoulder in agreement and checked the guy's pulse. "He is breathing. I forgot just how strong and capable you are, son."

"Frankly, so did I."

Sergeant Gittens of the Royal Barbados Police Force ran up to the scene. He was fluent in English, so that was helpful. First, he checked the vitals of the creep lying unconscious and called for the medics. "Now, who can tell me what happened here?"

"I'll be glad to explain it. As my parents and I walked down the boardwalk, I noticed how tightly this man was holding onto that little girl over there with my mother," he said, pointing. "She had a look of terror on her face and she was crying. I cautiously, and in a friendly manner, approached the man, pretending like I knew the little girl and wanted to say hi. He got combatant fast and pulled out a knife and started thrusting it at me. I kicked it out of his hands and ended up beating him until he was knocked out cold.

"Look, I'm really sorry. I have just left a young lady who

described the horrors of child and adult sex trafficking, and I lost it. What type of person can look into the eyes of a child—or woman—and do such wicked things and enjoy it, no less? Of course, you will have to take my statement and arrest me for assault, and I'll go with you peacefully. My parents, I and our team have been hired by your government to conduct studies and research in the Caribbean and Atlantic, is why we are here. Here is our temporary address while we perform our duties."

"Thanks. This is a first, not dealing with a hostile suspect. Hold on a minute. Officer, please stand guard over this victim/suspect. The medical services should arrive very soon. Now, let's go see what the little girl has to say."

As they walked up, she hid behind his mother and held onto her like life depended upon it.

"Hello little girl. I'm here to help you. This nice lady will stay with you. Now, what is your name?" He translated it into her language. She whispered to Melana.

"Aaralyn," Mom replied.

"Do you think you could get her to tell us what happened?"

"I will certainly try," Melana replied, giving a look of sympathy to Hagan. After a few minutes, Melana spoke. "She was with her mom and the mom was paying for their lunch at a food stand. Aaralyn was sniffing flowers and walked out of her mom's sight, is my interpretation of her explanation. Then that man grabbed her, putting his hand over her mouth and ran. Before he took his hand off her mouth, he warned her that he would kill her and the mother if she screamed. I'm struggling with interpreting her language."

"Would you mind accompanying this girl to the station in the back of my squad car? She seems to trust you."

"I would love to right after I get her an ice cream cone. We'll meet you there."

The sergeant called the station to see if the mother reported her missing. He was a little worried about that because in past cases, a lot of children were sold to these monsters by their own parents who didn't have the means to take care of them. In his mind, it was appalling.

"A relief, Mr. Bennett. The mother is at the station in bad shape. She is out of her mind sick with worry. You and your father ride with that officer over there and we'll get you back to your home afterword. I'm really sorry to have to take you in, but I think this will turn out in your favor once we compile all the necessary information. Try not to worry.

"Look, I see remorse in your eyes. I want to thank you for taking the action that you did. If it weren't for you, this little girl would never be seen again. I have a little girl her age, so your reaction is understandable, and everything in my power will be done to get any charges dropped."

"Thank you. That means a lot to me. Truthfully, I am just not that kind of person who loses it. It's just that...hearing the tragedies of the victims is unspeakable pain." He lowered his head to hide the tears.

"I can see that, but remember, you saved that little girl. Look at that face. Look at it! Now, picture some awful man taking away her innocence. You did the right thing and I will testify to it. Let's just hope we can break this man and find out where he was taking her."

He and his parents sat in an interrogation room waiting for the sergeant. He finally walked in.

"Well, looks like you're all free to go, but stay around until the case is complete and you are cleared of any charges. Oh, yeah, the suspect is conscious and suffers with a concussion, but he'll be fine. And he is pressing charges for assault and battery against you."

"Of course he is. He's a criminal, and I bet I'll be convicted for assault and battery."

"Not in my precinct you won't. I got your back, man. Try not to worry."

They shook hands, and he thanked him. Hagan wasn't a flight risk, the sergeant found out as they dug into their background and found his statement of the work they do here in the ocean to be true.

That evening, he called Drake to see how he was holding up. Not too well. He was blindsided by meeting Jorie and having a difficult time moving on. Very strange after meeting someone for a short period of time. Magic. It has to be. But before we could carry on a decent conversation someone knocked at Hagan's door and they had to end the call.

"Come in," he answered.

"We had a good idea," his dad said. "Why don't you work with us tomorrow? We'll stick closely together. I think it will do you well to go to the one place in the world that brings you happiness."

"Now, that's a plan. I'm in." He patted Hagan's shoulder and left the room.

Hagan's attention was drawn to the bookshelf that hid the treasure Chantara gave to him. A glow was coming from it. He walked up close and the moon water was swirling with the colors of Chantara. He swore it formed into her face momentarily. Cuckoo, cuckoo, he knew. He was hypnotized by it. Maybe a little delusional, too. It was an absolute reflection of her and would always help him to remember her, depending upon his decision, which was frightening. Moon water is a part of her; looking at it was as spellbinding as though he were looking at her.

Chantara's transformation was beyond words or imagination. As far as science and anatomy were concerned, it's inconceivable that she could be both human and fish. It just wasn't logical that her tail could become legs and vice versa. But his eyes saw it. If truth be told, Hagan and his parents had wondered why God didn't give life to him as a fish, because of how precious time in the water was to him.

Every evening, he would walk out to the end of the pier and

leave scrumptious snacks for Chantara. Before he stepped off the pier heading back to the apartment, there would be some token of incredible value sitting on top of where the snack was left. So he walked back and lifted it, cherishing it because it was from her. It was a ritual between them.

# Chapter Thirty-Seven

Hagan was in his element. He and his parents conducted their research, gathered samples, and performed all the other necessary tasks. A glow started growing from the corner of his eye. Turning in that direction, it was astonishing at how bright it became. He wondered if the sun fell into the ocean, it was so bright. Of course, not like there hadn't been enough chaos in his life, he clipped a lifeline to his belt and waved to his dad indicating his intentions and direction. Ten fingers held up signified come and look for him in ten minutes, if he didn't return. His father nodded.

As Hagan got closer, the water was calmer and clearer than it had ever been. It was his observation that what lay beneath was not volcanic or manmade, but where was that glowing, bright light coming from? It was a hole or portal in the middle of the ocean, with no rocks, sedimentary, or even sea plants surrounding it. This hole was right out in the open. A ferocious whirlpool encircled the portal, but below it smoothed out into a peaceful, calm, magnificent mixture of colors like an artist's palette. Following these colors, the glowing, bright light led into an area that wasn't in view.

Like that first day, what-lay-beneath thoughts were driving him wild. He still couldn't identify this feeling as being terrifying or intriguing. For all the craziness he'd been through, it still felt uncomfortable relying on a feeling. And once again, the hairs on the back of his neck stood up like being electrocuted.

It got even stranger when he was able to swim right up to the opening. From what he could see, it looked like an entrance into a very expensive, posh gated community, but better, with a natural array of colors. The crazy thing was that you had to get right up close to see this and guess who was the first person to get this close? That's right. Him.

Bad, bad move. Was it a trick to allow him to get so close? The water became violent and stirred up so many bubbles and sea particles that he couldn't see anything. Big, huge fish—he thinks they were fish—were bumping into him. His lifeline snapped in half and he was in trouble. The Littoral transport picked up and swirled him into whirlpools. It felt like he was in a wash machine, swishing back and forth but faster. No questions asked, this was serious trouble. A swirl of colors came into view before he drifted into the current and blacked out.

Hagan's parents and teammates saw the disturbance and tried to find Hagan, but it was impossible. So they swam up to the boat to take necessary precautions. To their shock and surprise, Hagan was lying inside the boat, unconscious.

Thomas called for medical services to meet him back at the pier while another member of the team drove the boat. Hagan became conscious, but didn't move.

"Son, can you hear me?"

"Yes, Mom." Hagan tried to sit up but became very dizzy and nauseous, and his head ached terribly, so he fell back in place with a thud, rubbing the back of his head as a bump began to grow.

Before they could discuss what happened, the medics arrived at the pier and immediately transported him to the hospital. While checking his vitals, the medic used words he knew well: *bends*. Translated means a severe case of general barotrauma. He heard them refer to it as Caisson sickness several times. They worked to maintain his blood pressure and administered high-flow oxygen. Then they placed him in a left-side down position and the head of the bed tilted down. Honestly, he felt more horrible than at any time in his life.

They rushed him into the hospital and placed him in a high-pressure chamber immediately where nitrogen is driven back into its liquid form. This could take hours.

When he was brought to a room to be monitored until they felt it was safe to release him, his parents were there waiting. Before closing his eyes and getting some sleep, like he desperately wanted, his mother held a pink diamond in her hand. "Where did you find this rare stone?"

"I have no knowledge about it."

"The medic handed it to me in the ambulance. You were clinging onto it."

"How weird is that." It must have slipped his mind until he cleared it and remembered seeing a swirl of colors coming his way before losing consciousness, realizing there was no way to tell them where it came from without compromising the safety of the merfolk. Did the word "merfolk" come from his thoughts as if they were factual beings? Hagan saw them with his own eyes; didn't he? Could he have had a nervous breakdown and imagined all of it?

Unconsciously, he rubbed his forehead, feeling another monster headache starting. Thankfully, his parents dropped the questions and a deep sleep took hold of him for almost two days. It put his parents in a state of worry, but the medical staff had explained to them that he was just exhausted and needed serious sleep. Besides, all the fluids and everything needed was pumped through him like he was an incubation doll. No wonder he didn't want to wake up. We've heard of voodoo dolls, well meet the incubation doll, decked out with all the features and tubes filled with fluids to bring hours of fun to any "not" normal child—*The Addams Family* type of children.

Lifting his arms, he counted the tubes.

Once he was released into his parent's care, he had to go on office duty. He'd take a root canal any day rather than the boredom of office work. His mom was right; there are reports needing completion that college professors were waiting on. Filling out written reports was painful for him, any kind of office work. Ugh! Could he trade in this duty for that root canal instead?

Since there was nobody else in the office, his mind became infatuated with researching the anatomy of a merman. Diagrams popped up on the screen and captured his total interest. Detailed illustrations—someone's guess since it wasn't common knowledge that merfolk exist—on how they could change back and forth from merman to humans with actual legs. Impossible, but he saw it with his own eyes. Chantara was that proof he always required; hard, cold facts and evidence, and feelings can't dispute that.

Missing her was as though it was only yesterday. His heart was hurting from being away from her and all the hesitation in the world wouldn't change that.

"What is this all about?"

He tried catching his breath because his mother startled him. "What are you doing here?"

"Other than the fact I work in this office, you mean?"

"Yeah, other than that."

"My son is supposed to be filling out reports, and it doesn't appear he has accomplished any of that necessary work, but instead, he is looking at the anatomy of mermaids. Your turn."

"Sorry, but I was scrolling around and found these diagrams and found them quite interesting," he said, wondering if she bought into his avoiding telling her the real reason.

"The professors are emailing me, looking for this information. You are late in getting it to them and with no excuse."

"Don't you know by now that office work is like torture to me? Talk about making me face a firing squad. Can't someone else do this?"

"Absolutely not. We all have just as many reports as you do to complete and we get it done. Now focus." He dropped his head and sighed in annoyance, not at his mother but the office work.

"Who really gives a darn about plate tectonics, or the interaction of seawater with the atmosphere and seafloor?"

"The professors and students relying on this information to learn how to become an oceanographer; that's who."

"When you're right, you're right. I'll have it done before the end of the day, submitted through email and copied to the folder. You know what I was thinking, though?"

"What?" she said in a voice that made it clear he better think twice before trying to avoid completing his work, arms crossed, a foot tapping the floor.

"After that episode with the man I almost killed, it may be a good idea for me to fly home for a few days and talk to Pastor Knoit. He still laughs when I call him Pastor Knowit All." His mom cracked up.

"That's a very mature idea. I sure miss not being able to go to church all the time."

"Me, too. Skedaddle Mom, so I can get done, but first I'm making reservations."

"See you at home, Son."

Hagan lucked out and got a ticket for tomorrow morning. Completing and emailing the results of his report, like he promised, and, mind you, in a very professional and well written report that his parents were quite happy with.

# Chapter Thirty-Eight

Hagan arrived home and drove straight to his pastor's church, after telephoning him while driving in his wonderful car. He couldn't help it and pushed down on the gas pedal while he had his foot on the brake.

"Hello, Mrs. Angeloni. I'm here to see Pastor Knowit All." She laughed.

"How great it is to see you. How are the folks?"

"Fabulous, as always. Doing very well and as always very busy."

"So, what about you? How did you manage to get time off?"

"I had an accident and needed to take time off to recover."

"Oh, my."

"No worries. I'm fine and will be back to work in a few days."

"Glad to hear it. Wait here and I'll let him know you're here."

The pastor came out of his office with a wide, welcoming smile and embraced him. "I am so happy to see you. You look good, strong and handsome as ever."

Blushing, he thanked him. "Hey, you've lost some weight. Looking good yourself."

"Thanks. The wife has been on my case since my 'checkup'." His face had the expression of dread, making Hagan wonder if he had to eat cardboard-tasting foods. "Come on in and take a seat. Now, I remember what a tight schedule you keep so you probably want to kick this conversation into full gear."

"You know me too well."

"Forgive my manners. What would you like to drink? Coffee, water, soda, gasoline?"

"Still the jokester, I see. Nothing, thanks, but I'll take some gasoline for the road—get it?"

He laughed like it was one of Johnnie Carson's jokes.

"Okay, Pastor. I suggest you buckle up. It's going to be a wild ride." He pretended to snap a seatbelt around his waist.

"Sounds like that gasoline will come in handy after all."

Hagan just shook his head. "Don't worry. I can handle what it is you want to talk about."

"This, I'm afraid, is nothing you've dealt with, so I'm a little skeptical that even you will know how to help me."

"Whoa! Slow that horse down, son. I certainly don't claim to have all the answers, so we'll just talk and see where it leads us and see if the Lord has anything to say about it." He prayed before they got started.

"Well, if I'm riding a horse, you better forget about giving me gasoline." He chuckled. They both shook their heads at how ridiculous their attempt to be humorous was going.

"I can't tell you much, because it will jeopardize this person's safety and anybody else who has knowledge will be in danger. Now, I want you to throw out any normal person's reasoning. What would you say if I told you fairy tales, aliens, etc....are real?"

"I'd say you need to get some rest or seek mental therapy, but enough about my thoughts. Go on, because my curiosity is flying in outer space right now."

"Let's just say for argument sake that there are worlds out there and beings that are more than myths. Would you think I was crazy?"

"One hundred percent. Kidding aside, I have known you all your life. You are the most level-headed person I have ever known, and I say that in truth and affectionately. Having you as one of my congregation members all these years is sentimental to me. Maybe not in agreement with your logic, but your reputation exceeds you, so there is always room for the benefit of the doubt where you're concerned."

"That means more to me than you'll ever know." Hagan worked hard to hold back the sentimental tears, embarrassed to look the pastor in the eyes, trying to act like something in the room caught his interest. This man has always been one of the best people he'd had the pleasure of knowing and admired him greatly.

"Now that you managed to bring me to tears, I'll continue. I'm sure you know Dani and I broke up, but that part is okay. It needed to happen. We love each other but we're not in love. But that's not what I came to talk to you about. When we broke up and how we broke up affected me so badly that I went on a cruise to try and work through my pain. Without any desire and by a complete accident, the most beautiful woman in the world slid into me in the midst of a storm. To get straight to the point, it's not from rebound, but I am so in love with her. We're talking flutters, tingling, and all that romantic fluff.

"Here is the tricky part. She escaped a sex trafficking and a human/animal experimentation facility. These monsters are looking for her and will kill anyone with information, and possibly her, also. She asked me to stay with her. It would require moving to a different country altogether. And it will literally, mentally, physically, and any other way, change my life. I can't go into details and my parents don't know this part yet.

"Pastor, I can't get her out of my mind. My gut is telling me to do it and be with her. Here's her picture."

"Wow! You aren't kidding. She is beautiful and has a kind, sweet, angelic aura about her. Is she an angel?"

"Right? If you could meet her, that would be an easy assumption to make. Look, I cannot tell you anymore. What do I do?"

"That's it? That's what I get to work with?"

"I'm afraid so. I'm afraid so."

"Okay then." He paused momentarily. "Marriage and God. You know what He says about choosing your spouse. It's basic Bible 101. Don't dismiss His words of wisdom on the matter. You already know them, so it would be a good idea to revisit them. I'll look up verses and text them to you."

"I have to say, the way this whole thing started, that completely slipped my mind. This should make for an interesting discussion."

"Now, as far as a belief that myths and other worlds could exist is not something I have found in His word, however, I am not so wise to dare and believe God could not have created secret worlds apart from ours or that Satan wasn't involved in foul play. To me, I don't see it, but I'm afraid heaven awaits that answer. There is no possible, and to me, logical way to accept such a thought.

"Truth is, I've been reading L.A. Marzulli books and they are along these lines and quite mind boggling. I find it hard to be critical of his findings, even though they sound bizarre. I'd bet he would like an audience with you.

"There isn't much more I can give you and I fear I'm a disappointment to you."

"Not in the least. I can't think of any other person who would have not taken the opportunity to lecture me. Thanks for approaching it so humbly and sensitively. The one thing I recognized all these years is that you are firm in your Biblical beliefs and teaching. You are not afraid to teach them to us, but you also allow us to share our opinions in disagreement without trying to intimidate or make us feel foolish.

"On the other hand, I have seen righteous anger from you in situations requiring you to take a firm stance. I appreciate how you have had the courage to teach your congregation everything a person deals with in life: romance, job choices, politics, education, salvation and all Bible truths. These traits are admired by your congregation, because they all form together into one incredible man."

"Now I'm blushing. Is there anything else you needed to speak to me about?"

"Like this isn't enough, but, yes, there is more."

"Lead the way."

"Since I have dealt with the traumatic results of sex trafficking, I have a raging anger toward people who participate in it." The pastor had a quizzical look about him that showed his curiosity in hearing more. "Walking down the boardwalk in Barbados I encountered one taking place." Pastor raised his eyebrows at that remark. Then Hagan went into detail about the whole story, top to bottom.

"My angry actions scared even me. I didn't want to stop hitting this horrible person, and he most certainly is not made in God's image, I'm sorry to say. If Dad hadn't stopped me, I probably would have killed him. His face was bleeding, swelling and bruising. This isn't the kind of person I am. How can I prevent this type of outrage to consume me?"

"Officially, you have become my most challenging counsel session, so thank you for that," he replied satirically. "One of the Ten Commandments comes right to my mind: 'Thou shalt not kill'. To go a step further, killing him makes you no better than he is. Allowing the justice system to convict him and go through the proper channels is the right means. And I am aware that even the justice system has been corrupted in places, but God's Word stays the same, whether righteous judgment is administered or not.

"I get it, and that is righteous anger, but murder is murder. You had a split decision to make, and just knowing what his intentions were for this little girl is just sickening. Say a quick prayer before you find yourself in a predicament like that. Too much happened to you in such a short period of time. You need to recover before allowing yourself to get back in those types of situations.

"By the way, were you charged with any assault charges and given permission to come back to the US?"

"Yes, the suspect did press charges against me, but the officer is backing me up and the man I beat up is just fine now. The authorities gave me two days to come back—heading back in one day."

"The Hagan I know has a good head on his shoulders. Follow the Lord's guidelines and then follow your heart."

Hagan put his finger to his mouth and squinted his eyes. *Where have I heard that before?*

"God gave emotions to help us in our struggles, but He also provided clear and simplistic guidelines to direct us in making the right decision with those emotions."

"How is it I always feel better after talking to you?"

"Because God's word is simple and you love Him, plus our *manly*—he emphasized the word with a toughness in jesting—affection for each other is mutual."

We stood up and embraced in a *manly* hug then Hagan left.

# Chapter Thirty-Nine

I t was another moment of truth, and this was the first time he'd been back to his apartment since the breakup. No matter how in love with Chantara he was, the hurt of what happened in his apartment that day will always be a devastating memory. He'd lost his girlfriend of a three-year relationship and his best friend all in one lousy day.

He pulled into his parking spot and chatted with several neighbors on the way in. His car always made for great conversation. In his opinion, that was a good distraction. Before opening the door, his heart rate sped up, and he took a deep breath, automatically turning in the direction of the living room, where the world's-best couch was now gone. That was the most unbelievably comfortable couch he'd ever owned. Such was life. His thoughts shot directly to merfolk lives. *What do they sleep on and sit on?*

The feeling in his apartment was like being in a haunted house. He cringed and knew it was impossible to remain here much longer. Wisdom directed him to take a walk on the beach, one of his fondest memories and loves. Anything near the water gave him a peace of mind. He couldn't have wished for a more

241

perfect day. The sky was the prettiest blue color. Temperature in the seventies, and the water shimmered like diamonds.

The breeze blew his hair all over the place and sort of tickled. Seagulls were squealing and scouting the ocean and beach for food. Hagan put his hand up to cover his eyes, searching for Flopper. He wondered why God hadn't made most birds, fish and animals of the same species look different from each other. He would ask God about that when he meets Him one day. Surely He has been asked stranger questions than that.

Drawing in the sand with a piece of driftwood, he drew a sketch of what was on his mind: Chantara. She was ever present on his mind. With his legs crossed over and elbows resting on top of them, his hands held the weight of his head. If only they could hold the weight in his heart. So many things to think about that require so much emotion. As he stared in La-La Land at the ocean, thoughts of her were so powerful that this breathtaking angel captivated his very being.

Not fair for his mind to go to his parents, sister, nieces, plus his family's dogs. It brought reality to light. *How could I ever leave them? Would I be able to see them again after transforming into a merman?* Never thought he'd think those words in his mind. The decision was too great and complexed. Chantara was proof they can become a human anytime and visit family. Could the transformation work or could he die? He was too young to die.

A hand rested on his shoulder. He looked up and an older woman with a kind face looked down at him. "Follow your heart, even if love takes you to the stars in the heavens or down into the depths of the sea. Make a splash."

She smiled and walked away. He had never seen her before in his life. *There's that saying again.* What she said kept playing over and over in his mind. Does she know something, or is she trying to advise him how to make the toughest decision of his life? He walked back to his apartment deep in thought.

Validation and grief struck hard as he opened his sock drawer and pulled out the engagement ring to return to the jewelry store tomorrow on the way to the airport. Since it was too painful to hang around his apartment, he spent most of the day on the beach. The sting of too much sun just added to the sting of reality in making a decision that sounded psychotic. The best thing for him was to get the heck out of Dodge. So he drove to his parent's home and stayed there until the morning.

The next morning, he stopped at the jewelry store before heading to the airport. Plopping the ring and receipt on the counter was loud, embarrassingly loud. People turned to see what made the noise, glued to, in his mind, a pathetic and shameful face. A face that depicted failure. The jewelry sales associate walked over.

"I need to return this ring, please." His voice was low, trying to avoid anyone from hearing, even the sales associate, apparently, since he informed Hagan he couldn't hear him and he had to repeat it.

"I'm sorry to hear that. Is the ring defective or something? Maybe a different style?"

"No, thanks. We ended our relationship." Like it's any of your business, Hagan wanted to tell him. Now he was mad at himself for wanting to take it out on this employee.

"I'm so sorry, sir. I'll take care of this for you right away."

Riding in a taxi to the airport, his feelings were all over the place. It was a mishmash stew of feelings, but it was good to be heading—he almost said heading home, because it was feeling more and more like home in Barbados.

Mom and Dad were waiting for him at the airport. They hugged and discussed his counseling session with the pastor and how returning the ring went. He wasn't in a very talkative mood and they picked up on that. They drove to the apartment in silence until Mom remembered something.

"Son, I almost forgot. Here is mail from the Royal Barbados Police Force." She handed it to him and watched every tear he made to open the envelope, and even followed his eyes as he read the document. Hagan could see her through the corner of his eye. A glint in his eyes, a mischievous thought came to him. He could have some fun with this. He needed to have some fun, even at the expense of his dear parents.

So he dropped his head in a solemn manner and slowly said, "I only have a couple of days before they bring me in."

"Oh, dear!" She sighed placing a hand on Dad's shoulder. "We should get an attorney and fight this," his mother commented in a panic.

Then he repeated what he had said with just a few additional words that would complete his sentence. "I only have a couple of days before they bring me in to sign my release papers from any criminal actions. Charges have been dropped and I'm cleared of any criminal charges." He pulled his head up, revealing a mischievous smile.

"That is not funny one bit," Melana scolded.

"I'm sorry. I just couldn't resist. You looked so serious and worried, it was all I could do."

"I didn't buy into it for a minute," his dad added.

"Really?" Hagan replied in disbelief. "Not for a minute?"

"Okay, half a minute." They all chuckled.

Hagan's telephone alerted him to an incoming call.

"Hello."

"Mr. Bennett, this is Sergeant Gittens."

"I'm glad you called. I just read my release document. Thank you for your help."

"It was an absolute pleasure to assist you. But that is not the reason I am calling. Normally we don't follow up with a case, but it seemed the right thing to do in this instance, since it was you who led the way for us to find the criminals involved in the trafficking crime in the first place.

"It was tricky finding the traffickers in question, because they usually don't stay in one location very long. This is only a drop in the bucket for the large amount of trafficking organizations out there to discover, but one drop is so much better than none. Thanks for your help."

"Anytime, Sergeant, anytime." They spoke for a few more minutes and ended the call.

When they got to the apartment, Hagan ran straight for the pier. Why Chantara wouldn't make herself visible was concerning, but maybe it was a protection strategy. He strolled back to the patio area. As they sat around the patio table, he informed them about what the lady on the beach said to him.

"That's an odd thing to say from someone who doesn't know you from Adam," his mom said realizing her mistake. He just ignored it so they didn't have to discuss "Adam". This was where the-rubber-meets-the-road.

"I have something to tell you that is going to blow your minds, cause you to admit me to a mental asylum, and probably never take me seriously again. And you can never speak a word of it to anyone. Promise me this before I go any further."

"You've managed to scare the wits out of me," Melana exclaimed, "now please continue."

"I'm on board with your mom, but we promise to keep your secret."

"Remember when you said something was different about Chantara?"

"Yes," Thomas replied.

He held his arms out as if he was going to be handcuffed. "She is a mermaid." They didn't flinch nor speak. Then, after careful consideration, Thomas spoke.

"We actually talked about this possibility between us. The thought was already there. It is still difficult to wrap our heads around such an unscientific notion, but I fear the same thought has brought us together in unison."

"Wait...what? My parents, who have no imagination whatso-ever, believe me?"

"Guilty as charged," Melana added.

"There's more. She wants me to live with her in their underwater realm. Her father will transform me into a merman and I can always turn back into a human anytime. They can't stay out of the water five full days or they will remain a human, never to be a part of their people again. I am leaning to go with her. She is constantly in my thoughts. And just think how much better working arrangements could be for me—all of us.

"You know what? I just had a revelation. When I was escorted to the hospital that day by medical services for treatment from the Bends, I saw that mystical area again. That is where they live. It has to be. Of course, they have to protect themselves against intruders, especially humans. Could you just imagine what would happen if they were discovered? There would be endless research, exploration, bad and unsafe exposure. Their lives would become a circus. That spot can never be invaded by humans."

"Hagan, everything about them screams fantasy, myth, something. Even the way she spoke had a harmonic melody to it, just in normal conversation. Then those magical tones of her skin, I mean, come on, who in their right mind would not have questions? We will never breathe a word ever. You can trust us. Your decision is something only you can make. There will be no interference from us in your decision. It will be hard for all of us, but we will not try and influence you either way," Melana stated sincerely, but yet her eyes revealed a little sadness. The thought of him leaving and what if the transformation doesn't work; could-he-die thoughts, were pounding inside her emotions, he guessed. She just held a look momentarily that meant a whole lot without saying it with words.

They hugged for an extended amount of time. It sort of felt like a I'll-miss-you hug. Hagan turned his head and walked away, teardrops falling down his face. They probably saw him wipe the sniffles from his nose that seemed to drip constantly.

# Chapter Forty

D rake sat in his apartment gloomy and all out of sorts. His head rested against the couch, legs crossed out in front of him and eyes closed. He could not make sense of anything. Why was he so enamored by a woman he met once? This was the type of a reaction someone would feel after breaking up from a three-year relationship, not a three minute one. And now that she was engaged, it was completely hopeless.

On his phone were texts from friends asking him to come and hangout. Family gatherings, he skipped; go to dinner with his coworkers, he skipped too. The only thing he could hear was his thoughts yelling at him to get out of the apartment. *Go for a walk; go get a bite to eat; go to the coffee shop down the block; GO SOMEWHERE.*

Shockingly, he listened to that little voice and went to the coffee shop. The shop was crowded and loud, with clanging and clatter, grinding and humming noises, but it didn't matter to him. He was oblivious to it all. Drinking a hot cup of a bourbon roasted coffee, he scrolled through pictures of Jorie. "Let me give my friend a call. That's a great idea," he convinced himself.

Hagan answered his cellphone. "Hagan, it's Drake. How are things?"

"The same, I'm sorry to say. Haven't seen Chantara or Jorie in weeks. They say no news is good news," he remarked.

"So they say. Are you anywhere close by?"

"Nope. My parents and I are still working on our assignments in Barbados. It's starting to feel more like home than Fort Myers."

"I wish I could find some time to get over there. It is a beautiful island, but I would probably get fired for taking time off so soon."

"What I love about my job is that it feels like we are on a permanent vacation."

"Well, I'm envious."

"Are you doing okay with the notion you will never see Jorie again?"

"Truthfully, no. I feel like a fool blubbering over a young woman I met for a short amount of time. You can laugh all you want, but it feels like I'm under some weird spell."

"Laugh? You hit the nail on the head. I, as well, can't quit thinking about Chantara. Here's why this is strange: I feel like I'm under some spell with Chantara and as incredible as Jorie is, I don't think about her like Chantara; and you have the opposite spell with Jorie. Maybe they handpicked us to be theirs and torture us with a lovesick life. Maybe it's a curse they put on us."

"We certainly do have a big imagination."

"Hey man, I need to go, but I'll call you soon." They said their goodbyes and ended the call. Drake kept looking at his pictures not paying attention to anything going on around him. That's when an ice cold chill ran down the back of his neck. He rubbed his hand behind his neck and felt a sticky liquid substance. Holding the hand to his face, the substance dripped on his shirt.

"Just what is the meaning—"

"I am so sorry," came a sweet voice from behind.

He started to stand up and turn, holding his sticky, dripping hand up with a menacing glare.

"How did... How did I cause this silly accident?" he asked stuttering and in complete stupefaction.

"Please accept my apology and let me help clean that mess off of you. You must not have realized it, but you jutted your leg out as I passed by and clumsy me tripped, spilling my ice peppermint cream Frappuccino down your neck." Her face expressed humor and horror at the same time.

"Please, it was all my fault. Let me buy you another one of those things and would you join me at the table? I just need to clean this off of me because I'm feeling like a frozen, sticky marshmallow. I'll be right back."

"I'll join you, but not at this table." He looked and immediately moved his coffee to another table, notifying the staff of the accident that needed to be cleaned up. But before he walked away, he stood staring at her in disbelief.

"Is something wrong?"

"Just that you look so much like someone I once knew." He snapped out of his trance and said, "My name is Drake Evans." He extended his sticky hand to greet her.

"My name is Jor—"

Before she could finish introducing herself, he gasped. "I'm sorry, Please reveal your name again." After hearing the beginning of her name, he lost all thought.

Looking at him curiously and a little nervously, she said again, "My name is Jorine Chambers." She shook his hand and crinkled her face at the sticky handshake, opening and closing her fingers from the sticky substance, lips forming downward.

"This is so crazy. You look so much like this beautiful lady I once knew, and her name is Jorie. This is a delightful, crazy coincidence. Silly me, why don't we head to the restroom and clean up. Before we do, a boyfriend, fiancé, or husband isn't going to stomp through the door and knock my lights out, is he?"

She snickered and replied, "Nope, I'm single."

"Well, I'm glad, and I am single as well."

They started seeing each other, and Drake quit thinking about Jorie. This new development had to be shared with Hagan.

"Hello," Hagan answered with a somber tone.

"Whoa, you sound terrible."

"Well, thanks for that vote of confidence."

"You okay?"

"Sorry. I have a lot on my mind, like a life-changing decision I need to make, and it's not an easy one. Before you ask, I am not at liberty to tell you anything about it and it's not bad."

"Seriously? You're going to leave me hanging with that explanation, 'James'?"

"Good try, there, but double *O* anything is not the clue. No mystery spy puzzle. So tell me what's going on. I can detect a good change in your voice."

"It is so unsuspected, just like when I met Jorie. I was in that coffee shop, *The Mystery of Coffee Cafe*."

"That's such a cool name for a coffee shop; isn't it?"

"Why yes, it is, and they're opening up a chain of them around the country. Some of the flavors are quite mysterious, if I say so myself. Anyway, in the coffee shop this lady spilled coffee accidentally—my fault—all down the back of my neck. We have been seriously dating since then. You'll never guess who she clearly resembles."

"Jorie," Hagan replied in a "duh" voice.

"How'd you guess? Never mind. You're not going to guess this: Her name is Jorine. How's that for a coincidence?"

"You had me going there. This isn't coincidence; it's fate. I'm happy for you," Hagan said sounding insincere, but really was happy for him.

"Tonight is a big one. Meeting the parents. I think she's the one, Hagan. You have to stand up in my wedding."

"Wedding? When you fall, you fall hard."

"It may seem ridiculous, but I wondered if it was just an infatuation with her because she resembled Jorie, but the more I'm with her, Jorie doesn't come into my mind. I really think I'm in love, and we are so good together. I'd follow her to the stars in the heavens or down into the depths of the sea. Truthfully."

*Where have I heard that before?* Curious, indeed. "Look, I need to go, but keep me updated. I'm really happy for you."

"You bet. Keep me updated on your decision, also."

We hung up the phone and the glow from the moon water grew bright in its hiding spot. Hagan picked up the bowl, studying it, and immediately fell into a trance at the mystery of how much it represented Chantara. Probably all in his mind, but it swirled into a heart for just a second. Remember that old commercial that says something about how at times you feel like a nut and sometimes you don't? Well, his sometime moment was now. He went to the pantry and found a candy bar, and munched on it.

In the living room, he found Melana watching a movie. His dad had to run an errand. "Any chance we could talk, or I'll come back later. I don't want to interrupt the movie."

"Don't be silly. I'm just watching it to pass time and relax." She was watching *Splash*, ironically. "This is a perfect time to talk."

"Good. I really need some direction with my life. Chantara is constantly on my mind. The truth is I'm terrified at the thought of physically transforming into a merman. I would be the first attempt—victim—fool—stop me anytime."

"Nobody can make this decision but you. Frankly, I'm terribly concerned about the transformation failing, too, but that's because I am clueless to their whole world."

"That's another thing. What if I hate their world?"

"The boy and now man who swears he should have been born a fish? That man?"

"Good point. The truth is, I can become human anytime I

want. It just takes time to get to that point, and looking at their anatomy, it's virtually impossible."

"Is it really? You have seen Chantara in human form and as a mermaid. Do you think we could see them? I can't even imagine."

"No way. That may take some time. You realize it is never appropriate to talk to anyone about this EVER." She pretended to zip her lips.

"One more thing, I brought this comic book of this merman character with me because I wonder if it is serendipity," he said, handing the comic book to Melana.

Her hand went to her mouth with eyes that looked like golf balls. "I'm looking at you. It's as though you modeled for this picture. Did you?"

"Nope. Now, see what I mean?"

"Serendipity it is. In that case, don't wait so long that it ends up breaking your heart like with Dani. Don't wait this time. You have to make a decision. It's almost funny how my comic book nerdy son is about to become one of them. My very own comic book hero."

"How cool is that! I didn't give that much thought. But you're right. I am in full agreement and this decision can't be put off any longer. If I mess this up, I'll pound my own self into the ground."

"Hagan, what are you waiting for? You have what millions of people only wish they had. Complete spellbinding love, a job that you love more than anything and can still have. You now have what your dad and I have. It's true. We love each other deeply. You are so strikingly handsome, you love God and have high morals and values. Sometimes I cry when I talk to God, thankful for you as my son."

She broke out in tears but smiling. He hugged his mother and dropped some tears himself.

"Mom, I'm turning into a mush of a man. Have you ever seen me cry so much?" he said wiping tears from his face.

"All you've managed to do is soften your macho image by

showing compassion. That's a good thing. Now, try and get some sleep. That attractive face is showing unattractive purple bags under the eyes. It is all going to work out. I feel it in here," she said, gripping her fist over the heart.

Now, that is a feeling he believed in. Her intuition had always been magical.

"Good night, Mom. I think I'll take your advice and get some sleep." Kissing her on the cheek, he then headed upstairs.

But that darn portrait started the same thing again. He was there, in the portrait, and then he wasn't. Maybe it's a sign to make the transformation. What else could it be?

# Chapter Forty-One

The next morning, jogging down the stairs, I was met with a frantic father.

"Son, may we speak to you?" His conduct was of distress and uncertainty.

"What's wrong, Dad?" he asked, placing his hand on his shoulder.

"A report from the FBI came back. You're not going to believe this. The bodies of Prince Raiatea, his crew, and a house full of men and women were savagely killed. They were torn to shreds. I was told it looked like a herd of sharks attacked them, but that would be impossible. What was most strange is that they found this like 10-foot fish that had human aspects to it but it was too torn up to really tell. At the lab, they still couldn't identify it. Looks like another cold case. Scientists wondered if this thing was from a group of whatever it was that killed all of these people. Those teeth and claws could definitely shred someone to pieces. I have a sneaky suspicion of what it was that killed them."

Hagan thought back to when Chantara attacked him, clawing his arm. *I didn't realize it then, but she must have taken it easy on me. I'm grateful she didn't use full force.*

"Cetus." Hagan didn't mean to say out loud. The dead merman was him. It was clear to him who killed these people, and he was so relieved that Chantara can live in peace now. Someone had to end this cruelty.

"Excuse me. What did you say, son?" It wasn't a secret any longer between them, but he forgot and decided to keep that information to himself.

"Nothing. Sorry. Please continue."

"The poor women and children survivors were rescued. What was quite odd in this report is that several cages were filled with huge ponds—very strange, but I think we both know why they were there. A cook was the only survivor and is happily working with authorities. She was a prisoner, herself, and also the person who called for help."

He looked at me sadly.

"That's not all. It is so disturbing, I am having a hard time explaining it. These people were conducting human and animal experimentation. There were corpses of dead mutants all over the place, including jars and jars of an experiment gone wrong. They actually have found some specimens alive but will have to keep them out of the public. It's like a real live *Frankenstein* movie. There was another part of the building that had burnt corpses and all sorts of dead bodies waiting to be cremated.

The women and children were drugged and dealing with withdrawal symptoms. Get this, the women and children were kept in topnotch shape to please their clients. Their clients paid dearly for their sick fantasies. If a child or woman was resistant to perform their duties..." Thomas had to stop and catch his breath. Tears flowed down his face. He embraced him, because Hagan felt the same pain for these children and women.

"Son, it's not just the poor, unfortunate illegal aliens who are raped and abducted, but this happens all over the world, in our back yards. It's a huge profit-making industry. It sickens me."

He cried more tears. Melana kept quiet the whole time,

because she couldn't begin to speak even if she tried, it was all so upsetting.

"One more thing, son. That fellow named Brutus washed ashore, murdered with a gunshot to the head."

For some reason, that was not shocking to him. It was just a matter of time before the power-thirsty squire got rid of him. With evil minds like those people, one would wonder if they weren't wolves in sheep's—people's clothing.

An unexpected relief flooded his soul. The report was disturbing in every way, but the result of the massacre was easy to predict. This was a huge, secret facility. The prince certainly became rich from the services and cruelty he provided, and now that money will go to helping these women and children be reunited with their families or be adopted, since there are families who sell their own children. The intervention they will go through will probably be a life-long treatment. The live animals will get treatment and be provided with adoptions, set out into the wild, or whatever will be best for them.

What makes him furious is that there is just no reason to have such evilness in the world. How perverted someone must be to get enjoyment from such atrocities.

After watching some comedies, Hagan was able to take his mind off the report and sleep soundly knowing Chantara and her people, these children and women, and even the animals found in cages are alive, rescued and safe.

# Chapter Forty-Two

Hagan awakened from a great sleep, finally, and walked casually out to the dock stretching his arms and yawning. His yawn caused his mouth to open so wide, it felt like it would remain permanently in that position. He finally was able to release this position and wiggle his jawbone around to reconnect the joint. It felt that way anyway.

In his mind, he had made his decision already and was starting to feel the excitement of what his future would hold. Grabbing supplies for the work they needed to do today, as he walked out to the boat, there was a loud squawking and cackling. Shovel was in a tizzy sitting on the handrail of the boat. When he looked inside the boat, Flopper was lying on the floor, barely moving. The supplies dropped from Hagan's hands, rattling or banging as they hit the boat's deck, and gently he gathered him into his arms. Flopper was in bad condition and there wasn't any time to waste.

Flopper didn't even struggle, and Hagan guessed he wasn't getting much oxygen. His mom helped him to place a towel around the seagull, and then they searched for the closest animal hospital that cared for birds. Thankfully, one was found just minutes away. He ran to the car with Flopper and sped down the road. Melana called and informed the clinic that he'd be there shortly and that it was an emergency.

Hagan almost tripped walking into the clinic, being so upset and not paying attention to his surroundings. His hand quickly braced the wall for balance while the other held Flopper in an embrace. Poor Flopper didn't even react to the shakeup.

"Hello. I am Hagan Bennett. My mother called to inform you I was bringing in this injured bird. This is an emergency. He can barely breathe."

The woman stared at him for a moment because he spoke so fast, but then his name must have connected the dots and she answered.

"One moment, sir, let me see if I have any rooms available."

"Please. I don't mean to be pushy, but this bird is in serious trouble. He needs immediate attention."

"Remain calm. I will be back quickly."

He was having a hard time understanding her attempt to speak English, but at least she tried.

"Sir, come on back."

Flopper was laid on a table and the assistant came in to check his vitals. In very poor English, she attempted to say, the doctor will be right in. Since he knew some of their language, he spoke his concern in Bajan. When they first arrived, he was too rattled to think about using it. The assistant smiled and thanked him. Pacing back and forth, Flopper was weakening.

"Don't they understand what an emergency is?" His foot tapped impatiently on the floor. Now anger was setting in, so he swung the door open, looking for someone. He swung it so hard the swish sound was loud. The veterinarian was walking toward him. He'd be lying if he said it wasn't disturbing to watch his casual approach. What part of *emergency* don't they understand?

"Doctor, please save this bird. His friend, a pelican, is panicking and I fear will not survive without him. Please help him."

"Let me take a look at him." He opened Flopper's beak and looked down his throat. Next, he leaned over and listened to his breathing.

"We need to take x-rays right away. We'll be right back."

More pacing with occasional breaks for a prayer, it seemed to be taking extra-long. The door opened and the doctor and assistant walked in with Flopper.

"Mr. Bennett, I have good news and bad. The good news is that we can save your bird."

"He's not my bird. He lives in the wild, but please continue."

"The bad news is that he needs surgery now if he has any chance for survival. A type of plastic is lodged at the bottom of his throat. He can barely breathe. Surgery is always risky, I'm sure you know. It's the only option at this point." His accent was strong but understandable.

"Certainly, please make sure he survives. Even though this is a wild bird, he means a lot to my girlfriend and his pelican friend. Doctor, he has to survive and recover." He must have looked a pathetic mess because the doctor gave him a concerned look and patted his shoulder to offer support.

"This bird will get our utmost attention, and we will do everything in our power to save him. This may take hours, so why don't you head home and I'll call you as soon as surgery is completed."

"That's a great idea. I am way too antsy and need to check on his buddy, the pelican. Please call me as soon as you are done. Thanks, Doctor."

When he got back to the apartment, he ran down to the pier and Shovel was just sitting there, quiet, unmovable. The poor thing looked to be in a state of a deep depression. "Hey there fella. Flopper is being taken care of. He is in good hands."

Who knew that birds and animals could feel sadness and become depressed? He could honestly say to anyone disputing such facts that he'd experienced it firsthand.

There was a bait shop on the same road driving home, so he

stopped and got some minnows for Shovel. He threw them on the pier and they bounced off into the water. Lucky break for them today. Shovel wanted nothing to do with food. It was a very pitiful and sorrowful scene. He let the other minnows loose and watched them slip under the water and swim away. Shovel was such an emotional mess, so he walked up to this pelican, who had captured his affections, and softly brushed his hand over his feathers.

He looked down at his one eye that was watching him while the other one faced another direction, snuggled up close to him and spoke softly. "Shovel, I am doing everything I can to save Flopper." He turned his head to the other side and looked at him with the other eye at the name of Flopper. "I'll keep praying and come back and check on you."

# Chapter Forty-Three

D rake sat at his desk, preparing for a conference. Getting this company's business could put him in line for any upcoming promotions. He scrolled through his phone, looking for a particular photo taken for this presentation. How he stumbled upon this photo, he didn't remember, but it would be the break he needed for a promotion.

While scrolling, he passed Jorie's picture. No matter how well his relationship with Jorine was going, the hypnotic trance of looking at her picture would always affect him. He stared, completely in a trance, remembering her enchanting face and the melodic sounds that she made. "Nobody could forget such a vision of magic and intrigue. You'll always be a very special memory to me."

His assistant stood at the door, listening before she stepped forward. "Who are you talking to?" she asked, humming the sound from the music of *Strange Things in My Closet*.

"You startled me, Katarina. Just talking to myself."

"Do you need me to take you on a little drive to Rosebloom Lane?"

"That sounds familiar. Now I remember, that's the institution for mentally challenged people. I know you don't mean anything insulting by that remark. Nowadays, everything everyone says is blown out of proportion, so no offense taken on my part. But, hey?"

"They say talking to ourselves is a symptom of something much deeper."

"To be honest, take a look at this picture and tell me she doesn't cast a spell over your mind." He handed her the phone to view Jorie's picture.

"Oh, my goodness! You're not kidding. Is she real or a doll?"

"She's the real deal. I met her on a cruise but found out she is engaged. I feel like I've had a spell cast over me ever since."

"Maybe she's a witch."

"No way. If I had to choose, I would say she is an angel. Being around her is like a feeling of floating on clouds. Don't worry, since I met Jorine—"

"And that's kind of strange, too. Jorine looks so much like her, without all the enchantment and imagination. Even the name 'Jorine' is making this a little weird." She moved the picture up close and back, observing it from all angles.

"Like I said before, you interrupted me. Since I met Jorine, Jorie is no longer on my mind. Who could ever forget someone like Jorie, but I truly love Jorine. Actually, it is because of her that I met someone who has become a good friend to me: Hagan Bennett. You would swoon over him, but his heart belongs to another angel. Don't say anything, because this weekend I am proposing."

Katarina jumped up and down in joy. They hugged.

"Did I tell you the dream I had last night?"

"Nope, you didn't. You have been glued to your computer getting ready for the conference."

"I just have to tell someone. The dream felt so real that I wonder if it stems from meeting Jorie. In the dream I was walking in a wilderness area and came up to this cabin hidden deep in the middle of this forest. The cabin had a small castle flavor except that there was junk and mildew on and around it. It was not kept up at all. Not those seven elves home, or whatever they are called, that's for sure." She looked at him squinting one of her eyes with concern and attempted a one-sided grin.

"Then I saw something sparkling in the window. It was mystifying and intrigued my curiosity. I walked up closer and almost collapsed looking at it. A woman twirled inside this room that looked to be barred up preventing her to escape. She was the most beautiful, fairy-tale woman I have ever seen; that is, evenly compared to Jorie.

"The thought that she is an angel was profound and a sensible conclusion. I wondered to myself how you would keep an angel prisoner. Superheroes can't function around certain substances, and maybe her tower was surrounded with brimstone, something she can't break through."

"Okay, mister. I'm taking you for a ride to see the beautiful roses on Rosebloom Lane."

"I'm just adding my own spin on the dream. The next thing that happened was someone called her name. It was Talia."

"That is actually an amazing dream."

"It felt so real, as though I was really there. But it was just a dream, so lighten up. We need to finish getting ready for this presentation. This could be the one that puts us in line to win the race."

"That is why I came into your office in the first place, to make sure you're prepared."

"I was looking for the winning photo when I stumbled over Jorie's. I'll be ready in ten minutes." Katarina left his office and his cellphone alerted him to an incoming call.

"Hagan, what a pleasant surprise." He laid his head back on the chair. "I only have two minutes to talk because a very important conference begins."

"Not a problem. Just checking to make sure you're doing okay."

"I'm doing better than okay. My plans are to propose this weekend."

"No kidding. That is great. I mean it. It's good to see you overcame that spell that hovered over you."

"What about you? Did you come to a decision?"

"The verdict is just days away, and I believe it's the right one."

"You think I'm a fool, don't you? I know the decision has to do with Chantara, and I also know it is for her safety that you can't tell me anything about it," Drake said. "No worries. I'll never tell anyone anything that could compromise you and their safety. You'll still be in my wedding; right?"

"Absolutely, but based on the outcome of my decision, I may only be able to be there for a couple of days."

"Perfect. I'll keep in touch. I don't know why, but a thought came into my mind: Follow your heart. Follow it, Hagan. It's the right choice."

More confirmation. They both hung up.

# Chapter Forty-Four

At the apartment, Hagan's cellphone buzzed.

"Hello," he answered in anticipation.

"Mr. Bennett, this is Doctor Cumberbatch. I wanted to give you an update." Hagan couldn't speak. "Flopper is in recovery and removal of the obstruction blocking his oxygen intake was successful, however, he is still sedated. We will watch him around the clock to help him recover. His cage is nice and toasty, and all necessary fluids are being administered. Someone from my office will call you either later today or in the morning about his recovery outcome. It's just too early to tell. He was really weak when we performed surgery and it concerned me. We came close to losing him, but whether it had anything to do with his recovery or not, one of my assistants kept whispering Shovel's name to him. He seems to be recovering well, but it is just too soon to make that prediction."

"Doctor Cumberbatch, thank you for everything. It means so much to a lot of people and to his buddy, Shovel. You wouldn't believe it, but Shovel is in bad shape. He won't eat and just sits on the pier. I believe he is in a state of depression."

"And who says animals don't have feeling, right?"

"My thoughts exactly. I'll be waiting for that call. Thanks again. We hung up the phone.

~

Hagan and his parents sat around watching television. Popcorn and cookies sat on the coffee table untouched. No one was in a talkative mood, so they all sat in silence. It was about 7:00 p.m.. His cellphone rang and he jumped, startled. His eyes stared at the number for seconds, and you could see the hesitation in his face. There was a fear of hearing the words, *Flopper didn't make it*. His stomach felt nauseous, and he gently placed his hand on his stomach before answering. There was just no way to avoid answering.

~

He sat up and lowered his body downward, avoiding eye contact with his parents, speaking softly. If it was going to be bad news, who knows what emotions may transpire, so this was a tactile move. "Hello," he said quietly. His parents stared at his face or tried to, he could feel, and when he glanced over in their direction, that feeling was spot on.

Thomas and Melana were analyzing his expression to prepare themselves for the verdict he feared desperately to hear. Frustrated, not able to see his face, they bent down, moving their heads around.

"Mr. Bennett, this is Dr. Cumberbatch's assistant. I am calling to inform you of Flopper's recovery." Her voice didn't alter one way or the other, so he impatiently listened, toes tapping.

"Flopper is doing well. The recovery has been successful. However, the doctor would like to keep Flopper for a couple days to help speed up the recovery before releasing him back into the wild. You can call or stop by tomorrow. So, we'll see or speak to you then."

"Thank you. Until tomorrow."

Thomas and Melana were anxious, not being able to unravel the mystery of his expression, nor the words spoken, leaning toward him.

"Flopper did well. He's going to be fine." Relief flooded his soul, and his eyes watered. "I have to go give Shovel the news."

Hagan ran to the pier and found Shovel in the same spot he'd left him. Poor fellow. "Shovel!" he said with much excitement. "Flopper is going to be okay. Flopper is good." Speaking with a wide smile so that he could hopefully relate his words and features together. It didn't seem to work.

An idea popped into his mind. "I'm taking you to see Flopper in the clinic tomorrow. You'll see." He bent over and very tenderly squeezed him. Shovel wasn't certain how he felt about the squeeze and shifted his body.

The next morning, Hagan grabbed a cage and put Shovel in it to transport him to the clinic. It was easier than he thought. Shovel didn't put up much of a fight. They entered the clinic and Flopper must have smelled Shovel's not so pleasurable scent and began squawking in the back. Shovel heard him and started making it clear that he wasn't going to shut up until he took him back to see Flopper.

"I'm really sorry. This poor thing has been so depressed wondering about Flopper. I thought it would be a good idea for them to see each other and maybe this way Shovel, this pelican, will start eating again. Could I please take him back there for just a moment?"

The receptionist seemed to be lost in thought staring and cast a sweet, flirtatious smile at him. "Sure. Follow me," she said with a gleaming smile.

Both birds started squawking and clattering like crazy. Hagan held the cage up to Flopper and they both jumped around excitedly. Not a good idea for Flopper to get this flustered so he ran Shovel out of the room and left him in the cage by the receptionist, then went back in and tried to calm Flopper down.

Shovel was by no means relaxed. He wanted to be with his buddy. He asked the receptionist if it was possible to get Shovel a checkup since he had him here and would probably never be able to get a chance again once Flopper was released into the wild with him. She checked the schedule.

"Looks like you're in luck, Mr. Bennett. We just had a spot open up."

"Oh, wow, thanks."

"Certainly. Follow me, please." There was that adorable smile again.

They walked into the examination room and he waited for the doctor. An intern came in and apologized that the doctor had an emergency surgery to perform.

"Please, no apologies needed. The good doctor was gracious enough to perform emergency surgery on the seagull I brought in yesterday. I am more than grateful for you to conduct this examination."

With a few wiggles and disapproving squawks, the checkup was completed with a bill of good health. Hagan paid the bill for both birds. "You two better be thankful I actually care about you after paying this bill. I'm just kidding with you, fella. I'd do anything in the world to keep you and Flopper safe."

Shovel made a honking sound like he responded to his statement.

"Besides, where I'm going, money is insignificant and useless." He couldn't believe he just made that remark without hesitation. "In a few days, this decision will be made, or my name isn't Hagan Bennett," he mumbled quietly.

Driving back to the apartment, he pulled into the bait shop and bought some minnows for Shovel. It was the least he could do. As he walked up to the bait shack, Adam walked out of it.

They stared and stood looking like they were in a standoff, inadvertently.

"Hagan, I'm actually glad we ran into each other. I've been sick to my stomach since that lousy day." He listened intently.

Adam broke down in sobs, a hand covering his eyes in embarrassment. "I'm truly sorry. I never intended things to turn out this way, but that makes absolutely no difference. Losing my best friend in the whole world, well, trust me, I deserve that. But it torments me what I've lost. You will always be my best friend, but I know how foolish it would be to wish you could forgive me and move on. Dani and I had been spending a lot of time together, and it just happened. It wasn't planned. Don't worry, I accept full responsibility for my horrendous actions. It is difficult to try and express to you how much our friendship means to me and ruined because of me.

"You know me and food, well that's all over with. I can't even eat." It did look like he lost a lot of weight—too much weight. He sobbed again, and it was gut wrenching to watch. Adam turned momentarily embarrassed, trying to gain control.

Hagan placed a hand on his shoulder and gave him an authentic smile of forgiveness. "Your apology is accepted. It may take some time, but I'm certain we will get back to the way things were between us. The one good thing that came from this is that I realized I wasn't in love with Dani after all. I'm in love with someone else, and it happened accidentally, literally, but can't get into any details. She's not married or anything like that and lives nowhere near us. If we marry, we'll have to move away, far, far away, where they don't have cellphone service. It's a long story, but when I get to return for a visit, I'll get in touch with you. Here is her picture."

Adam's eyes bugged out of his head. "I'm speechless. She's— Wow! I'm really happy for you. Are you happy?"

"Let's put it this way, I have been miserable since we have been apart. By the end of this week I plan to rectify that."

"Hagan, I am so sorry for betraying you. Forgiving me is something I never expected, so thank you and you have my word nothing like this will ever happen again."

Shovel started ranting and raving. "I have a hungry pelican in my car. I need to get him home." Adam looked at him curiously. "What are you doing here in Barbados, by the way?"

"My parents bought me a getaway ticket to work through my shame. I totally forgot you were here. Take care, and I mean that." He hugged me and dropped more tears on his way out, unable to form any words. It felt good to resume their friendship and let bygones be bygones. His eyes were a blurry mess, too. After getting back his manly composure, for whatever that's worth, he went into the shop and headed home fast because Shovel was getting anxious.

Melana and Thomas were overjoyed by Hagan and Adam's reunion, so much so, that it caused Melana to cry.

"I have a great idea. Why don't you hire Adam to replace me when I'm gone? He can always be sent to another one of our locations while we work together."

"Son, are you saying you made your decision?" Thomas asked.

"After speaking with you and Mom, I plan to decide by Sunday one way or the other. Maybe we could have Adam work with us a few days to see how it will work out, depending on the choice I make. One thing I've learned, anything could change at any time."

"That's a marvelous idea. I'll set it up," Melana answered. She stared at him without his knowledge sadly, happily, beyond pride in him and thankful to God for giving her such a wonderful son.

That week Adam worked with them for a few days. It was like old times. If you didn't know any better as a bystander, you would never have known that something so horrible happened between Hagan and Adam. It was a glorious thing to see. Flopper and Shovel became acquainted with Hagan's family and teammates. Now, someone would always be around to take care of them.

# Chapter Forty-Five

Dani walked out to her mailbox, sulking at the way things had turned out in her life. She missed Hagan's family more than she missed him. A very bizarre letter fell to the ground, and as she picked it up, the name of the company resonated with her. It had been months since she mailed them an application, even before the breakup.

Fingers sweating and trembling with nervousness, she opened the letter. Her face lighted up and she let out a gleeful shriek. After making a call and accepting the position, she packed quickly. She would send for her things as soon as she found an apartment. There was nothing to keep her in Florida, so she drove to Rhode Island. A new wardrobe would be purchased. Flip flops and shorts certainly wouldn't suffice in cold weather.

She found the perfect apartment, and she grabbed it. It was cozy with a fireplace and all the modern amenities she adored. After a full day of orientation, she decided to find a coffee shop and review the five-hundred-page manual. Just maybe she could keep her eyes open in a public setting. Her mouth dropped open and she let out a lengthy yawn. Now that her furniture arrived, it was evident she would fall fast asleep on the couch or bed reviewing this ridiculous binder.

A coworker recommended this new coffee shop that just opened that had the most amazing coffee flavors but couldn't remember the name, so she gave Dani the directions instead. As Dani pulled up, she was at a loss for words. Eyes wide and mouth open, the sign read: the Grand Opening of The Mystery of Coffee Cafe.

She walked inside and recognized a face behind the counter immediately. "Hello there. I recognize you from Southwest Florida. I just moved here from there. My name is Dani, and I used to come in the Florida shop with my boyfriend," then mentally kicked herself for bringing that touchy subject up.

"Right! Hagan and his friend, Adam?"

"Yes, that is correct," she answered. Her eyes darted around the room looking for something to talk about besides her past relationship, but thankfully customers were lined up and he was too busy to discuss it any further.

"Well, as you can see, business is booming and we are short of help not knowing how much business to first expect. By the way, my other brother and some cousins are opening up shops in other parts of the country. We are going to keep them family owned and operated. Now, what can I get for you?"

"That chocolate, bacon and sea salt flavor sounds promising. I'll take a large with just cream."

"We'll have that for you in a moment."

Dani sat down in the noisy café, wondering how in the heck she would be able to concentrate. She carefully lowered her lips to the cup and took a sip, eager to try this new flavor. Quickly, she pushed the cup away, licking her lips and squinting her eyes from the scalding hot pain. Blowing in the cup she resumed the task at hand. After taking a small sip, she sat back and licked her lips more, staring in oblivion and then realizing with a wide smile, *Hey, this actually tastes just like the ingredients. Amazing and wonderful!*

Next, she reminisced over the past, since she and Hagan frequented this establishment quite often, trying desperately to focus on the giant-sized manual haunting her mind. Then she took out her notepad and wrote a note to self: reconnect with family. It's about time.

She studied, yawned, studied, yawned, and the pattern went on just like that. The next thing she knew, an ice-cold chill ran down the back of her neck. She made the shrill sound of someone experiencing the shock of something freezing coming in contact with their body. Shuddering, she stood up and said in a shivering voice, "What...just...happened?" Her teeth were chattering.

"Please forgive me, miss. You must not have realized your leg jutted out as I passed by and I tripped, while my iced coffee found its way down your back. I'm really sorry."

She turned slowly, steaming, shoulders pushed upward, face with glaring eyes, trying to gain control and stopped abruptly looking at the good-looking man apologizing to her. His eyes were concerned and sincere. That softened her raging temper.

"It's all my fault. I should be apologizing to you. This needs to be reviewed by tomorrow. Tomorrow!" she repeated pointing to the manual wondering how in the heck that could possibly happen.

"No wonder. They really expect you to study all that, I assume, in one day?"

"Yes, yes, they do. Isn't there some sort of overburdening-new-employees-with-such-nonsense therapy group I could join?" She chuckled.

They connected immediately. As days go by, they will evolve into a serious relationship with a marriage proposal close by.

# Chapter Forty-Six

It had been days since Adam worked with Hagan. The realization that he was going to move away seemed to hang over everyone's minds. Now that things were back the way they should have been, knowing Hagan will be leaving brought him great sadness.

"That had to be the reason Fernando, Kent and several other of our friends hung out last evening. I'm sure of it. We had such a blast, kind of like a bachelor party, without making it the official title." He spoke to himself in trying to console the soaring emotions.

He drove around, trying to distract his mood. A walk on the beach was relaxing and serene, but only made him think about Hagan leaving more. They practically lived on the beach. Still driving around, he came to The Mystery of Coffee Cafe. This was a common hangout for them. Thinking this was a bad idea, he went in anyway and chatted small talk with the owner before ordering his coffee. Sitting at a table, scrolling through picture after picture of them and all of their friends, loneliness started mocking him. The next thing he knew, something hot scorched his skin down the back of his neck, running down his back.

"Ow!" he yelled out, grabbing the back of his neck. Then he tried to soak up the coffee with some napkins, certain he would turn around and punch whoever was stupid and careless enough to do such a thing. As he turned, body rigid, face scowling, he spouted like a teapot that reached its boiling point.

"Do you happen to have any idea how much pain—"

But before he could complete his sentence, he stared into the tearful, apologetic eyes of this cute-as-a-button young lady, decked out with the cutest freckles you ever saw, with a darling just-below-the-chin hairstyle. Her red hair, with a mixture of blonde highlights, was the perfect color and length for her features. Then she spoke.

"Mister, I would be more than happy to take you to see a doctor and treat any burns. I am deeply sorry for my clumsiness. You see, as I walked past you, your leg jutted out and I tripped with my coffee spilling down your back." Her Southern drawl captivated him, and her slouching body and blurry eyes softened his demeanor.

"You know what? It is all my fault. I was lost in thought, not paying attention, but are you all right?"

"Yes, yes, I am." He was overtaken by her southern charm and accent.

"Would you accompany me? I'll get you some more coffee. That is unless you have a husband or boyfriend."

"No, I am single, but I feel that I should be the one to buy the coffee."

"Absolutely not. This is all my fault, but I have a sneaky suspicion that it could be fate." She smiled shyly, lowering her eyes, which added to her charm and made his heart pound.

After cooling down his skin from the scalding coffee, he handed her a coffee and they talked and talked and talked. "How is it that someone as attractive and sweet as you is single?"

"Well, I could ask you the same thing," she said, face a light pink, covering her smile with her hand.

"You are an absolute delight. Truthfully, I haven't found the right person. What about you?"

"My situation is a tad bit different. I thought I found that somebody and we dated for three years. My ex felt we needed some time apart and started dating. This position came available and I jumped at it. It was too good of a job to pass up and the timing couldn't have been more perfect."

"Three years is a long time. You said you are from Tennessee?"

"Born and raised."

"What about your family?"

"They're still in Tennessee. They never liked my boyfriend and are happy we broke up. Having an opportunity like this only comes once in a lifetime, and my parents are thrilled for me to accept it. Now they get to visit sunny Florida on vacation. It's a win-win."

"I'll say it is. I hope I'm not being too forward, but I am being completely honest with you about not dating anybody. Wasn't any interest. But now, there is nothing I'd rather do than spend some time getting to know you, if you agree. You can speak to the owner over there and he can verify my reputation as a good guy. No murderer, criminal, playboy, nothing like that."

She smiled in that adoringly, innocent, shy way. He felt like a snowman in Florida, because she melted his heart.

"I would love to get to know you."

They started dating and it turned into a serious relationship, where an engagement ring was purchased.

The mystery of romance in this establishment has to be related to the cafe's name. There must be something mysterious about that coffee.

# Chapter Forty-Seven

The week went by in a flash. Every evening, Hagan would walk out to the end of the pier and leave the most delectable snacks, and Chantara would leave him some incredible piece of a treasure. Cotton candy was still her favorite.

Going down the steps headed to the kitchen, a bright ray of the sun lit up the family portrait. This time, Hagan stared in shock because he was not in the picture. Completely gone. No fading in and out, just gone. "Mom! Dad! Come quick!"

He could hear the tapping of their footsteps as they ran. "What is it, son?" Thomas asked, face filled with worry and placing his hand on Hagan's shoulder.

"Look at the portrait and tell me if you notice anything unusual." Melana and Thomas stared into each other's eyes before looking at the portrait.

"Hhhh!" Melana gasped, grabbing Thomas' arm to steady herself.

"I'm not in it, am I?"

"How is this possible?" Thomas asked, scratching his head.

"I wonder if it has anything to do with what my decision will be. Maybe God is showing me what to do in a very startling way.

Whatever my decision will be, I will never abandon my family. You won't get rid of me that easily. But it does make sense that I will be leaving the world as we know it."

They looked back at the portrait and Hagan was in it once again. A strong cup of coffee was needed. "I smell coffee. Don't you hear it calling? Thomas, Melana, Hagan, I'm ready." He extended his arm out and his parents laid their hands on his arm and they recited: "Family first and always."

Every evening, he stared at the moon water. The substance swirled and molded into what always looked to be a heart shape. He stared, confused and amazed. The moon water would never allow him to forget Chantara. It was a reflection of her. She was the greatest treasure he would ever find or need. A treasure men around the world could only dream about. It was the proof of who she was.

Day and night, Hagan would walk out on the pier, casting his eyes around the water to find her. Unknown to him, she would sit below and watch him.

"*I love*. She always used those two words. She loves everything," he said out loud, picturing her in his mind. His world has been turned around and his thoughts to what is really important in life. It's not a job, not money, but love. *I love*. "I'll never, ever forget those two words."

He mulled over what decision to make. It had been months since he had seen her and that strong feeling was burdening him to take action before he chickened out, or heaven forbid, she lost interest. Another Dani and Hagan story in the making.

What if the transformation doesn't work? Could he drown?" He looked like one of the games at a fair where the steel ducks walked back and forth before getting shot down.

To be fair, these concerns would hold anybody back from jumping into a decision. There were legitimate reasons for the uneasiness he felt. But, what if he hated their lifestyle? He couldn't stop thinking about her. So much to think about.

His thoughts were in constant turmoil. Each day, his parents watched, knowing the decision was his own to make. It was painful for them to watch. They would support his decision, regardless. After all, he would still be able to work with them in the oceans, and in better circumstances than they ever could.

One evening, after returning to the pier to see what token she left him, he found it empty. The snack he left for her was still sitting where he left it. He nibbled on his fingernails while looking out over the ocean. The next evening, the same thing. The snacks he left were untouched.

"I'm too late. No!" he screamed while grasping his hands over his head in despair. "You fool!" He kept yelling those words. Thankfully, no one was around to witness this disparaging scene. There was some kind of taste of the town event happening, and it seemed that he and his parents were the only ones not attending the event. It would always be around midnight when he came out to the pier, so it usually was abandoned of any people, except tonight. It was still daylight, heading into the twilight portion of the day.

His parents watched the scene from the balcony. Tears fell down their faces. Memories of this moment would haunt them the rest of their lives. *How do you comfort someone who was warned and waited until it was too late? The way he was reacting, there would never be another relationship in his future. He would bury himself in his work*, were thoughts racing through Melana's mind. Thomas pulled her into a very caring embrace and allowed her to cry until she could regain her composure.

After a while, she ran inside, and a bright glow came from Hagan's room. She entered the room slowly, hesitating, and finally walked up to the area. Her hands moved some of his things and she found the bowl of moon water. The colors swirled, and they were the exact colors that reflected from Chantara. Melana quickly covered her mouth with her hand. *What's going on? What am I looking at?*

She ran back to Thomas to tell him, but froze at the scene below. Both hands covered her heart and her face lowered with tears dripping like a running faucet. She couldn't bear to see any more of this.

Hagan started yelling in distress, "Chantara! Don't give up on me. Please." He put his face in his hands and sobbed as his knees dropped to the sand. His parents continued to watch with tears pouring down both of their faces. They tried to walk away but just felt glued to that horrific display of doom.

No answer from Chantara.

Thomas and Melana watched for about thirty minutes when they had taken as much as they could take of this devastating scene. They slumped onto the couch, silent, watching television, but not. Their thoughts were anywhere but on the television. They both had a look as if they were in a trance. It was just too tragic to speak about.

An hour later, Thomas walked up to the window that overlooked the beach. Hagan was lying in the sand, face down. Tears dropped, and he grabbed Melana and suggested they head to bed.

"I need to help him. He needs us. We can't leave him out there alone." Every word she spoke was accompanied with sniffles.

"No, I really feel he wants to be alone. We need to give him space to deal with it all, with his emotions."

She dropped her head and her hand covered those eyes filled with tears. The door to their room closed softly.

The next morning, Thomas arose before Melana. He softly walked out of the room so he didn't awaken her. He noticed Hagan's bedroom door open, and when he looked inside, it was obvious Hagan never slept in the bed. Almost tumbling down the stairs, he hurried out to the beach. The breeze blew hair in his eyes. He kept moving the hair from his eyes in search of Hagan. Hagan was lying on the sand with no movement. Fearful of what he may find, he walked up and gently touched his arm. Startled by the touch, Hagan jumped up in a sitting position. Sand covered his cheek, and it fell from his body as the breeze blew. His tears dried on his face, filled with beach sand.

"Son, are you okay?"

Hagan dropped his head. Barely audible he replied, "No, Dad. Not this time. I'm going to head over to the new Madagascar project and complete our work. I need to be alone. There is nothing I can say, or nothing you can say that will matter. This is one time I really don't want to be around anyone. I'll work every day and send you emails of my progress. Do not send anyone to work with me or to check up on me. I'm serious about just wanting to be left alone. Please understand."

Thomas nodded but remained speechless. Hagan jumped up, wiped the sand off his body, and ran inside to get his stuff. After making his flight preparations and gathering everything he needed, the doorbell rang. He walked down the stairs with hands full of luggage. Melana couldn't quit crying. Thomas' eyes were a blurry mess. Hagan stopped in front of them, emotionless, face blank.

"It's best this way. I'll keep you informed of all details necessary for this assignment. Not sure how long I'll be gone. I love you both."

And just like that, he walked out. No hugs. No kisses. He needed to escape fast without any words that he feared to hear. After all, he already felt like a loser, a self-inflicted loser. He didn't even look toward the beach. His heart was broken. The way he felt inside, his heart had to have physical tears because the pain was physical as well as mental.

Hagan sat back in the seat on the plane, eyes closed the entire trip. Like a zombie he gathered his luggage and supplies, checked into the apartment and diddled around making preparations for work tomorrow. It was now midnight and he had everything in order and ready for work.

Day after day, Hagan worked and entered data into his report, then emailing any results to the appropriate departments, including his parents. He actually was providing more inclusive information than expected. Work was all he did. No more socializing. He went to work and came home to an empty apartment.

His personality was changing. One of the professors was obstinate about his behavior in conversation with Thomas and Melana, which brought her to tears.

"Thomas, it's just not like Hagan to act like a jerk. You and I both know how arrogant Professor Alloy is."

But then they received more complaints from other clients. Hagan provided superior information and more than they requested, but his attitude with them was sharp, quick and tiresome, as though they bored him with their questions.

Thomas tried calling him but Hagan didn't pick up or maybe was working. He didn't know. Around 1:00 a.m., Thomas' cellphone clinked. He grabbed it and read the text.

"They're all being idiots. You saw my reports and can't dispute the fact they are complete with more applicable information than they requested of me. What do they want from me?"

"Son, they want you to talk to them like a civil human being. Your work has been exceptional, but even I can see a change in your attitude. Please don't change who you are as a person. Please."

Thomas waited for a reply but it never came. He lied back down and his body rolled back and forth, never able to find that perfect spot.

Hagan threw the phone on the counter and grumbled.

His heart was growing cold. Hard. Comic books laid around untouched. He watched hours of mindless television. Anytime a memory flashed in his mind about Chantara, he would blank it out. Women worked tirelessly to gain his attention, but it was all in vain. He wasn't even kind or caring in the way he dealt with them, almost always causing them to screech obscenities at him and walk away with heavy stomping, and sometimes in tears.

It was going on two months, and the only changes he made were in how he discussed his assignments with clients. They couldn't see him biting his lip and breathing heavy, but somehow he pulled it off over the phone.

The sound of his cellphone chiming angered him. He grasped it like a grenade and stared at the text. His mouth dropped. For the first time since he arrived in Madagascar, his eyes teared up. His hand went to his mouth. Automatically his fingers dialed Thomas's number.

"Hagan, it's all right. She's going to be fine."

"How...how did the stroke happen?"

"She's been under a lot of stress. It's not your fault so stop right there."

"Not my fault? How can you say that with a straight face? She has never been stressed out before. Not like this. Not so stressed that it caused a mild stroke. Stop babying me, Dad. I've caused this."

"Son, of course what you're going through is going to have an effect on us and yes, it makes us sad that you won't talk to us. It hurts us just as much as it hurts you. You're the one person who always takes everyone else's feelings to heart, and now you shut everyone out who wants to do the same for you. Son, it's time to come home and let family and friends be there for you, for once." His voice cracked and he could barely speak. "Please, Son."

"Okay, Dad. I'll take the first flight out. I have completed this assignment, so I was hanging around to avoid having to come home. I can see how my pain is tormenting you both. I'm really sorry about that. I have one condition."

"What's that, Son?"

"No discussing anything about Chantara or anything."

"It's a deal. Just come home. That's all we want."

"Tell Mom I'll see her soon."

～

Hagan entered his parent's house. His sister and family and Thomas jumped up and ran to him. They embraced, and everyone became emotional. Except for Hagan. His face was blank, not mean, not uncaring, not arrogant. Just blank. He walked up to his mother. She stood slowly and smiled tenderly, not able to speak.

"I'm sorry, Mom."

She reached a hand up and cupped his cheek. "You have nothing to be sorry about.

I'm just happy you're home."

He forced a smile.

They sat around talking about anything that wouldn't upset Hagan.

"Hey, Hagan. You want to come outside with me and throw the Frisbee?" his niece, Anna, asked.

He looked out toward the beach and turned his head back fast. "Not now. I'm really tired from the trip. Maybe tomorrow," he remarked, messing up Anna's hair.

"Okay," the girl replied with disappointment.

"Hey, all, I'm going to head to my apartment and check things out. Call me anytime if anything should happen. I'll be back tomorrow."

"Oh, son. I forgot to mention. We are heading back to Barbados next week. We would love for you to join us. There's been a lot of speculation of some activity around the hole you discovered."

"I'll think about it, Dad. See you all tomorrow."

When his car pulled out, way too slow from his usual screeching like driving a race car, Melana whimpered softly. Thomas and his daughter sat on each side of her holding a hand.

"Now that he is home, I'm sure he'll come around. We need to give him time. This is the most difficult situation he has ever been through," Thomas said.

She snorted in sniffles and replied, "That's not my son. He's completely different. Completely."

"Mom, just give him time. Now that he will be around us, I'm sure things will change.

He's lost a lot of weight. That alone is concerning. Maybe he's trying to create a new comic book character: Thin Man." His sister shook her head in distress.

"Look, we need to act normal around him. That's the only way he'll snap out of this depression, or whatever it is. It baffles me, too, to see such a change in him. We can't act like we're walking on eggshells. He'll pick up on that."

"I think you're right, Thomas," Melana agreed.

For the week, his friends stopped by and tried to get him to do things. He was never mean, just came up with excuse after excuse. His phone chimed, and he saw the name. His finger powered off the phone quickly. Drake was the last person in the world he could speak to, because they always discussed Chantara.

Hagan sat in his room watching endless television, refusing to go out on the beach or socialize. He visited his parents daily, but only stayed long enough to make sure his mother was doing okay. Staring blankly at the TV screen, the doorbell rang. His head dropped; eyes closed. Rising like he was carrying a truck full of cement, he walked to the door. The doorbell rang again. He grumbled.

Just as he opened the door, Dani turned around and sighed in shock, not expecting anyone to be home.

"You frightened me," she said patting her heart. "I wasn't sure if you'd be here, but I thought I'd check. I'm only here for a day. Could I come in?"

He moved back and waved her inside. She entered feeling really awkward. Hagan stood by the door not even trying to be civil. "So, what brings you by?"

"Are you sick or something? You don't look well."

His lips formed down and he replied: "Nope."

"Oh, good."

He crossed his arms. "What is it you want?"

She sensed his cold mannerisms and found it hard to speak.

"Please tell me my parents didn't send you here?"

"No. I haven't seen them. Seen anybody. I'm here on business, but I just wanted to check on you. Plus, I have something to tell you."

He sighed and just said what was in his thoughts. "You aren't going to try and get us back together, I hope." His voice was very cold.

"You know, you're being kind of a jerk. Heck no, I don't want us to get back together. I just stopped by to tell you that I'm getting married."

His eyes popped open.

"What about you? Are you still dating that Chan—can't remember her name."

"No. No one."

He extended his hand. "Congratulations. I hope you'll be very happy."

Her eyes squinted and she replied, "Thank you? Well, I guess I should be going. Take care, Hagan." She looked seriously at him. "Really."

He nodded.

Dani sat in her car replaying her time with Hagan. Nothing registered. He didn't look or sound like the Hagan she knew. She slowly pulled out of the parking spot and drove away feeling sad for some reason.

# Chapter Forty-Eight

The Bennett team worked together again in Barbados. Being around his family, Hagan was communicating much more and even laughing at times. Still a ways to go, but at least he perked up. However, he avoided the entrance to the "Mer" world. His work involved everything but that area. All the chatter about activity surrounding this hole was avoided on his part. Kept himself preoccupied so he didn't have to discuss it.

Several days later, a team member motioned for him to come and help. So he swam over to the spot. The water was crystal clear, and he saw another team member being escorted to the boat. Alone, now, he began to swim up, but something stopped him dead in his attempt. Chantara was swimming toward him.

His heart sped up. Eyes closed. When they reopened, she was gone. His head turned swiftly, looking for her, but she was gone. *Great. Now I'm hallucinating.* Moving up to the surface, he glanced back and saw a swirling of colors. It shook him up. Worried about his teammate, Hagan pulled himself into the boat and devoted all of his attention on his teammate. He was getting the "checkup". For some reason, Hagan chuckled. Greg smirked back at him.

Relieved that he didn't have to talk about what he saw, he asked what was going on.

"I saw this incredible swirling of colors, wondering if I just entered heaven's pearly gates. It was so amazing. Then something bumped really hard into me and pushed me away from that spot. I didn't realize I had drifted so close to the forbidden hole. Thankfully, Thomas was feet away."

"Did you see anything, Dad?"

"Actually, I saw colors in the water as they vanished. Other than that, nothing."

"You okay, Greg?"

He waved his hand down. "Just peachy. Now, can we please stop this fussing and get on with our work?"

Hagan sat staring into space. Melana and Thomas looked sympathetically into each other's eyes. They knew what Hagan was thinking.

That night in Hagan's room, he bowed his head and said a prayer. "Father, I'm so sorry for how egregious I have been in my treatment toward you, blaming you when it is my own fault for the heartbreak I feel. Forgive me." Tears dropped. Finally.

He leaned his head against the backboard of the bed and just sat quietly. Deep, deep in thought. Suddenly, he heard something, then thought, what is that gurgling sound? Pushing his body up from the bed, he headed in the direction of the noise. Tormenting pain had kept him from looking at the bowl hiding on his shelf. Couldn't bear to look. His hand moved books and whatnot away. The brightness of the moon water was reflecting in the whole room. Amazing, beautiful and vibrating like he had never seen before.

He stopped suddenly, and a thought came to him. His parents heard him run down the stairs and the front door slam shut. They ran around the house, looking for him to see what was going on.

By this time, he ran to the public pier. Just before entering it, a reflection of colors caught his attention. He ran down to the beach area and saw a heart made out of seashells. In the middle was moon water. His heart pounded with anticipation. After purchasing cotton candy wrapped with various colored cellophane, he wasted no time. He ran fast back to his parent's apartment but out to the beach area. Huffing, puffing. Just drained. He hadn't kept in shape and this time it struck him how badly he had let himself go. The bag of cotton candy dropped swiftly onto the pier. Slowly, he backed up. Waiting. Still waiting. His head dropped, and he turned to walk away. *How could I be so stupid?* Thomas and Melana watched from their bedroom balcony. Just as he stepped off the pier to their backyard, he heard a soft, angelic sound. It was so beautiful, but Flopper ruined it by cackling as he landed. Hagan smiled and ran his fingers over the feathers. Shovel joined them and he ran his fingers over his feathers, too. Then a sound like the breeze whispering through the trees could be heard.

"Hagan, I here."

He jumped up, scanning the water, wiping his eyes and nose, using the back of his hand. His face convulsed with tears, scared it was a hallucination.

"Where? Chantara!" choking out his words between sniffles.

"Here."

He saw her. The wind blew her hair all around and it made her look more and more like a storybook princess. The colors were the brightest and most beautiful he had ever seen reflect off her. He couldn't help but feel tingles run through his veins. Then a whiff of her scent blew through the breeze and that memory he placed into his secret chamber of Chantara memories came back tout de suite.

When he reached her, they embraced and kissed passionately. She melted in his arms.

"Chantara, I was so afraid I would never see you again. It felt like I was going to literally die. It hurt physically. Please tell me I'm not hallucinating." His voice was frantic.

"I no understand. I stay with you, Hagan. I not happy without you. My colors went away for a while. Father think I was dying and wouldn't let me see you," distraught in her voice.

"I'm so sorry. You can't stay with me, though. You can't live in my world, but I've been thinking. There is something I need to discuss with you. I had a counsel session with my pastor. The conversation made me realize how important my beliefs are." He tried to explain his thoughts.

"Pastor Knowit All—I just always have to add my affectionate name for him—has always been right about mostly everything that I can ever remember. Not that he's perfect, but close, very close."

After about twenty minutes, they hugged and laughed. His body was being tossed around due to the tide coming in, making it difficult to stand, and constantly fighting to keep his balance. Chantara was not affected. Seagull chatter had stopped, and a breeze picked up.

"Two more questions. If I will be the first human ever transformed into a merman, how can you be certain it will work and I won't drown or die in the process?"

"Everything my father do works out. I know you be fine. I just know."

"You can certainly understand the struggles I've been dealing with. Remember how sad you felt being taken from your family?" She shook her head yes with very understanding eyes.

"But you can see them anytime. You can be a people anytime you want, like I was."

"That is true."

"Do you and your people have some sort of power or spell you put on humans that draws us to you? Your fragrance"— He stopped momentarily and thought about it. *How did I not realize I have her fragrance, and she has mine.*—"your voice, your touch and even your appearance draws me to you. I can never quit thinking about you. Even Drake felt the same way about Jorie. Can you make us feel this way?"

"I part human, too, but I hear Cetus tell prince— I not sure if it true, but he tell prince that we can make people feel things."

"But, if Marin was your mate, you shouldn't feel this way toward me since your mate is determined for you at birth."

"I ask Father about that and he believe Marin was not my mate. I just liked him and want him to be my mate. But I love you, Hagan. I love you so much and I not stop thinking about you."

"Will you always feel this way about me?"

"Always, forever. My parents still feel this way about each other."

"When I transform"—her face lighted up with happiness at his remark—"will I still be able to speak in my language and will I still know my family and friends and who I am now?"

"I not know. It never happen before. You could talk with Father. He should know."

"That sounds like a plan. I'll do that but give me a moment."

Who could ever dismiss the fact that they were meant to be. He always loved and felt he should have lived in the water. He kept repeating that woman's words: "Follow your heart, even if love takes you to the stars in the heavens or down into the depths of the sea. Make a splash."

In that moment, he knew the decision had to be made once and for all. He stared at her and turned around and walked close to the shoreline looking up at his parents, knowing all along they had been watching, with a repeat performance many, many times, waves growing stronger, crashing into him. His balance was unsteady, and the tide was rushing in faster. Light from the sun was dimming. His thoughts were discombobulated, excited and terrified at the same time. Hagan's family and friends mean everything to him, so of course that is the main reason this is so hard. Even though it seemed he quit caring about them, frankly, it was a sink-or-swim situation. He had to keep his distance for himself, as well as their wellbeing, but the love he feels for them all is so very deep. As far down as the ocean goes. Fear of the transformation is no longer a deterrence. Just making the right choice; that is what truly matters.

But, after what he went through, now there isn't a doubt. His concern was for his mother and her health. "I just hope Mom will be okay. I certainly don't want to cause her more distress," he acknowledged to himself.

The one thing about Chantara he did know, *she love*.

His eyes stared them down, pleading for his parent's blessing. They both smiled affectionately and nodded their heads slowly, tears plummeting to the deck floor. Happy tears.

In his room, the moon water started to bubble and gurgle even louder, exposing a bright, mystic glow.

# Chapter Forty-Nine

Several evenings later, news organizations around the world alerted breaking news. An unforgettable display of fireworks exploded out of the Atlantic Ocean. Scientists were bumfuzzled and couldn't agree on any conclusion.

When the power of love unites the mind, body and soul so completely it seeks release.

They love.

~

**Don't miss out on your next favorite book!**
**Join the Melange Books mailing list at**
www.melange-books.com/mail.html

## THANK YOU FOR READING

~

Did you enjoy this book?

We invite you to leave a review at your favorite book site, such as Goodreads, Amazon, Barnes & Noble, etc.

### DID YOU KNOW THAT LEAVING A REVIEW...

- Helps other readers find books they may enjoy.
- Gives you a chance to let your voice be heard.
- Gives authors recognition for their hard work.
- Doesn't have to be long. A sentence or two about why you liked the book will do.

# About the Author

Linda Phillips moved back to a winter wonderland in Wisconsin until a sneaky sunray snuck through the overcast clouds and beamed down on her, pulling her right back to sunny Florida. When she's not daydreaming about a sweet romance story, she tends to Monster I and Monster II, affectionately known as Sprinkle Dinkle and Skittle Wittle, her two cats. *Marry Christmas* is her first book, with more on the way.

lindalouphillips.com

facebook.com/LindaLPhillipsAuthor
linkedin.com/in/linda-phillips-61347270